BETRAYED

JAKE CROSS

Print ISBN: 978-1-913419-11-0

PART I

Nate drove as fast as he dared and cut as many turns as possible, just in case they were still after him.

'Shut your damn screeching.'

But the woman in the back of the van screeched on, obviously in pain from her injuries. She got her loudest, predictably, as the van crossed Wandsworth Bridge, which seemed completely loaded with cyclists and pedestrians, even though it was past midnight. Up went his anxiety as they turned to watch the van pass by. Down it went again as his mirrors showed nobody running in pursuit or hauling a phone to dial triple nine.

'See? Nobody's going to help you. You're all alone in the world, you bitch.'

Twenty minutes down, he took a turn into a side street that was coated with brick dust. It dead-ended at a set of iron gates that led into a partially built housing estate. There were heavy machines parked within, the darkness giving them the appearance of frozen yellow dinosaurs. He turned in the road and parked with his ass close to the gates, so he could see anyone who came down the street. The dashboard clock said it was 00.32. He felt as if he'd been up and running all night.

The silence after he cut the engine was both welcoming and eerie. He looked round at the woman in the back. She had been sliding around on the slick floor, but had now rooted herself by clamping her good hand around a bracket that held a small fire extinguisher against one wall. Her head was resting on a wheel arch as if it were a pillow. Even in the dark, he could see her eyes were groggy, but focused on him.

She spoke, her words mumbled, like those of someone drunk. He worked it out after trying the same sentence on his own tongue, quietly. Her query: what did he intend to do with her? 'I'm taking you to get help,' he lied. Her head slipped off the wheel arch and clanged on the floor. She must have been using energy to keep her skull propped, and now had none left to do so.

Just then, headlights. Nate stiffened, feet moving towards the clutch and accelerator, hands towards the gearstick and ignition key.

A police car.

He quickly buttoned up his jacket to cover the red bloodstain all over his white shirt. The car slipped towards him like a shark and pulled up alongside, passenger side to passenger side, and the window came down. Nate powered down his own passenger window. A lone cop, forties, hi-vis jacket. He was bent down so he could look up at the taller vehicle, and Nate had to sit up straight to look down. He made sure he kept low enough to hide the stained portion of his shirt above the neck of his suit jacket. He waited for the guy to recognise him as a wanted man, then for all hell to break loose.

It didn't happen.

'Don't park here, pal,' the cop said. Nate kept his mouth shut to hide his smashed teeth and gave a thumbs-up. He started the engine, moved slowly away. In his mirrors he saw the cop car turn in the road. Now would come a slow pursuit as the cop followed to work out where he was going, all the time keeping up a commentary with his base. Other cop cars would converge on Nate somewhere down the line, and once he was surrounded, they'd attack.

Nate indicated left at the end of the street, already thinking about finding a place where he could leap out of the van and run. He was holding his breath. As he turned, the cop car slid into view through his passenger window.

It was at the kerb, reversing into the nice spot at the gates that Nate had chosen. Then it stopped and the lights went off.

He breathed. Just some cop who'd shifted Nate so he could have the area to himself to while away a boring night shift. Nate drove on.

The woman was sitting up now, but couldn't keep her head up. Like a tired baby's, it kept lolling. She was muttering incomprehensible stuff that Nate figured might be her native language, which sounded Turkish. Or it was just noise. At least she wasn't screeching any more.

Then she keeled over and was silent. Her head hit the floor hard, right where the laceration was, and started bleeding again. For five minutes, he kept glancing round at her as he drove, just to make sure it wasn't some trick. Busted arm or not, she could be across the van in a second and lay her hands around his neck. Didn't happen. She didn't move, and her eyes were closed. He felt bad seeing her face in a pool of her own blood, but didn't want to touch her.

And then he had to. Fifteen minutes later, he found a desolate side street and parked, and took his stolen knife from his inner jacket pocket. He stepped between the seats and into the back. He had to stoop because of the roof.

'Do you need help?' he said. She didn't respond. He stepped forward and nudged her head with his foot. Nothing. Then he bent and picked her head up by the hair. There was a ripping sound as her face came away from the drying blood on the metal floor. The wound started leaking again. It looked more ragged than earlier, maybe because of what he'd just done, or because she'd been rag-dolled in the crash.

'I'll get you help,' he said.

Eight minutes later he was parked outside a late-night chemist's, wondering if this was a good idea. It meant leaving her alone in the van. And it meant risking someone seeing the blood on his shirt. But he had no choice.

He rushed into the shop and collected supplies. The young clerk didn't look up from what she was doing, even when he dumped his goods on the counter. While she worked the till, a mobile phone laid beside it, he went to the door and looked out. The back doors of the van weren't wide open, so at least his prisoner hadn't escaped.

He was outside a minute later, and just in time. As he stepped onto the pavement, one of the van's back doors slammed open. The girl was right there, kneeling on the edge, looking as if she'd woken after a deep sleep. He rushed over and jammed a palm into her chest, toppling her backwards. He slammed the door and prayed nobody had seen–

'Hey.'

A shout from up the street – she'd been exposed for only a second, dead of night, but of course some asshole had spotted her. Nate spun and, sure enough, three black guys loitering on a corner about forty metres away were staring at him. One was on a pushbike, the other two leaning against a car. The two on foot started running this way while the cyclist tried to find his pedals.

Nate jumped in the driver's seat, started the engine, and tore out of there. The guy on the bike, after a slow start, had overtaken his pals and was just feet behind the van, then alongside before Nate could get the vehicle up to speed. But the guy seemed to have no clue what to do next and soon fell back. Nate watched all three receding in the wing mirror, still chasing, and didn't let out a breath until he'd turned the next corner. Even then he could still hear them shouting for him to stop. Because that always worked.

Then he heard movement in the back and turned his head to see the girl clambering to her feet against one side of the van. About to come at him. He twisted the wheel hard and she stumbled across the floor, falling, slamming her head hard into the other wall. She lay still after that.

He drove for fifteen minutes, then parked down yet another dark side street. This time he slipped on a knuckleduster before climbing into the back. The girl was awake, woozy, lying on her side and dipping a finger into her blood on the floor, and sucking it slowly free before repeating the process.

She said something as he approached, but the words were again incomprehensible.

He showed her what he had bought. Painkillers, plasters, superglue, and bottled water. There were more goodies in his pocket, but she wasn't allowed to see those. 'You don't deserve this stuff.'

She looked at him, then back at her finger. Dipped it in the blood. Slowly pulled it out. A little game to amuse a brain whacked back a few developmental stages.

He said, 'If you try anything while I'm doing this, I'll let you bleed.'

She rolled onto her back as if to show her willingness to be compliant. He approached cautiously, holding up the fist wearing the knuckleduster, just so she'd know he was serious.

She stared at his face as he closed the wound on her temple with his fingers and superglued it shut, then covered it with two plasters. He tried not to meet her eyes, but couldn't help it when he sat her up and fed pills into her mouth and held a bottle of water for her to drink from. *If she says thanks,* he thought, *God knows what I'll do.* He had considered her a beast in human form and any kind of humanity from her would fire his guilt chip. She said nothing, thankfully.

When he was done, she lay back down, gave a slight smile, and said something. It was blurred again, but he was sure it was something like: *Making me healthier so I can kill you, eh?*

He drove aimlessly. He had no plan and his head was too hazy to even begin to think about one. He needed to sleep, but that was a risky idea. But he couldn't drive all night.

He tried, but soon had to give up. He found a quiet spot near a small river in an empty spot of land behind a go-kart track. He hadn't paid attention to where he was going and had no idea which part of London this was. But it was away from civilisation and would do for the night.

The moment he turned off the engine, the remnants of his energy fled like rats from a sinking ship. That was him: a sinking ship.

His neck seemed to lose all input from the brain, and his head fell forward as if his spine had suddenly evaporated. It was an effort to raise his head again, and when he did it flopped backwards. He stared at the roof of the van. For some reason he thought about Artex ceilings and ashestos.

He went out, but not for long. When the world swam into

focus, he jerked around, one arm raised defensively, as if he were just in time to deflect a killing blow. But the girl was not standing over him with a knife and a sneer. She was lying in the back, shrouded in darkness.

Punching.

On her left side, with her right arm, the bad one, thrusting in and out like a boxer's jab, the fist clenched. Fast, hard.

He realised she was asleep.

He watched for a few seconds. Repetitive, like a cycle: in and out, in and out. Then, like a toy whose battery was fading, her arm slowed and stopped, and she curled into a ball with both arms against her chest. And was still. A strange dream acted out, Nate figured.

So, he closed his eyes again. And sleep came. He felt it pulling him down, pulling him into himself, condensing him as if he had a vacuum for a stomach. The feeling of slipping away felt good. *God, if only he could do this every night.*

Before he went out completely, he hoped that the morning might bring a clear head, and some answers. But mostly he hoped he'd wake back at home, and could tell his brother all about his horrible dream of fire and mutilation and death.

When his eyes opened, the van was still dark. If he'd slept, it had been jagged, sporadic. The girl had moved and was now on her front, lying on that busted arm. Not faking it, then. No way she'd choose a pose that surely hurt her.

He avoided looking at the dashboard clock. It would only piss him off if he realised only a short amount of time had passed. The same if he saw that it was nearing dawn, because his head hadn't cleared yet and he needed to be fit and well come morning, even though he had no idea yet what the next day was going to bring. Ignorance, then, was preferable. So he closed his eyes again.

He thought about training sessions. Lifting weights and how it felt afterwards, moving limbs no longer laden. Like everything was light, free, like you were weightless. He felt like that now, as if he could float right out of this seat. He felt wide awake. The van was still dark, though. Still early, or late, however you viewed it.

He got up. Floated up. Got up so quick he hit his head on the roof of the van. Walking felt like this after a long run with a rucksack full of sand on his back, a favourite training method back in the day. Like you were empty inside. That was how he felt.

He knelt on the seat and watched the girl. She was sleeping like a log. The dark was sluicing away, everything now grey, and he could see quite well. Alarmingly, her bomber jacket lay under her head as a pillow. She had woken up in the night and stripped it off. He was lucky she hadn't strangled him with it.

Underneath she wore a tight pullover of thin black material that hugged her breasts. It also showed him the strange square-ness to her dislocated right shoulder. The bad arm was hugged close to her chest as she lay on her side.

He sat again and checked himself in the rear-view mirror and saw his eyes. Great black pupils, making him look like a demon. He grinned, showing his jagged teeth, which completed the gruesome image. No more sexy smile from the girl at his local newsagent.

More dirt on his face, somehow. As he spat on his fingers and started cleaning his cheeks in the mirror, he found himself smiling. He felt better. The shakes had gone. The fear had gone.

Unusual, given the amount of paranoia he'd been experiencing. The drugs in his system must have worn off.

'I dreamed I stabbed you to death,' she said.

He jerked round so fast his neck hurt. She still lay on her side, and was staring at him. There was drool on her mouth and on the floor below where it had dripped. Her eyes were open, but heavy. He watched them slide closed, jerk open, then slide shut again. Her breathing became ragged.

Nate lay back and closed his eyes. Now, instead of feeling sleep overwhelm him, he felt as if he were plugged into a charger. Felt energy sparking into existence inside him. No way he could normally sleep, wired like this. But nothing about this night had been normal.

He dreams of being burned alive, and wakes into a nightmare far worse.

The burning part is real, though. It starts in his fingers, moves to his left shoulder, then consumes his face. Terrible fiery pain, surely the reason for the dream.

But over it he hears the purr of an engine, and then becomes aware of the soft vibration of the floor beneath him. His blurry eyes make out walls close by. A vehicle. A van. He is in the back of a van.

And then, somehow, he knows it is an ambulance. Something bad has happened, hence the overwhelming pain, but people with the right training to help have rescued him, so everything is going to be okay.

But that isn't a nightmare, is it?

The walls of the ambulance solidified into blank metal, no windows, no beeping electronic life-saving machinery. So not an ambulance at all. Just some van. He tried to move his arms and realised they were jammed under his back, so he rolled to free them. But then he was on his side, and his arms still didn't move.

A stab of pain from his wrists informed him that his hands were tied. Tied behind his back. He looked down. Bare arms pressed hard against the sides of his bare torso. Bare everything. He was naked.

He struggled to his knees to look around better. The darkness beyond the front windscreen turned the nightmare into a reality. Thick black vertical lines in the black air: trees.

Back of a van in the woods, tied and naked – so, the nightmare.

Now, voices. Muffled, behind him. He turned his head, but behind him was only the blank wall created by the closed back doors. No windows. Voices beyond, from behind the van. He paused and listened. The throbbing pain was vibrating his heart, and the van's engine was idling, but even over these noises he heard one of the voices laugh. That laugh was what slotted the final piece of the jigsaw into place.

Ten seconds ago he had assumed he needed only to lie and wait, and friendly professionals would fix him. Now he knew he had to get moving or unfriendly people would end him.

No way out of the van except by the back doors or the front, and the back exit would lead him right into the hands of the men laughing out there. No-brainer right there.

He slipped between the front seats, eyes searching the land beyond the windscreen. Nothing but darkness and trees. Creepy woods, God knew where, a thousand miles from home for all he knew, ten years after a coma. The driver's wing mirror showed him movement. He knelt on the seat and stared.

Black on black, so barely discernible. But he was sure he was watching two men a few metres behind the van. He heard thudding noises as they rose and fell like men bowing. *Digging,* he thought. It looked like they were digging.

Digging a grave.

He couldn't tackle two men with his hands tied behind his back, and he couldn't open any of the doors with his hands behind his back anyway. Yet, he didn't panic. Nothing to do with the lizard brain, not a fight-or-flight reflex. Just a knowledge that his options were singular. Like being trapped in a maze and facing a single path ahead that must be taken, regardless of the outcome. So, with nothing left to puzzle about, no more options to choose between, his brain got to the business of getting down that path in order to save his life.

Almost calm, he moved so he was sitting in the driver's seat. Now his eyes were accustomed to the darkness, and he could see everything. Standard gearstick, for instance. It was his antidote, his ejector seat, his paramedics all rolled into one.

He'd been a driver most of his life and all the basic movements were in his repertoire, like walking through your own home in the dark. But not this. This was a blind stroll through a stranger's house, and would need finesse and care. He had to visualise the actions in his brain first. Slowly he jammed the clutch down with his right foot, and lifted his left and hooked it over the gearstick like a monkey. Finesse, care. He jerked his foot to the right and back. Felt the gearstick engage reverse. More care and finesse as he swapped feet on the clutch, and then, like a tightrope walker reaching safe hands and a sturdy platform, he let out a loud sigh of relief.

All alien movements until this point, but now the hard part was over. Now light had been shed across that stranger's house. From here on it was just basic driving, and that was all muscle memory, no finesse nor care nor brain visuals needed, and he didn't require his hands, either.

Clutch up fast as the accelerator was pounded down. The idling purr of the engine became a shriek, like an animal stabbed. The shapes in the wing mirror jerked upright. He heard a voice shout something. Then his bare chest slammed into the steering wheel as the van leaped backwards.

He heard the heavy thump of something against the rear doors. A yelp a half second afterwards. The van rushed backwards a few more feet, then the rear dipped and it stopped dead, tearing him away from the steering wheel and throwing him hard into the seat. He heard another shout. In the wing mirror, a black shape pelting alongside the van, growing bigger. If he'd hit the men with the van, it had been only one, because here came the other.

Then he was at the window. A tall guy, stocky, with curly black hair and a thick black beard, and black eyes, although maybe that was a trick of the night. Exactly the kind of face you didn't want to see in the dark woods, especially wearing this guy's angry sneer.

The driver's door clicked, started to open. He yanked up his legs, toppled left across the centre console, and pistoned his feet outwards, straightening his body. *No way this is going to work*, he thought, even as he did it. But amazingly it did work. A scene right out of a Hollywood action movie. Feet into door, door into body, body onto ground.

But it wasn't over. The man was rising, cursing. The naked man sat up, turned, planning to escape into the passenger seat and then – what?

Too late. The guy was back. A hand grabbed his arm. The naked man pulled back, then thrust his head forward, striking his assailant hard in the nose. Down went the assailant again.

But the vice-like grip on his arm was still there, so the assailant had a passenger for his journey to the ground.

Before the guy under him could even start to struggle, the naked man pulled back and then thrust his head forward. All lizard brain this time, fight or flight, the amygdala forcing a reaction before his nervous system could even register the continued danger from a man who'd avoided Hollywood unconsciousness. Three quick headbutts, like a woodpecker, and it was all over. Over even before the naked man realised it was.

And the guy was out this time. On his back, one arm above his head, the hand clutching a short blade. Other arm tucked awkwardly under his back. The naked man rolled off and got to his knees. Heart thudding, breath rasping out of him. Then he started to relax, because the way that guy's arm was awkwardly bent under him was a sure sign the guy wasn't faking.

Then he remembered: two of them. The panic rose again, like bile. He struggled to his feet and staggered away, curving a semi-circle so he could angle himself to look behind the van, to give himself a second or two to think if the other guy came dashing out. He knew he should have turned, should have bolted, but he just couldn't turn his back on that dark area behind the van.

The van had hit a tree. Actually, not quite. Between the tree and the van, there he was, an unmoving black shape jammed there in a funny sideways position, as if he'd been caught as he turned to dart aside. Jammed real tight, so he was going nowhere, unconscious or not.

The heart calmed. The breath slowed. Danger over. For now. But he felt no better for it. One moment all had been fine in his life, and the next he was naked, tied up, and facing violent death and burial in the woods.

Why?

Because the danger was apparently over, the flood of adrenaline became just a trickle, and his calming brain got back to the business of sending a blizzard of pain signals. Fiery, overwhelming, inescapable. And with it, a lucid thought that he had to get out of here. But not while still tied up.

He found a rock jutting from the ground and sat over it, and used a sharp edge to cut the binds around his wrists. A cable tie. Effective, easy to apply, but just thin plastic, easily sawn through.

He looked at his throbbing fingers, putting them close to his face because it was dark, and went to the van to check his face and shoulder. Fingers: tips raw and red, prints burned away, maybe by acid. Shoulder: skin missing, flesh scoured rare, his old shoulder tattoo now a ragged mess with just fragments remaining. Face: bashed up, dried blood all around his mouth and his teeth broken, seemingly all of them, making him look like some horror film zombie after feeding on flesh. The pain was no surprise in light of this.

All his distinguishing marks gone. Clearly his kidnappers had wanted his body to yield nothing identifying should it be found out here.

Before he could dampen it, a bloom of anger sent him striding back to the unconscious guy on the forest floor. And with beautiful timing, because the guy was coming round, beginning to move and moan. Three hard stomps to the face, all rage-fuelled, sent him back into dreamworld.

Then the rage was gone, and in its place was again the urge to get the hell out of here. The guy jammed behind the van was not moving. He couldn't see the face because the head was lolling towards him and he wore a baseball cap. But that guy was going to offer no threat, even if he came round. He was wedged nice and tight.

He returned to the other guy and stripped him. It felt wrong, but being naked was worse. Training shoes, tracksuit bottoms, and a bomber jacket. All a good fit and in good nick, except that the jacket had blood all over the front from the guy's crushed nose and lips. Dark colours, good for a man who needed to be invisible in the night. And he needed to be – that was a feeling he couldn't shake.

In the jacket pockets he found two wallets, an economy Nokia mobile phone and a rusty knuckleduster. The phone got his immediate attention, but it had no signal out here in the woods. The first wallet was the guy's. No identification inside, just eight ten-pound notes and a crumpled receipt for a sandwich from a Tesco store. The second wallet was his own. Everything there, even the cash: nearly a hundred pounds in notes and coins. His driver's licence had a big dirty thumbprint on it, as if the guy had held it close to scrutinise it in the dark. Maybe to check they had kidnapped the right guy. But what did this pair of bozos want with a lowly security firm owner called Nathan Barke?

Nate transferred all the cash to his own wallet and dropped the other one and the knuckleduster into the dirt. Then he picked up the weapon again. He was loath to discard it, although he didn't know why he felt the urge to keep it. But he was reminded of that old saying about it being better to have a gun and not need it. So, the knuckleduster went back into one of the bomber jacket pockets.

Now to get the hell out of here. Since he didn't know where he was, how far from home, he decided to use the van. The engine had stalled after he'd crashed into the tree – and the other guy, of course – but while it started again, it wouldn't move. The nearside rear wheel was floating over one edge of the grave the men had dug, and the grounded wheel couldn't get enough traction to propel the vehicle forward. It just spun in the mud.

So much for that. He got out and looked around. Nothing that hinted at the way out, except for the van's tyre tracks. At least he could follow them and find a road.

They cut a semi-circle and then a straight path for a short

while, then turned left to go around a ditch filled with junk, then onwards again in the same direction. By this time he could hear traffic ahead, and this buoyed his spirits. Traffic meant people, and people meant help.

He exited the woods through a gap in a fence at the treeline, onto a busy road running left and right. He was about to flag down a car when he spotted a petrol station across the road, sixty or so metres to his right. It had a skip in the forecourt, where builders had been fixing part of the roof that had come down. He knew this because he knew that petrol station.

Putney Heath, Wandsworth. The men who'd kidnapped him had tried to bury him just a few hundred metres from his home.

His heart soared one second: he was close to home. Then deflated the next: being so close to home might mean the kidnappers had snatched him from the house. But home was shared with his brother, Pete, and they ran their security business from it.

What if they had targeted his brother, too?

Certain that the danger was far from over, Nate emerged slowly from the woods that surrounded Putney Village, eyes everywhere, seeking strange vehicles or pedestrians. He calmed his impatience. Home was now only a sixty-second walk away, but he couldn't afford to just go running there. Not while he was uncertain whether the two kidnappers had been acting alone.

The road was empty. No lurking pedestrians or cars parked in the shadows. He relaxed. Sixty seconds and he could be at home with Pete, kettle on the go. He spat on his hands and rubbed at his mouth to remove dried blood. He flattened his hair with a wet palm. He scraped dirt from the backs of his hands. Wouldn't be good to have the neighbours see him unkempt. He checked his handiwork in a car's wing mirror, decided he looked okay, and set off.

He made the turn onto his street with a casual walk, hoping to look like just some guy heading home after a routine day that didn't involve nearly getting killed.

And stopped dead.

The street contained large houses behind lawns and walls, and driveways barred by ornate gates. And was usually very quiet at night. Not now.

Some of his neighbours were on the street, all staring towards his house, some fifty metres along, near the corner. There was a guy on a motorbike by the side of the road and a car a short way ahead, near the crowd, both probably having turned down this street and found their way ahead blocked. The whole street was blocked. Outside his gates, filling the road, were emergency service vehicles, lights flashing like a vast alfresco disco. All three types. Police, ambulance–

And fire.

Now he noticed, even in the dark sky, great plumes of smoke rising into the air from above the trees that mostly hid his house from view. He stepped into the road, closing on the ragged back row of the people massed on the street. His legs wobbled as he caught a view of his home through the trees. He saw a blackened, busted window, and more smoke foaming out of it. He could hear the roar and crackle of fire gorging.

His house was burning.

The right thing to do was rush forward, barge through the crowd, grab someone in a uniform and tell his story. The police would take him aside, explain what they knew, ask questions, and soon this would all be cleared up. But he didn't do that.

Instead, Nate had a great urge to get away, even if it meant not yet finding out if his brother was alive, if his house was salvageable. He didn't know why. But he knew he needed to get away and come at this thing from a new angle. Some animal instinct deep within that wouldn't be denied, maybe.

So, he took a step backwards, and that was when a motorcycle with a black-clad rider swerved in front of him. It was the bike that had been parked at the side of the road. The rider flicked up his visor and Nate saw young eyes staring at him beneath curly blond hair pressed flat against his forehead by the helmet.

'Nathan, thank God you made it. Get on quick before they spot us.'

'Who?' Nate said. He was frozen on the spot, shocked by the appearance of this guy like a spectre. How did the man know his name? How did he know Nate would be here, outside, watching his own home burn to nothing?

'Quickly!' the guy barked. 'Before it's too late. They're going to kill you.'

The guy's eyes were full of fear, and that decided it for Nate. He didn't know this guy, but so what? He could find out that much once they were a mile or so away from whatever threat the guy thought was out there.

So, he swung a leg over the back of the bike and hugged the guy's chest with under hooks, and squeezed tight as the bike leaped forward, turned, and shot off. At the end of the road it swung a right and roared away.

'What's going on? Who are you?' Nate shouted into the back of the guy's helmet as they rushed by trees on their left and more houses on the right. In seconds the houses were gone and it was all trees, which blocked the moonlight and made the world dark. Back into the alien world. Nate realised then that the bike's headlamp wasn't on. He could barely see the road ahead, but the guy seemed to know where he was going.

'Someone with the same problem as you, Nathan,' the guy yelled back.

Before he could wonder where they were going, or how this guy knew what the hell was going on, the bike stopped. Fifteen seconds' riding. The guy pulled into the side of the road just before a junction, at a lay-by sheltered by overhanging branches like a canopy. There were no people or cars around, which Nate knew was always the case with this part of the village this late.

He hopped off the back and moved away. 'So, you know what's going on? That was my house burning. What do you know about it?'

The guy got off and removed his helmet. He was a good-looking guy with floppy blond hair and big white teeth, like a surfer. Maybe early thirties. 'I know it was your house,' he said. 'The people who set fire to it are the same ones who kidnapped you.'

'How do you know that?' Nate said, still wary. He took another step back.

The guy took a step back also, maybe just to reassure Nate, and pulled out his mobile phone. 'Just wait a moment, Nathan. I'm here to help you survive the night.' He typed a number into the phone and stepped further back.

Nate's eyes were seeking exits. The trees seemed the best bet, but he really didn't want to go back into the woods. Not now, not in broad daylight, not ever again.

'My brother, I think he was at home. Where is he? Is he okay? Who were those men and why did they kidnap me? I think I was drugged.'

'You *were* drugged, Nathan. And your brother is fine. I'll explain everything, but first I need to make this call so we can both get out of this city alive.'

'We need to go to the police. They burned my house. My brother might be kidnapped as well. They were going to kill me and bury me in the woods. How do you know my brother's fine? Tell me.'

'I know, Nate, I just know. Trust me. We'll be in a police station within twenty minutes and we'll meet your brother after that. But we won't get there alive if I don't make this call. Just a moment.'

Nate took another step back, away, and his feet hit the kerb. The guy was twenty feet away now. Holding his phone to his ear. One arm resting on his hip. Definitely not looking like he was about to launch himself at Nate. So Nate relaxed. Nothing else he could do right now but wait. He sat on the kerb, dropping hard onto his ass like a man who'd just finished a hard day's work dropping onto a comfy sofa. He let out a long, ragged breath. *Here to help, remember that.*

And right then the phone in his pocket started vibrating.

The one he'd taken from the kidnapper.

He looked at the biker, and the guy nodded at him, held up a finger as if to say *just a moment*. Nate's heart sank, and his fear rose. His eyes found the exits again. Surely this was a coincidence… Surely the biker couldn't be ringing the kidnapper's phone…

Nate slipped the old phone out of his pocket and, holding it low and shielded by his body, looked down at the screen without moving his head. It continued to vibrate in his hand. A number was listed there, but no name. He pressed the green button to answer the call. He prayed he was wrong.

The biker rubbed his nose, as if to hide his moving lips. Then Nate heard a low, tinny voice come from the phone.

'Damar, it's your lucky day because I just love to hear a nice fuck-up story. So, why don't you tell me how a dead man with his hands tied and his balls hanging free managed to get the fuck away from you?'

A dropping feeling, as if the ground had collapsed below him. The horror was real, then. Nate looked at the biker, who winked at him, surely a move designed to calm him, let him know everything was going to be okay. This guy was one of them, one of the men after him. But how had he known that Nate had escaped the others' clutches? Or had he been watching the house? Just sitting there and enjoying his team's handiwork, when along came the last man he ever expected?

The biker turned away, still with the phone to his ear.

From the phone: 'He turned up at his fucking house, Damar. Smartly dressed and not tied up and not dead. If I hadn't been there, he'd be talking to twenty cops right about now. What the fuck happened?' A pause. 'Hey, you there?'

The biker turned back to Nate. 'No answer yet from the people who are going to help us get through this, Nathan,' he called over. Nate heard his voice from two sides. 'I'll just be a moment and then we'll go to the police.'

Phone: 'Damar, is something wrong?'

Nate pressed the button to kill the call, his mind racing, his heart in his throat.

The biker looked at his phone, anger on his face, and put it away. He looked up and down the street. Still no-one around. He started walking towards Nate.

'Hey, my men will know where my phone is, and they'll track it and be here soon. We need to get off the road. Into the woods.'

Nate fought the urge to scramble to his feet. He didn't want to spook this guy before he got himself into a better position to flee. The guy stopped close and held out a hand to help him up.

'Okay,' Nate said. He slid the phone into his pocket, and left his hand in there. Suddenly the fear was gone. He knew what he had to do, and the knowing, somehow, made it seem easier. Single path in a maze. Nate took the helping hand and was yanked to his feet.

'Look, I found something that might help the police work out what's going on. Maybe you know what this is.'

He fumbled in his pocket. The biker's head bent forward, eyes on the pocket, mind all over Nate's words. What could Nate have found? Evidence that implicated him?

Nate pulled his hand out fast, twisting his body slightly to that side to hide the item until it was ready to be shown. Then he twisted the other way, purely to generate momentum, to pack mechanical energy into the knuckleduster that he powered forward with all the force in his shoulder. It was a devastating blow that sent a wave of pain along his forearm and hurt his elbow. So much so that he knew it was a done deal. Game over. The biker's head snapped backward and he went down so quick that he was a crumpled mess on the tarmac before Nate's arm had finished its swing.

He ran through the trees, knowing that the bike would never catch him. It could slip by the trees and negotiate the under-growth, but not with the dexterity that he was slaloming. Half a minute's running and he emerged onto an open space. Putney Heath cricket ground. He stopped to think. To the north, the area of Putney Heath where he'd been scheduled for burial, back west, past the village, was Richmond Park. South lay Wimbledon Common. A lot of nice hiding places if he so chose, but curling up in a bush that would get him no closer to finding out what the hell was going on.

And finding out if his brother was alive.

He needed to get to a police station. There were policemen swarming around his house, of course, but going back that way was not an option. The biker had been waiting there, maybe just to watch the show, or maybe in case Nate returned – which he had. Who knew how many other men were scattered around, waiting for him to show up? He had no idea how many people were involved in this, but it was too risky to assume it was just the three he'd met. So home was not an option. Hell, home didn't exist any longer.

Wandsworth Police Station was not much more than a mile west of here. Nate had been there once to retrieve his lost car keys, which some kind soul had found and handed in. It was good to know there were decent people around.

There had to be police cars around, too, surely at least one or two floating about somewhere closer than a mile away. Putney Village itself might be nice and pleasant, but this was still London at night, even though he'd once read that Wandsworth was the safest borough in all of London. Or was it just inner London?

Regardless, there would be cops about, and he needed one. His best bet was to keep going west. He'd meet the A219 soon enough and could jaunt south to the Tibbets Corner junction of the A3, and once there he'd surely happen upon a cop car before long. Or he could just flag down a driver for help. Or he could smash a window and wait for the cops to come get him. But first, get the hell off Putney Heath.

So, back into the cover of trees. His thudding heart was just fear and adrenaline, then, not exertion because he ran fast. He emerged from the woods into shrubbery and immediately ducked, holding his breath. There was a man directly ahead, also in the shrubbery, just three or four metres ahead and staring straight at him.

Nate's fingers clutched tightly around the knuckleduster. He must have pulled it from his pocket without thinking about it. Was this guy one of their team? How the hell could they have known where he would exit? How many were there?

Cars were zipping past along the northbound two lanes, which would have covered the noise of his exit from the trees. But then the cars vanished and the road was quiet, and he heard a strange rustling noise.

The guy ahead, a dark shape in the night because he was partway between two street lamps, turned and walked away. Nate raised his head slightly and saw the guy approaching a car parked in the bus lane. It was a taxi. As the driver turned sideways to walk around to the driver's side of his car, Nate saw him fiddling with the zipper on his trousers. The guy had been taking a piss in the bushes.

Nate pulled his wallet, waved it and shouted to get the guy's attention. A minute later he was in a warm seat, listening to the radio, his tale told. Since it was a Friday night, he'd been out on a stag-do with friends and had gotten lost. And beaten up. Lost guys should rendezvous at the junction where Wandsworth High Street met Putney Bridge Road, he'd been told. He didn't want to mention that he needed the police station, which was just off that junction. The driver accepted his story, or didn't, and cared only about accepting his fare. Either way, the guy drove, and that was all that mattered.

The warm seat hugged him. He felt his eyes start to close. He didn't fight it. Brain all mushy, straight thought impossible, body feeling twice its own weight – a little sleep would be nice. The bad guys couldn't get to him here.

He jumped as he felt the phone vibrating in his pocket.

The same number as before. The biker calling again, but

perhaps this time trying to reach Nate because he knew what had happened to his comrades.

He felt a wave of fear, then damped it down. It was a phone. The guy wasn't about to reach through it and grab him around the throat. There was no harm in answering the call, and he might be able to get some information from the guy.

He pressed the button to answer the call, but said nothing.

'Nathan, what's going on?' the biker said.

So he knew Nate had the phone. Nate said nothing.

'You can't go running about on your own. They'll get you, Nathan. Where are you? I hear a radio, so I'm thinking you're in a car.'

Nate said nothing. He looked at the driver, who was just watching the road.

The biker laughed. 'Fair enough, Nathan. You worked it out. Yeah, I'm one of the bad guys. How did you get away? And get my man's phone?'

Nate said nothing.

'Keep running, Nathan. That's all you can do, because you can't go to the cops on this one. Give it up now because we'll get you sooner or later, and later will be worse for you.'

Nate said nothing.

Angry now: 'Okay, Nathan. You just keep running and we'll keep tracking you.'

He remembered the biker's words about phone tracking. Nate killed the call and took the battery out, then snapped the phone in his hands and tore the sim card in half. He didn't know if the kidnappers had the ability to track this phone, but he wasn't going to take that chance. He saw the driver looking at him, puzzled, but the guy said nothing. Not his business.

Nate stared out the window. When the trees on both sides ended and gave way to civilisation, he relaxed a little and cleared bad thoughts from his mind. They were leaving Putney Heath behind, finally. He wound down his window and tossed the phone pieces away. He put his head back, trying to think.

Can't go to the cops. What did that mean?

The radio was a low chatter of background noise against his racing thoughts. But when Nate heard Putney Village mentioned, he perked up and turned up the volume.

'Hey, you don't touch,' the driver said. He moved to turn the volume down, but Nate grabbed his hand. He cut off the next protest in mid-word by slapping a £10 note into the driver's hand. Cash and protests were gone two seconds later.

Breaking news on a Wandsworth radio station: *'...receiving reports now, some from residents there, that a mansion is burning on Bakersfield Crescent, Putney Village. People at the scene claim the police believe it's a suspicious fire, started deliberately...'*

Deliberately? Nate felt the nails of one hand dig into the back of the other. A fire started on purpose?

'...apparently, police are questioning residents about the owner of the house, who was seen driving away in the few minutes before witnesses saw smoke emerging from the mansion...'

Seen driving away? Nate understood. His last memory before waking up in the van: he had been heading out of the house. He must have taken his car, which meant the kidnappers must have captured him out on a street somewhere. Pulled him over, maybe, and dragged him out and folded him into the van.

'...neighbours heard a car racing away fast...'

Dear God. Now he remembered. He and Pete had had an argument and Nate must have stormed out of the house in anger. All still vague memories because of the drugs in his system, but the story was there. Pete had made him a drink and Nate had thrown it at him, and knocked over the kitchen table in anger, and then thumped out of the house. He remembered a sound of screeching car wheels, the G-force as the car turned fast out of the driveway. But surely the police couldn't think that he had–

'...*wish to trace Nathan Barke, forty-two, of Bakersfield Crescent, Putney Village, with an eye to providing answers about the possible cause of the fire...*'

And there it was. Undeniable. Nate felt bile trying to claw its way up his throat. This was what the biker had meant. Some witness at the scene had told the cops that Nate had driven away from the house just before it caught fire, and now they thought he might have been responsible. That he had burned down his own house.

'*The public are advised to report if they have seen this man or know where he might be, but not to approach him...*'

Not to approach? Every time the police said 'not to approach' someone, it was because that person was considered dangerous.

Nate couldn't prevent it. He jerked forward, opened his mouth, and splashed vomit all over his trousers and the floor of the taxi.

The driver was screaming at him, but Nate couldn't hear anything more than senseless noise, because his mind was overwhelmed with one thought. He had no memory of what had happened in the house in the moments before he fled in anger, but he knew one thing: he had been with his brother, Pete.

So where was Pete?

The driver stopped the car and told him to get the hell out, and Nate was glad to. He paid the soiling surcharge to make sure no police got the story, and heartily apologised. The driver pulled away with a long honk of his horn, whatever that was supposed to achieve.

Nate was on Wandsworth High Street, a few hundred metres

away from the police station. But it might as well have been a million miles, because that place was out of the question now. No way he was going to the cops while they considered him an arsonist.

He was near St Thomas à Becket Catholic Church, and there was a left turn onto Santos Road just ahead. He took it. Anything to get off the main road and away from people. He had a horrible feeling that someone was going to recognise him and call the cops, and he didn't want the police around until he knew more about what was going on. A tale of kidnappers wouldn't go down well unless he had proof.

Santos Road was lined with three-storey Victorian double-fronted houses and he walked the pavement looking at each of them, not really sure what he was seeking until he saw it. A sign in a window saying 'Cedar House rooms available' in neon.

The jacket he'd stolen was dark and the bloodstain on the front had dried, so now it simply looked as if the garment was dirty. He sniffed it, but didn't think the odour was clearly that of blood. That meant no-one else would recognise it, either. He straightened his hair and clothing. He could see that his earlier attempts to clean his hands of mud hadn't been adequate, and had to spit and rub again. It hurt his raw fingertips. Then he tried to clean his face again, again using a wing mirror to see if he'd done a good job. Any damage to his gums when his teeth were being broken had been minimal because the wounds hadn't bled again.

No-one answered his knock, but the door was unlocked. He stepped into a hallway with a child gate barring access beyond an inner door. A tiny bell rang and a middle-aged lady in pyjamas and slippers materialised from a doorway in the hall. He held up four ten-pound notes.

'Wife booted me out. Argument. Need one night, no breakfast. I'll go straight to sleep.' He spoke as best as he could without moving his lips, to hide his animal teeth.

If she saw, she didn't care. She snatched his money like a monkey grabbing a sweet, but after that was slow and precise about making him fill out a form, and show his driver's licence, and if she saw the bloody thumbprint on it, well, she didn't care about that, either. Formal lark done, she plucked a key off a row of them on pegs and rubbed it on her pyjama trousers before handing it over, but didn't let her end go until she'd run through the rules: no visitors, no TV after one in the morning, and if he had to smoke, it was in the backyard and he'd never be welcome here again if he stubbed out his fag end in one of her plant pots. He promised to be a good boy and thanked her and went up to his room.

He didn't even check out the room, or even turn on the light. In the dark he crossed to the window and stared out over a leafy garden. Similar houses beyond the backyard blocked his view of everything, which was good. If he could see London, it would remind him of his predicament, and he didn't want that. He wanted to sleep and tackle his problems with a rested brain and sun-warmed cheeks. The houses helped him feel locked in and contained and secure.

So he lay on the bed, fully clothed. No way he was going to undress when he didn't know what might happen. He wondered if he'd ever be able to undress again. Maybe it was now a phobia.

That thought brought a rare smile to his lips.

The bedside clock had glowing green digits. Almost ten o'clock.

It also had a radio, which he turned on. He spent some time dialling through channels, and soon he found what he wanted. It was a local news program, and, with movie timing, it was all about him.

'*...body found inside. A police spokesman said that there are* injuries beyond those caused by fire and that there are suspicious circumstances surrounding the death...'

Pete.

Nate had a strange sinking feeling, as if his bodyweight had just tripled. He couldn't move his arms. His head was suddenly hot, as if he'd been holding his breath too long. In the dark, staring at glowing green lights on the clock, his anxiety tripled.

Pete. Dead?

He closed his eyes. Darker than ever, of course, but his lids were like great steel shutters that locked his aching brain away from the horrible world. And it helped. The neon fear instantly started to fade. But only a little.

Pete. Dead.

The next time he looked, the green digits said 11.31. He must have slept, amazingly. He remembered no thoughts or dreams this time, but during his out, his brain must have quietly been working on a plan. Because he sat up with a clear idea of what he had to do. And forget the sun – he knew he had to do it now.

He found the downstairs empty, except for the landlady. Through the living room door he could see the back of her head poking above the backrest of a wide armchair facing a TV. Quietly, he went past and into the kitchen, which had a laminated A4 sheet pinned to the door that said 'GUESTS OFF LIMITS'. The door creaked as he opened it, but since he could hear the TV still, and she was right in front of it, he figured she hadn't heard.

When she didn't come running, he went all the way inside. And straight to a magnetic strip on the wall above a worktop that held knives of varying lengths, all with green handles and all pointed downwards. He selected the middle one, which was long enough to make a good weapon and short enough to hide comfortably in his clothing. As he turned to leave, he saw a mobile phone near the kettle and pocketed that, too.

In order to convince the police he was innocent, he needed proof. The phone he had taken off the bad guy might have worked, if the police could extract information about past calls and texts from it. But in a moment of fuzzy thinking he had tossed the phone away.

However, in a moment of clarity, he had a better idea: a confession. Admissions of guilt – always welcomed by the police.

Before he knew it, he was heading out the door. Scurrying along the deserted street. He could hardly believe he was doing it, as if his body was being controlled by someone else. But doing it he was. Heading back.

Back to his gravesite and the men who had tried to bury him.

'Emergency services, which service please?'

Nate had checked out police procedures for identifying burned bodies and knew that the go-to method was dental records. But the bad guys would have smashed up Pete's teeth, same as Nate's. And probably Pete's face, so any kind of trick with bone-shape recognition was out of the question. Costlier, more time-consuming, was DNA, the last resort. Undeniable. Unless the body was completely destroyed, DNA could be extracted from intact organs, deep in the muscles, the remains of the brain, bone marrow – and from smashed teeth. Pete had had the option during his army days to store his DNA, for identity purposes, but had refused – Nate remembered his brother liking the idea of being the unknown soldier. So Nate didn't think

Pete's DNA was on file anywhere, not even after the HyperX fiasco four years ago. So, the cops would be stuck.

Unless they got help.

'Police. It's about the house fire in Wandsworth,' Nate said quickly, his tone high, a cheap form of voice disguise. 'Tell the police that Pete Barker had sesamoiditis, left foot, piece of bone removed. That will help them identify him.'

Pete. Outwardly, a tough guy. Former Marine army sergeant, heavily muscled from a lifetime in the gym, and tall, and handsome, his curly hair still shiny and his teeth still white despite approaching the big five-O, even though he kept a big beard streaked with grey. A funny guy, even though his wit was all sarcasm, and a hit with the ladies, even though he liked men. But inwardly, still the fragile older brother Nate could remember from as long back as his memories went, prone to all sorts of ailments, always ill with this or that. Always first to get a cold, and last to lose it, easy to cut, with bones that broke under pressure that shouldn't be a problem.

As a teenager, he'd had two spontaneous pneumothoraxes, hypothermia, ulcers, gastric problems, his illnesses reigning and abdicating like kings: always one at a time, but the throne passing from one to the next without pause or gap. Until he hit his thirties, when he started to carry them in two and threes. He was forty-eight and currently had elbow bursitis and nasal polyps, and ragged eczema on his back, but Nate didn't think evidence of any of this would have survived the fire.

But the sesamoiditis, that was different. Missing piece of bone – surely the pathologists could use that defect to help identify a body ravaged by fire. Not concrete proof, but good enough. They thought it was Pete, and if the body had a specific fault that Pete also had...

Better yet, if it didn't...

The operator was asking questions, but Nate hung up. He

bust apart the handset and tossed the pieces into a bin on the forecourt.

Under the crumbling roof of the petrol station, he watched the woods across the road. No movement, but he wasn't sure what he expected to see. Men hiding behind trees, just the whites of their eyes showing?

He had no idea if the police would try to trace the call, or even if they could, or if the woman on the switchboard had even understood enough of his rapid words to contact the people involved. He wasn't even sure his information would do any good. Maybe the authorities had clever, secret technology that allowed all sorts of easy ways to identify a burned body. Just because the cops hadn't yet said they'd identified the dead man, it didn't mean they hadn't. Maybe they were holding off for some reason. He just didn't know. He only knew that he wanted to see a news item tomorrow claiming that the dead man in the house was not Pete, but some other hapless bastard's brother.

And that three men had been arrested.

On the taxi ride here, while googling burned bodies, Nate had been all up for going into those woods and getting a confession from the kidnappers, but not now. He had no idea what he might find within that realm of darkness. If the biker had discovered what had happened to his men, it would mean he had probably been here. Might still be. All three of them, just waiting for him to show up.

But he had to go in. Quickly, he crossed the road and entered the woods some way down from the point at which he'd exited earlier. He moved slowly, keeping low, listening, watching, but seeing and hearing nothing. And he held the landlady's kitchen knife tightly in his hand.

A few minutes later, he saw a patch of white off to his right and moved towards it. Soon that patch of white took on the shape of a van. Nate paused behind a tree. Waited.

No movement. The van was in the same position, and a shape at the back told him the squashed guy was still there, same position, still jammed in nice and tight.

But the other guy had gone.

From this angle, he could see the back of the van and the driver's side, the black hole of the grave, and the empty spot on the ground where the guy who owned the wallet, the phone, and the knuckleduster, had been stomped into oblivion. But that spot was empty.

Maybe the guy had tried to move the van and, like Nate, been unable. Then what? Unable to free his friend, unable to call for help because he had no phone, what had he done? Cut his losses and run? Or was he around here somewhere, maybe off seeking a branch to use as a lever to help unjam his pal?

Nate waited. His head told him ten minutes had gone past. If the guy was still around, he would have returned by now. So, he was gone.

Nate moved forward, slowly. He was wary of the remaining kidnapper. The guy might be awake, might have a gun. He circled around to come in from behind the tree the guy was jammed against, using it as a shield. Ten feet out, he paused, listening. No sounds from the kidnapper. No movement from the arm or leg he could see poking out beyond the trunk.

Nate move past the tree. Careful, distant, just in case. And the guy's head turned and looked at him.

Nate was shocked to see him move, but glad, too. It meant he hadn't killed the guy, and it meant the guy could now tell his story to the police.

Nate was also shocked to see that the guy was no such thing. The guy was a woman.

The ball cap had fallen off. She had neck-length blonde hair and the same dark skin as the other guy – Damar, the biker had called him. Her eyes were dark and her age somewhere in the early thirties. Nathan thought she would look attractive if all spruced up, perhaps in a dress instead of grubby jeans and training shoes, and a bomber jacket like her partner's. He felt a moment of guilt, then slapped it aside. Woman or not, attractive or not, this was one of his kidnappers. His would-be killers. Her good looks were probably used to get men to trust her, like a siren.

Ten feet between them, the girl trapped, but still Nate was wary as he stood there and showed her the knife and said, 'Where's the other guy?'

A slight shake of the head. She barely had the strength for it. She had been lucky: if the van hadn't hit the hole and stopped, it would have crushed her to death against the tree. But she hadn't gotten off unscathed. Nate saw the right arm bent all wrong between her and the back doors of the van, and knew it was maybe broken or dislocated. The space between the tree and the van was slight, maybe eight inches, so there was probably a bad torso injury there, maybe a broken rib or ten. And he could see a big laceration on her temple, which had leaked blood down one side of her face. Luck for her, and some for him, because in this condition she was not going to cause him any problems. His plan to get her to a police station could work. But he needed to get her out of there. Now he wished he'd kept the landlady's phone. He could have called the cops and scarpered while they came to get her.

His fuzzy brain not thinking straight again.

'We're going to the cops,' he said. 'You and me. And you're going to tell them everything. They'll love your confession. So, I've got to get you out of there. Don't try anything once you're free. Understand?'

He showed her the knife again, turning it to try to catch the moonlight, just so she would understand it was sharp and deadly.

The girl shook her head.

'One of us is going to jail for murder, bitch,' he said. 'And let me help you on that one. It's not going to be me.'

He stepped forward and, always watching her, started kicking earth removed from the grave back into it. His plan: fill the hole so the back wheel of the van would have traction. He knew it might take a while.

The girl made a noise. No, not noise. Speech. A word or two. Sounded like she said, *Bring help.*

'This is all the help you've got,' Nate said. 'Just me, the guy you tried to kill. You'd die out here if not for me. Understand? So in return, you'll tell the police why you tried to kill me.' He stopped, glared at the girl, fighting a sudden urge to hurt her. 'And why you killed my brother.'

The girl's head dropped. Too much effort to keep it raised to look at Nate.

Nate continued kicking. Continued to stare at her, in case she was playing possum. Soon he had created a kind of causeway under the van's back wheel, from there to the edge of the hole. Kneeling, he grabbed handfuls of dirt and packed it around the wheel.

He prayed this would work. He jumped in the driver's seat. The keys were still there. He started the engine, put it in first, and gave the accelerator a little push. The van shook and moved slightly, so he pushed the pedal down hard and prayed. And the van shot forward.

He slapped the steering wheel in triumph.

He went back to the girl. Freed, she had tumbled into the grave. She was on her back, that busted right arm bent awkwardly under her waist. She was moaning, and this time it was just noise, not words. The moonlight caught her eyes. Glazed, blank, like a daydreamer's. Concussion, he figured.

Nate stepped into the grave and grabbed her under the arms, which elicited a loud grunt of pain that made Nate feel good. He could smell a battle between body odour and perfume. He dragged the girl out and laid her flat, then opened the back doors of the van. A small light in the roof blinked on, giving a weak grey illumination to everything.

The first thing he saw was his clothing, piled in a corner near the wheel arch. His suit. Somehow he'd missed it before. Seeing it, he suddenly felt dirty in the kidnapper's clothing. He stripped quickly. Naked for a couple of seconds, the trepidation returned, as he'd feared. Then he dressed in his own gear and tossed the kidnapper's clothing into the van. He was going to keep the guy's stuff in case the cops needed DNA evidence. The suit was creased, but not torn or dirty or bloodstained. The shirt, however, was red all over the front, probably blood from his mouth, and some of the buttons had been torn away.

Next, he dragged the girl closer and sat her up, then lifted her, sat her on the edge and pushed her backwards. And there was a little slice of anger in the way he pushed her. No resistance from her as gravity pulled her hard onto the metal floor, cracking her head with a clanging sound. No moan of pain from the blow to the skull, but she yelped when Nate folded her legs inside, which made her roll onto that bad right arm.

He was about to shut the door when he spotted a duffel bag. He dragged it close and opened it. Inside was a newspaper and a clear glass bottle that he assumed was the acid used to remove his fingerprints and tattoo. And a knife, bigger than his own.

And a battery-operated circular power saw. Immediately an image popped into his head. Him, naked, tied, lying unconscious in the grave, but waking with a scream as one of the kidnappers started cutting him with the saw. Had that been their plan, to cut him into pieces before covering him with soil? He shuddered and fought down the urge to pound the woman lying in a heap right in front of him.

A noise from way off. His head perked up like a cat's. It sounded like an engine, and it sounded close. Too close to be on any of the roads around the woods. Inside the woods.

He remembered the words the injured woman had croaked, the only two she'd managed. Not 'Bring help', as in *Please bring me some help*, as Nate had first thought. But 'Bring*ing* help'.

As in my friend is bringing help.

He shut the back doors and ran around to the front of the van, looking everywhere. The engine noise seemed to be all around, as if bouncing off trees, so he couldn't place it.

He jumped into the driver's seat, thankful that no interior light came on when he opened the door.

Ahead he saw a shimmer of black in the woods, a moving blob of darkness coming his way from the north, the route the van had taken. Not some kid out playing on a dirt bike, then. But someone coming here, following the van's tracks.

He bent over the steering wheel, low, and watched through the windscreen, and soon enough the moving blob reshaped into a large motorbike. Not an off-road machine. The machine was dark and the rider was dark, and in the night it would have been impossible for Nate to recognise the guy as the blond biker who'd picked him up, except for one thing.

What meagre moonlight filtered through the trees stood out starkly on the skin of Blondie's pillion, because he was half-naked. Nate had taken his clothing. He could see dried blood all over the guy's chest, but his busted face had been cleaned. The guy called Damar.

Nate clutched the steering wheel hard as the bike entered the clearing and stopped. Five metres away. Nate held his breath, fearful that they might somehow hear his breathing through the van's metal body and over the night noises and the bike's engine.

Then a second bike entered.

This was an off-road machine in bright colours. Nate saw a glowing yellow dragon's eye on each of the handguards and a fiery spiked tongue along the front mudguard, which combined to give the appearance of a face. Again, two men sitting astride the machine. They wore jeans, thick jackets, and black helmets.

Nate could picture how it had all gone down. Blondie, hearing no news from his pals, had returned to a pre-arranged meeting point and waited, and then Damar had arrived with no clothing and a smashed nose, and minus his girlfriend, bearing a sorry tale of how their prisoner had escaped. Blondie had then called in backup, and now here they all were.

Blondie jerked back hard, knocking Damar onto the ground. Clearly the leader of the kill crew, as Nate had suspected. He got off his bike and removed his helmet. The other two guys got off and all four started walking towards the van, with Damar leading the way with a dejected gait, like a man who knows he's in for some suffering soon.

Nate had sat in silence, frozen, praying that these guys would arrive and see the girl was gone, and just turn and ride away. He cursed his stupidity. That damned drug clouding his brain. Of course these guys would investigate the scene thoroughly, and of course they'd want to take back their incriminating-evidence-loaded van. How ironic that he now might end up as buried pieces of flesh after all, because he'd *chosen* to come back here.

His brain reacted before he knew what its plan was. He twisted the ignition key, threw the gearstick, stamped the accelerator, and the van leaped forward. For the second time tonight, the guy called Damar had to dive aside to avoid being slammed by his own vehicle. The two new thugs behind him had a little more time to think, and they darted aside with a little more grace, moving away from each other like parting curtains. Blondie, at the back, had all the time in the world to simply step out of the van's path, and was helped by the fact that Nate had already twisted the wheel to aim the van at the track through the woods.

Someone banged the side of the van as it blew past the kill crew. Then the vehicle was enveloped by trees. Nate slapped on the headlights. Behind him, even over the van's roaring engine, he heard the scream of a bike coming in pursuit. Not Blondie, because he didn't have the right machine for a chase through the woods. A glance in the wing mirror confirmed it: the silhouette of the dirt bike behind him, bouncing over his tracks, a single rider aboard. Nate saw only one black arm on the handlebars, the other raised, pointing at the van. *Gun*, he thought.

The track, some old walking trail, was barely wide enough for the van, and certainly not ample enough to permit the bike to come alongside. But come alongside it did, off to his right, the black shape weaving this way and that to avoid trees, bouncing up and down over fallen branches and other forest detritus. Just three metres away. He saw the guy try to aim his gun, but there were too many trees flashing past and his ride was too bumpy to give him anything but a blind luck shot.

Maybe the guy thought himself a lucky chap, because Nate heard a gunshot, but nothing came of it, or maybe a bird in a tree somewhere fell dead. Another shot, and this time Nate heard a clang on the side of the van. Then two more loud bangs, no clangs, just shredded bird or bark.

Nate remembered the junk-filled ditch just in time, and turned the wheel even before he'd put his eyes forward again. The van's right-side wheels dipped as the ground fell away beneath them, then rose into the air as they bounced off the far side of the ditch. The van rocked as if hit by something heavy. His head smacked the side window. Behind him, he heard a moan as the girl was thrown across the floor and into the side of the van.

Then he was back on the track, nice and neat, and staring ahead at a vertical slash in the trees. The main road. Fifty metres. Nate saw the blip of cars rushing by behind funnels of light.

The gunman was ahead now, but he slowed and turned left, probably having spotted the fence that blocked his path. Nate realised his intention: cut in behind Nate to join the track and use the gateway, since cutting in front would be too dangerous and he wouldn't know which way Nate was planning to turn onto the two-way street, and he wouldn't be able to aim his gun behind him.

Nate aimed straight ahead. A moment before the van blasted through the gateway, he glanced in the wing mirror and saw the black shape of the bike emerge from the trees and take the path just a few metres behind him.

Then the walls of trees were gone and the world was wide open, and Nate was washed in light. Light everywhere. Vehicles rocketing towards him from left and right.

The gunman would expect him to turn, but Nate didn't turn. Too fast for that, and not his plan anyway. He slammed on the brakes. The van skidded across the westbound lane and stopped in the eastbound lane, blocking it. A car bearing down on him skidded with a blare of horn, but the driver was living in a dreamworld if he thought this collision could be avoided.

The blow was hard enough to shunt the van a few feet. Nate barely held onto the wheel hard enough to avoid being wrenched out of his seat as the vehicle tried to jerk away from under him.

Behind him, the gunman had also had to stop, right in the

westbound lane. Shit end of the stick for this guy. Nate got a car, but the gunman got an open-backed van loaded with scrap metal, lots of it. The van's driver crushed his horn and his brakes. Dreamworld.

The cargo van disappeared behind Nate's vehicle. Over the blare of horns and screech of brakes, Nate heard the crunch of a biker having a bad day. Bowling ball and skittle. Out of the passenger window, Nate saw biker and bike go bouncing down the road in a tangled mess, and for sure neither one was going to be fit for purpose after that.

Horns and screeching tyres all over the place now. Pedestrians flocking. Cops and ambulances soon en route. Newspaper columns soon to come. Nate restarted the stalled engine, twisted the wheel, stamped the pedal. He was blasting east seconds later.

When he woke again, the girl was mumbling. But not in pain. Anger. She was sitting up, leaning against the back of the van, feet near the dried puddle of her own blood. And staring at him with clear eyes in a face full of rage. Good job normal people didn't have Superman's laser eye-beams, or he'd be a charred husk right now.

One of her palms was on a wheel arch. Her good hand. Laid there flat, as if she were testing it for heat. Except, she was trying to pluck it free with her other hand. Two fingers moved, but that was it.

Christ. A memory. He had woken in the night again and gone in the back because the girl was stirring. And he had superglued her left hand to the wheel arch so she couldn't bite out his eyes while he slept. He could now see a clear and solid mass all over her skin, in between the fingers, as if she had slapped her hands into jelly.

'Where's my partner?' she said. Now her words were clear, her accent unmistakably foreign but her English good. She was still trying to free her glued hand, but was forced to use her bad arm and couldn't work the fingers very well or generate much power.

He tried to stand and smacked his head again. This time he caught the rear-view mirror. He slapped it in anger and by chance it flicked into a position that allowed him to see his face. Normal eyes now. Pupils no longer like dinner plates. Fully charged body. Back to normal, it seemed. Apart from his smashed teeth, of course. There was a spot of blood on his lower lip, maybe from catching it on his own teeth. He took mouthfuls of water from one of the bottles he'd bought and spat until the water was no longer tinted pink with blood. It took six. He felt happy enough to swallow numbers seven, eight, and nine.

'Hey! Where is he?' the girl shouted at his back.

Nate knelt on the seat and faced her. There was no sympathy in him. Just anger. 'The imbecile called Damar, you mean? He left you. Left you to rot and ran away.'

'Sure he did. I can't wait until we get to bury you again.'

'Again? You messed that up the first time. And you should forget him and worry about what's going to happen to you. Because you're the only one who will.'

Now, only now, did he notice the bright world beyond the windows. Morning, at last. *Hello, my old friend.* Something he hadn't expected to see ever again. But there it was. Lovely daylight. The world was always a less scary place while the sun shone. Most of the bad people in the world had slunk into dark recesses like insects.

He fished the knife from his jacket and showed her. 'I kept

you alive for a reason. Time for you to earn it. Time to give me some answers.'

He thought he looked all menacing with the knife, and did not expect her response.

She laughed.

'My God, was this why you kidnapped me? Your big plan was to get me to spill all the beans, so you could then go to the police and have them sort it out and you could go back to your life? You idiot.'

Clearly she did not fear the knife, or at least did not fear the man holding it. 'Okay, fool, I'll talk. I'll tell you everything. Ready?'

He didn't speak. Was she serious? Was this a lark? Stalling for time? His head spun.

'Damar, the guy who's going to kill you, asked me to do him a favour. Here's a postcode and a house number. Be there at this time exactly. Sneak into the back of the property without any neighbours seeing. There will be a car with a drugged dickhead in the boot. Drive that car quickly away and bring it to our meeting point, a warehouse in Enfield. I'll meet you there and we'll kill the dickhead and bury him, and go spend £5,000, which was what we were being paid. Then we thought it would be a bit of funny irony to drive you all the way back and bury you five minutes from your house. But first we, er, *carefully* removed your distinguishing features. And you know the rest. And that's it. That's all I know. I don't know who paid Damar to do the job, which means I don't know who torched your house or killed your brother. Sorry, I don't have the kingpin's name and address for you. So that's your great plan out the window. So, what's your next move, cowboy?'

Nate's head throbbed. His assumption that he'd been out driving when he got snatched – wrong. If she was to be believed – and he believed her – then her job had been only disposal. Unknown others, maybe including Blondie and his biker friends, had performed the actual kidnapping and drugging part.

At his home.

It made sense. His last memories before waking naked and tied up had been of being in the house, not out driving. And those memories had been warped. Instead of shouting at Pete, he must have shouted at the intruders who burst in. He must have thrown the glass, not at Pete, but at those guys. They must have tackled him, which had seen the kitchen table knocked over. And as for the memories of driving away: nothing more than the groggy sensation of movement as he rode in the boot of his own BMW.

'You don't have any clue how to proceed from this point, do you? Now your dream is shattered. You're a damn novice. What are you going to do now?' And that damned grin was still there. Before he could stop himself, he was across the van, grabbing her throat. He slammed her head hard into the floor. But even as it connected, her foot came up, heel cracking into his knee, staggering him. He stumbled away and she tried to launch herself at him like an angry pit bull, but her glued hand locked her in place like a leash. Nate leaned against the back of the driver's seat, breathing heavy, ignoring his knee in order to pretend that it didn't hurt. If she thought he was injured, she might try another attack. He didn't think the blow had caused any damage, but it damned well hurt.

Her grin was gone, at least. Anger had taken its place: 'That silliness got you no closer to your brother's killer, did it? Do something productive. Not just trying to attack incapacitated women. Make a move. Don't just stand there looking dumb.

Your brother's dead; you are supposed to be; and whoever set it up is going to get away with it because you don't have a brain or any balls. Do something!'

Just words, he told himself. Words couldn't hurt unless you let them. So, he wouldn't. Unfortunately, he couldn't ignore the content. Had he really expected her to give him the kingpin's name and address, so he could send the cops wailing round there? She was right: he had no idea what his next move should be.

'Unfortunately for you, I used satnav and paid no attention to street names, so I don't remember where the warehouse where we left your car is,' she said. And then she started laughing, her face smug.

He didn't care. She had just unwittingly given him a way forward. His car. It could hold clues. He raised the knife and stepped towards her.

'Don't try anything this time.'

He grabbed her jacket from the floor. She watched like an inquisitive child as he patted it down. Just like Damar, she carried no ID of any kind, but she did have a phone. Of course she did. She and Damar would need to keep in touch. He was thinking how daft he had been to not have already searched for one. She could have called for help. Damned drug addling his brain.

'That's mine,' she hissed as he extracted her mobile.

'I know: it was in your coat.' He pocketed the phone and bent forward to check her hand was still firmly fixed to the wheel arch. The heel of her palm and two fingers had come loose. He took out the vial of glue, bent close carefully, watching her, and dribbled the fluid around the edges of her hand. She didn't try to stop this, or even object. He didn't like that. Did she have an escape plan?

He emptied the last of the glue onto the floor. She watched in puzzlement. While she was in this docile moment, he quickly grabbed her head and twisted it down, slamming it into the floor. Second time. And for the second time, she hit back. This time her bad arm snaked out and her fist got him in the balls. He staggered back again.

'You fucker,' she yelled as she tried to sit up and couldn't. Her hair was caught in the glue. She tried to look at it, and he stepped forward and planted a foot on her wrist, crushing it into the cold metal. Pinned at three points.

His other foot stamped onto her hair, squashing it into the glue. He pulled his foot back before it could become stuck, then bent and placed a palm over her ear and pushed, and kept her head there. She tried to thrash, but her awkward position, with her outstretched left arm bent back because of the height of the wheel arch, didn't allow her to generate much leverage. He held her there until he was sure the glue was dry, then stepped back. She tried to drag her head free, but it clearly hurt too much.

She didn't stop cursing him for a full ninety seconds after he'd retaken his seat. And then only because he said, 'I'll glue those bloody lips together if you don't stop right now.'

She glared at him. He turned sideways on in his seat, feet on the passenger seat. This way he couldn't see her, but would see movement if she got free and came closer. Now, more than ever, he expected her to try to come at him.

'Now sit quietly,' he said, grinning. The grin was false. He was shaken inside. He wasn't used to hurting people, and this was the first woman that he'd been violent towards. It helped to picture a naked and tied-up moment from history. To picture this woman with a spade in her hands.

'You are so dead,' she said, already calmer.

'Looks that way.'

He focused on her phone. Brand new, cheap, and with a spare battery glued to the back. No numbers or addresses stored, and cheap, so just a temporary thing, probably designed to be used last night and then discarded. But a call had been made, just the one. None in, but just that one out. A mobile number with no name. Made a few hours ago.

While he'd been sleeping.

Damar, he figured. She had tried to call Damar, but of course his phone was broken. Why hadn't she called anyone else? She had had a fine opportunity to escape, yet had seemingly given up after failing to reach her friend.

But he put that thought aside. Checking for contacts in the phone wasn't his reason for wanting the device.

She had said she'd used a satnav to find the warehouse. Nate's BMW had satnav. But she had also said that Damar had given her Nate's *postcode*, which meant she had used a route-planning device *before* getting hold of the BMW. Either she had carried a satnav between vehicles, which he doubted, or...

He clicked on a route-planner app in her phone called Traveller and accessed the history. Only two destinations. Nate's postcode was there. But the most recent entry was the one he stared at: Saturn Printworks Ltd. Riverside Street, Ponders End, Enfield. Jackpot. He showed her and said, 'Let's go for a drive.'

'Go to hell,' she said as he clicked on 'revisit'.

'In one hundred yards, turn right,' said the app's female voice.

'That's how ladies should talk,' Nate said to the girl, and she cursed at him again.

In Enfield, ten minutes out from the destination, Nate came

across a McDonald's and used the drive-thru to buy two burgers and two teas. Cash, of course, because a favourite trick of cops hunting fugitives was tracking their bank cards. He had planned to hide his face from the people at the serving windows, but didn't need to bother because they didn't even look at him. Not even when he asked for the free wifi code.

He parked in a far corner of the car park, facing a billboard with a negative photo of a cornflakes box. He stared for a few seconds, then looked down at his phone. Surprisingly, an after-image of the cereal floated across the phone and his legs. A neat advertising trick. When the ghostly cornflakes box was gone, he logged on to the Internet. He typed his own name into the search bar. While the results loaded, he tossed a burger to the girl. It landed near her face.

'How am I supposed to eat like this?' she said.

News items were listed above web pages, and impatiently he clicked the top one. A local Wandsworth paper's online edition. He threw a glance her way and saw she was unwrapping the burger with her free hand.

There was a picture of his burning house, and below the story, bottom of the page, a news ticker crawled along repetitively:

–ire deemed deliberate, body found inside home, police hunting missing local man. Cause of Wandsworth mansion fire deemed del–

A play icon in the picture denoted a video. Nate pressed it. The paused fire came alive.

A video seemingly taken from someone's mobile phone, given the shaky picture and bad sound. One of his sweet neighbours thinking about YouTube hits, maybe. A voiceover: some guy explaining when and what. Then the picture changed as time leaped forward. The voice's owner was at the scene with a microphone. Facing the camera, with the house in the background. The street looked serene now, the crowds gone, the fire gone, but a few emergency services vehicles were still in place, and he could see a large plastic tent across his front door so the crime officers could come and go in peace. Crime scene tape was strung between the driveway gateposts like a giant yellow spiderweb.

The reporter was a pasty-faced young man with a glow in his eyes that said he loved the big-time, now that he was reporting on major stories, not just dogs that could sing or funny-shaped cucumbers. There was a slight grin on his face as he recited the facts: the cops looked with suspicion upon the fact that, of the two people registered as owning the house, one was possibly dead and burned and the other was nowhere to be found.

Nate couldn't deny it now, could he? Before, just rumour. Now, the charge was there in all but official paper. The police thought Nate had killed his own brother, if indeed that body was Pete's. The girl was watching him intently. He couldn't help but glance at her. She had clearly heard the video.

'That's a bit of a pickle,' she said with a grin he wanted to smash off her face.

The reporter introduced someone and the cameraman panned to a cop who had been standing just out of shot, waiting for his moment on TV. The reporter asked him the score. The cop looked nervous, as if knowing his bosses were watching. This guy added little more to the revelations of the news ticker below him. Then the reporter asked what the cops were doing to find Nathan Barke, and the cop said they were trying to locate people who knew Mr Barke, in the hope that someone might know where he was – in other words, *We think this guy's shacked up with a pal, and we're going to search all their houses to find the bastard.* Known friends and employees at Acorn Security, the firm run by Nathan and his brother, were being sought.

Nate was a popular guy with a busy social life. Monday was bowling day, Wednesday was pool night at his local pub, and every second Sunday he and Pete could be found at Filey's restaurant in Whitechapel. A lot of people to chat to. A lot who would say Nate was a stand-up guy, decent, wouldn't hurt a fly. But he wondered how many might give the him a bad review. How many might say, 'Makes sense now, always thought that guy was dodgy, something cold in his eyes...'

He waited for the cop to mention clues given by Nate's friends and employees, but the cop simply said this line of enquiry was in the early stages. Good political answer that answered nothing. Nate took it to mean that they hadn't yet found these people, or that those they had questioned had unloaded nothing of use.

All fine and good and expected, of course. But then the reporter thanked the cop and stepped aside, and the camera panned to follow him, as if the cop could now fuck off, and that was when the bombshell was dropped.

The reporter mentioned that their office had received a call from the parents of one Achala Kaushal just before they came on air. Apparently Kaushal had not returned home from college yesterday evening, and that was very unlike her. No friends had seen her since she'd gotten in her car in the college car park. And her mobile was turned off.

The moment the family had heard about the fire, and heard Barke's name, they became concerned about their daughter's lateness. Because Nathan Barke had once caused her 'mental anguish' and 'threatened her'.

Nate couldn't believe what he was hearing. Achala Kaushal, a young Indian woman, had worked for him for nine months, four years ago. The 'mental anguish' had resulted from a security job she'd been on: the nightmare of HyperX. He had feared that one long-ago night would come back to haunt him. And here it came. The cops would now look into Achala Kaushal, and that meant focusing on Nate's past, and HyperX was lurking back there, about to leap out at them. And when it did, no-one would doubt Nate's guilt. Great.

He remembered Kaushal well. Good worker, but the HyperX thing had mentally battered her and she had soon quit the job. Her parents had blamed Nate and Pete, as her bosses, and threatened to ruin their business. And Nate had threatened them back. Not in the way the reporter had cleverly hinted at in order to captivate viewers and make Nate seem more dangerous. He had simply threatened to kill her job prospects if the family tried to blacken his company's name. Tit for tat. Before last night, the cops would have laughed the Kaushals off the phone for such a complaint. Different now.

'Look on the bright side,' the girl said. 'At least I know you didn't kill her. Take that as comfort.'

The police might think that Nate was two bodies into some kind of kill rampage, but he wasn't concerned about that at the moment. Finally, he had a clue. Achala Kaushal. Missing and presumed hurt, according to the newspapers. Missing and involved in this up to her neck, according to Nate. Four years ago she had been a sweet young lady, innocent, wouldn't hurt a fly, but the HyperX thing had messed her up. Maybe enough so to set her on a violent payback against Nate and Pete even years later. Arson and murder seemed beyond her, but Nate knew nothing about those in her circle. He doubted her family would be calling news stations if they'd had a hand in this lark, but what about someone else? Someone who was immensely protective and loyal and totally unhinged in the head. Someone who was told a plan of bloody revenge and said, 'Sure, why not?' Someone with the cash or clout to knit together a kill crew.

Achala Kaushal. Had to be involved. No way it was coincidence that someone he'd wronged had gone missing on the same night that hell washed like a tidal wave over Nate and Pete's lives.

He now had something to go on. Things were looking up.

A minute later, they looked straight back down.

When he went back to the main page, it refreshed and a brand new news item appeared at the top, and the words:

Arson murder suspect's car found abandoned

He clicked on the item with such ferocity that he almost knocked the phone out of his hand.

He listened in shock as a radio news jockey with a bored tone told the tale. The police had just released new information. Literally just. Nate's car had been found, with the driver's door wide open, in a long-term car park near Heathrow Airport's Terminal four. Empty, clean, according to the police. Now the assumption was that he'd fled abroad. The police were checking the airport's CCTV to see if they could spot him sneaking aboard a plane. Anyone with information was invited to call the police in confidence. And, of course, no approaching. Dangerous. The police were a hair's breadth from pronouncing him a murderer, even though the headline of this report proved that the media already believed it.

Nate dropped the phone.

'Someone's in biiiig trouble,' the girl sang. 'Can't run to the police now.'

He didn't even hear her. The truth was finally taking root in his brain. This wasn't just a case of mistaken assumptions on the part of the police, based on the fact that he was missing from a crime scene. The dumped car was the final piece of unshakable proof for Nate.

He had been set-up. Kaushal's people had wanted to make sure that Nate got the blame for the arson murder, and had done a stellar job of dropping him head first into a vat of shit. And it now made perfect sense why. Leave two dead brothers in a burned house and the cops are going to search for people who might have held a grudge, and eventually hear your name. Leave one brother dead and make the other look like the culprit, and the cops never look your way.

Nate took a few seconds to let his mind settle. And a question popped in there. 'What did you do with my car?' he shouted at the girl.

Now her eyes registered – not fear, but at least surprise. Shock that he thought she could be so deeply involved. Her tone was almost pleading when she said, 'Hey, we left it at the ware-house, as instructed. I don't know anything about who took it after that, or where.'

Pleading, but not scared. Not in fear of reprisal. Just injured pride. Upset that she'd been falsely accused, nothing more. And he believed her denial. She was just someone on the payroll, low down on the ladder. He needed the people at the top. He was beginning to worry that this girl would not be able to help him climb towards them.

'Are you going to eat that other burger?' she said.

He wasn't. Appetite gone. Still angry, he turned and threw it at her. It struck her shoulder and landed six inches from her face. She grabbed it.

'Now you have no clue what to do, do you? We were all over that warehouse, but I bet my people cleaned it up. A million pieces of evidence that could tell you why they did this to you, all gone.'

He started the engine. Eight minutes later, he turned into a residential road. Where the houses ended, the road surface worsened and metal palisade fencing took over on both sides, wild scrubland beyond. Fifty metres later the fencing halted and the land opened up: the industrial park. Nate pulled up to the kerb. No-one around. He climbed into the back, carrying the two teas.

'No sugar or milk,' he said as he put a tea near the two empty burger wrappers. He stood right over her, staring down. In profile, she looked handsome. Rounded chin, sharp nose, and a bottom lip that stuck out a little further than the top one. He noticed she had a tiny portion of the right earlobe missing right at the bottom, as if an earring had been violently ripped away a long time ago.

He sipped his tea, staring down. Her eyes turned to look up at him because her head had virtually no movement, already twisted far to one side because she lay on her front.

'God, you're not going to masturbate over me, are you?' she said.

In his pocket, the hidden goodies from the chemist's: cotton wool balls and acetone-based nail polish remover. The idea to restrain her with glue had appeared while he was leaving the store with painkillers and plasters.

He put down the tea and knelt by her head. He laid cotton balls on the floor and poured the nail polish remover over them. She watched, realising his plan. She said nothing as he mopped at the hair stuck to the floor, except to hiss in pain as he twisted and scraped and peeled and plucked at it with his fingernails, until the glue came away and she could lift her head from the floor. Hair got left behind. The rest was soaking wet. Then he backed off and pulled out the landlady's knife.

He waited until she had calmed down. When she had, she grabbed the sodden cotton balls and worked her glued hand, wrenching the fingers slowly, until she could raise them enough to dab beneath. Then beneath her palm. Minutes passed. The going was slow because of her busted arm. Nate said nothing, just watched. The girl ignored him. She got impatient near the end and ripped her hand free, which left skin behind and caused a yelp of pain.

But then it was done. His enemy was free. She arched her aching back and gave him a look like she was trying to burn him up by telekinesis.

'Don't get up or try anything,' he said, waving the knife. He backed up to the seats.

She glared at him, then seemed to relax. Or to realise she didn't have telekinetic powers. She examined her injured hand, then tried to run her good one through her hair. But it was crusted solid in bends and twists and folds. She looked like Medusa. She started to mop at it, crushing cotton balls around a tangle of strands and massaging, dissolving the glue. While she did this, she used her teeth to bite away jagged icicle-like glue from her hand, pausing after a minute to say:

'Damar–'

'Going to kill me for this, I know.'

He watched, she worked. A few minutes later, she stopped. Used her jacket to dry her hair as best she could, then tossed it aside. She clenched her frozen fist and glue dust fell away. Nate watched. It was fascinating, for some reason. She picked up the tea and drank it in one go. The empty paper cup bounced off Nate's stomach a second later.

'Now that you've had some food and a nice cup of tea, we're going inside. Try nothing. Give me your back.'

She didn't seem to understand. He held up a cable tie taken from the glove box, spotted when he'd put his supplies inside. One of a bunch. It was going to feel good binding her with the same item she and Damar had used on him. 'Turn around.'

'Your mother know you treat girls like this, does she?' She shuffled around on her knees, and for that he was glad. Because there was horror and shame on his face, and he didn't want her to see it. The mention of his mother had put her in his mind. He hadn't thought about her since this had all kicked off. His father had left many years ago and Karen had been on her own since then, living back up in her Scottish hometown, where she knew people. It was a small community, and he wondered how they were treating her. For sure she had heard what had happened. How were they reacting to the news that one of her sons was a hunted man, possibly a mur–

Pete. He cursed himself. How could he worry what she thought about Nate when she feared Pete might be dead? And by his brother's hand.

The girl turned her head and stared at him. No mirth in her expression, though. 'What's wrong with you?' she said. A genuine question. Real curiosity.

He cleared his head. This was not the time to dwell on family affairs. 'Put your hands behind your back.'

The left hand made the journey just fine, but her dislocated right arm barely moved. He knew the injury was real, but so was her desire to escape him. So, he grabbed both of her wrists and tried to force them together. She yelped.

'This won't work, you damned idiot. You'll have to tie them in front.'

'Shut your mouth,' he snapped. He pulled her left arm tight across her back, as far as it would go, and secured it to her left hip by slipping the cable tie through a belt loop. As he tested the bond by yanking, her left hand gave him the middle finger. He grabbed it tight in his fist and gave a little twist that elicited a barrage of insults.

He opened the back doors and got out and hauled her with him, using that offending finger. She came willingly. On the ground, she winced against the bright morning light. It was an industrial district of daytime workers, but he couldn't see anyone around. Heavy machinery thunked and whacked somewhere, and he could hear a revving car engine. He hugged her close to him, on his right side to hide her tied arm. Hopefully, to any distant viewers, they would look like a loved-up couple. For the first time, he noticed she was only a couple of inches shorter than his six-one.

He waited for her to scream for help, but she didn't. He figured she wanted the police involved just as little as he did. Probably a career criminal. They started walking. Again, she went willingly. Too willingly. He recalled something she'd said earlier, which she'd had no reason to share with him: *A million pieces of evidence that could tell you why they did this to you...* His anxiety upped a level. 'You're too eager,' he said. 'Slow down. Maybe we should forget this place. You're right. There will be nothing here that can help me.'

She turned her head and her eyes were ten inches from his. He saw the concern in them, and the last jigsaw piece slotted nicely in.

She wanted him here, wanted him inside that warehouse. It was why she'd been so willing to give this place up. Not outright, because that might have made him suspicious. Instead, she had given him the satnav clue like a piece of bait and waited for him to snatch it and work it, and think he'd been clever.

And why? Was Damar here? Maybe their plan, if separated, was to get back to the warehouse and wait for the other, no matter how long it took. So, in they'd go, and Damar would be there, and he would be on his guard because a separation meant a problem, and two minutes later Nate would be naked again and cursing the day his mum met his dad.

He hauled her to a stop.

'Don't you want to find out who killed your brother?' she said. Clear worry in her tone now.

He looked at the warehouse. A new day. Would Damar have waited around all night? Would he have sat around in the dark, not knowing if the cops might turn up instead of the girl? And if he was still awaiting her, surely he'd wait outside, so he wouldn't be trapped if a team of men in blue came for him. That would be the way to do it. That was how Nate would do it. And there was no-one outside the warehouse.

He had no choice. They had to go inside.

'I bet this brings back memories,' he said, and yanked her and started walking again.

The warehouse was a squat block on the riverfront, three parts rust to one part corrugated metal sheeting. Fun could be had seeing who was first to spot a window that wasn't broken. The riverfront was lined with warehouses, but it seemed as if all the others were in good nick, and the biggest gap between them was right here, as if the others had shifted position to get away from this eyesore.

Out front was a road cutting between this row of warehouses and a football pitch on the other side, both barred by a chain-link fence. The gate for Saturn Printworks was a sliding affair whose wheels had slipped their runner, but thankfully some soul in the past had used muscle or maybe a bulldozer to open it a perpetual eight feet. Around one of the gateposts was a remnant of police crime scene tape, so they weren't the only ones to have chosen this place for nefarious undertakings.

The road to the front door was broken and pitted. Same bulldozer entering, maybe, or that long-ago crime had been some kind of artillery warfare. The BMW got itself six months closer to a change of suspension by the time it stopped before the big twin doors, also corrugated metal sheeting.

Once the doors were open, the car entered and turned and stopped parallel to the front wall, and the driver got out. The driver was met at the boot of the car by someone else.

'You dead yet?' said one, slapping the man inside the boot around the face. The man stirred, moaned, tried to rise. In his hand was a spanner. He swung it, but the two people standing over him stepped back in plenty of time because his attempt to crush their skulls was weak, slow.

'Out you come,' said the female of the pair. She slammed a fist into his face, then both grabbed him and yanked. The man fell hard onto the dusty concrete floor, and the spanner skidded away.

Nate kicked the spanner with his toe and watched it skid away. He then tripped the girl to the ground and barely held back from kicking her. He still remembered that punch she had thrown at him, although it had somehow been hidden in his memory's recesses until this very moment.

'I'm going to fucking kill you,' the girl hissed, staring up at him. For someone with her hands bound behind her back, she got to her feet surprisingly quick. He grabbed her hair at the temple, hard enough to make her yelp, and hard enough to dig sharp glue remnants into his palm, and dragged her deeper into the warehouse.

Three floors. Stairs in two of the corners. Pillars throughout. Nothing but dust and debris. There were square patches of torn-up concrete where print machinery had once been mounted. Against the left wall was a full-width mezzanine raised on steel pillars with a box-like office on top that reached almost to the roof, like a package jammed on a shelf. Underneath the mezzanine, the floor was gone and Nate could see a grid of metal girders, like an exposed skeleton. And by the foot of the stairs leading up to the office there was an area laid with plastic sheeting, whose corners were held down by breeze blocks. He dragged her close and tripped her at the edge of the plastic area, staring at what sat in the centre like an ornament. A moulded plastic garden chair, each of its legs jammed into a hole in a cored house brick. It set his pulse thudding.

Nate was lifted and dumped onto the chair. His head was spinning, and he knew he'd fall if he tried to stand. But the bearded guy was holding him in place, so there would be no standing. And the woman was tying his ankles to the chair legs, and then his arms behind his back, so there would be no standing for a while now. If ever again.

'Who?' he managed. That was it.

The bearded man got on a mobile phone. He paced, and the girl stood before Nate, folded of arms, smug of face.

'We're here,' he heard the man say.

Ninety seconds later, both were standing before Nate, looking down at him. The man had collected a duffel bag from the back of the van, and it was at his feet now.

'Distinguishing marks,' he said.

The guy undid Nate's trousers and pulled them down, exposing everything. Had a good look, then pulled them back up. Next, both of his captors undid his shirt and threw it wide, then checked his arms and chest, and leaned him forward to check his back.

'Just this,' said the woman from behind him, tapping his shoulder tattoo.

He was hugged hard by the man and held tight while fire exploded in his hands. Things went vague again here, but he remembered screaming, then biting on a cloth forced into his mouth.

'This little piggy went home and burned in a house fire,' said the girl from behind him.

Clearly, nine kin of that piggy rushed into the burning house to save him, and also perished. After, when the man moved away, there was a whirring noise, and this time it was the shoulder, the tattoo. The guy grabbed him again. Fiery pain paid another visit. Finally, he went out.

But no. Or he was back. Both stood before him, grinning monsters, the engineers of hell. The girl held up a pair of lineman's pliers, thick ones, industrial types. Wicked jaws. She put a hand on his groin.

'Big here. Maybe we should pull this off. Might be a distinguishing feature.'

And laughter.

And after the pliers were forced into his mouth – blackness.

There was dried blood on the plastic around the feet of the chair, and on the chair itself, stark against the pale blue seat. Behind the chair, sections of the plastic sheet were melted. Acid, dripping from his scorched fingers, trying to burn through the world. He strode over to where the girl lay and grabbed her hair again, two fists this time, and dragged her to her feet. He heard her hair crack and remnant glue snapped.

He dragged her under the mezzanine, to the exposed skeleton of some buried iron giant. It was flooded, the grid of girders creating six square pools in two rows of three five feet across, like the iron giant's abdominals.

He was going to dump her there. Kill her and dump her in the water. Beyond the scope of whatever evil lay in him, but he was going to do it anyway. At the edge, he tripped her, meaning to drop her into the first pool on the left, but she leaped to the right at the same time as she fell and toppled into the pool on the right. She sank, resurfaced after a couple of seconds, and faced him. The water came to her waist.

Right then, he realised, he was not the first person to have had this idea.

They cut him loose. She dragged him by the feet across the dusty floor, into the gloom under the mezzanine. The bearded man was following. Then the man bent and they both lifted him, and the world spun, and he landed with a splash.

He struggled to his feet, breaking the surface. He looked up. The girl had the pliers in her hand, and she threw them hard at his head. He managed to twist aside and heard them splash next to him. Then she was laughing. She raised the battery-operated sander that they had torn up his shoulder with. Raised it up high, as if for a hammer strike. He saw blood and bits of skin and meat on the sandpaper. She turned it on. Blood flew off the spinning blade. The whine hurt his ears.

But then: 'Shit. Wait.'

Girl: 'What's wrong?'

'Blood.'

The sander shut off. Nate and the girl looked at the bearded man at the same time. She still had the sander raised above her head in both hands, like a sportsman showing off a trophy. The bearded man was staring at his fingers. There was a dark smudge on his cheek, as if he had wiped it.

Girl: 'You'll live.'

'Shit, it could be anywhere.'

He started panicking, looking on the ground around his feet and along the path he'd walked, as if seeking something he'd dropped.

Girl: 'What are you talking about?'

'DNA. Shit.'

They bickered. The girl was eager to get Nate all dead; the guy was concerned that a body found here would set the police searching, that they'd find his blood drips on the floor, and that they'd get all excited that they'd found their killer when that blood didn't match the victim.

'I'm in the shitting system,' was the deciding cry.

And to thank: a fragment of tooth turned into a missile when it broke away. Hit the guy in the cheek, it seemed. Nate hadn't noticed.

Nate glared hard at her, and she looked right back up. He wanted to crush her face with his foot. Her way presiding, Saturn Printworks would have been the final resting place of one Nathan Barke. But he lifted his foot and stepped back, turned away and stared at the ground just beyond the mezzanine. Signs of vicious movement in the dust.

'This is where you should still be, asshole,' she hissed at his back. 'Dead and rotting. We won't make the same mistake next time.'

He didn't look round. 'You're going in the water and never coming out,' he said back, softly, still staring at the disturbed dust.

Dragged again. Wet and hurt, and dumped next to the plastic. He watched the van reverse towards him. He was uncuffed and stripped, and cuffed again, and thrown into the van. Words, threats, each designed to sting, to instil fear. The doors slammed. He welcomed the darkness. Despite the pain, despite the threat of doom, some part of his brain still associated the dark with a time to rest, sleep. So, amazingly, unbelievably, he slept.

And woke. The van was moving. He saw two heads up front. Heard a voice.

'—on his doorstep.'

That was the woman. And the man laughed. Another great idea from this pair, then. They were going to dump his body close to home.

'You still got the saw in the back?'

Man: 'Yup. Exactly why I brought it.'

'His back garden, eh? So, the police will be walking right on top of him without knowing it.'

Her again. Nate had assumed she was a sidekick, but no. No, no, no. This girl had taken charge. All the pain and anguish, all the torture, all down to her. Angry, he turned to her again. He realised she was in the same pool. Pool on the right, where they'd dumped him. Fitting. If only he had a weapon to raise over his head like a sportsman's tro–

In an instant, one arm came free, no longer locked behind her, and her hand smashed into the side of his knee. He buckled with a yelp, tried to step back, but that leg didn't hold his weight and he crashed onto his ass. She was up in a second, on her knees, driving that hand again towards him, the target this time his head.

He took the blow and fell back, and in a nanosecond she was over him, holding his hair, and holding something close to his eyes. He recognised the pliers. Same pair that had splintered his teeth. He saw her own teeth as she grinned. The pliers had been in the pool. Pool on the right. Used to cut the cable tie. He had been fooled.

'I told you, didn't I?' she said.

She twisted his head so he was staring into the murky water. *Hello again, old friend.*

'This time there's no escaping.' She cracked him again with the pliers. Everything spun. Just before he went out – again – he felt the cold water snatch him in an old friend's embrace.

Back.

He woke with a heavy something on his chest and side of his face. It took a few seconds for him to realise that he was the weight itself. He lay on the floor, face and chest, hips on a girder, legs hanging in the cold water. Twenty feet away, the girl was sitting on the plastic chair, facing him. Just sitting there, slouched, and he would have thought she was dead if not for the eyes, which were wide and staring, although glazed, maybe seeing nothing. This had to be another dream.

Something bumped his legs as he moved them to try to haul himself from the water. He turned his head.

There was a body in there with him, floating on its back, dead eyes staring up, sliced throat gaping wide and filled with scummy black water. Nate would have scrambled away like a terrified cat if he'd had the strength. Instead, he just stared.

Damar.

Whoever had killed him must have weighted down the body, and it had shifted loose when Nate went in the pool. For the second time.

Finally he got the strength to crawl out. He watched the girl, sure that she would launch herself at him in one final, lethal assault, but it never happened. As he rose to his feet, she didn't move. As he walked towards her, dripping wet, limping because of his bad knee and staggering because of his dizzy head, she didn't move. He fell to his knees off to one side of her, ten feet away. In this condition, he could not run and could not stop her killing him if she so chose, so why not just kneel here a few feet away and get his bearings back?

She still had the pliers. He watched her twisting away pieces of glue from her hand. Spit had dribbled out of her mouth and hung from her chin. Water still dripped from her and onto the plastic.

Strangely, he felt sorry for her. Maybe that was purely because at the minute he was feeling the same pain of loss, or maybe it was something else. A portion of attraction, undeniable between men and women sometimes, despite the negativity of their history? A desire to seek the company of someone, even someone who had tried to kill him, during this dark period of his life? Maybe it was simply because she had finally had her best chance so far to end him, and hadn't seized it. Whatever. It was what it was.

'Who was he to you?' he said.

Her look was one of shock. Maybe she had expected him to kill her, and she didn't care, or might even welcome it. Maybe she had waited here for it and was confused by his hesitance.

'Just a friend,' she said. 'But he took care of me. I was supposed to do the same for him. You need to go. They might be back.'

'Then so should you.'

'It's not me they're after.'

He looked back at Damar, and she saw him do it. 'You sure?' he said.

She didn't respond.

'Why didn't you kill me?'

Now her look was one of anger. 'They want you dead. I'm not giving them what they want.'

Of course. They had killed her partner, so she was hardly their best friend or loyal employee any more.

He said, 'Then we should both go. They might come back here and kill us both.'

She didn't speak. Just played with the pliers and the glue.

'How many of them are there?' he asked. The question grated on him. He knew he was using her weakened state of mind to get what he could from her. But he owed her nothing, and himself everything.

'I don't know. Damar had all the information. I only heard one name from him. Lazar.'

'A guy on a bike?' He was thinking of Blondie. She nodded. 'Is he the boss?'

'Me and Damar were low-end. Top dogs have buffers between them and the scum.'

'So this Lazar was a buffer? There's people higher up we need to get to?'

Another look, but this time suspicion. 'We?'

It took that word, 'we', for him to fully realise what he'd just announced. A partnership. More than siding with someone who had tried to kill him, he hated the idea of continuing alone. He needed this woman's help. Her brain to work things out, her memory to help him navigate clues. Even her damned arms to help lift things. Every bit of her. Right now he could count his friends on the fingers of his third arm, and beggars couldn't be choosers.

He tried to convince her with: 'Do you want to let them get away with Damar's murder?'

'They killed him because of you.'

That struck like a hammer. 'Because I had the gall to try to escape a violent death? You chose to hook up with these people.'

She didn't respond to that.

'You need me if you want to get back at them. And I need you. We can help each other. Or go it alone and start getting in each other's way.'

She seemed to think for a moment – or was spaced-out still. 'You've got the police after you. Your movements are restricted. Mine aren't. I don't need you.'

Not exactly a refusal. 'Yet you let me live, and I don't think it's just because I'm your enemy's enemy. You know it makes sense. Admit you need me and this will go smoother for both of us.'

She couldn't meet his eyes. Wouldn't. 'This changes nothing between us.'

And just like that she was in. But not because he had convinced her with a good argument, or because she refused to help her new enemy achieve their plans. She needed his help. She just had a problem with admitting it.

He said, 'Right, then we do this together.'

'And what can you bring to this party?'

Good point. He had no money, no contacts, no information, no superpowers. For two seconds he just stood there, and that was all the time she needed to get her answer.

'I am not your helper, understand? You are mine. We do things my way.'

'No,' he said, almost snapped. 'You're forgetting that I'm the guy at the centre of this damn thing. I'm the important one. We do it my way or we go separate ways. I don't care.'

There was defiance on her face, which gave him the impression that she wasn't someone who was used to being bossed about. Or she was finding it hard not to respond with rage and violence. Certainly violence was a normal way of life for her. But the defiance subsided. He took that as an agreement.

'Then let's go,' he said, making for the door. Halfway, he heard her chair scrape as she got up. But when he got to the door, she wasn't behind him.

She was under the mezzanine. He watched as she dragged Damar out, using just her good arm, and used her own sleeve to clean his face, then zipped up his jacket so it covered his ragged throat. And kissed his forehead, and spoke to him. And then she let him slip into the water like a ship and pushed down on his head, and he sank and stayed submerged. Only then did she come towards Nate.

From the rage on her face, he was glad she was now on his side. Sort of. For now.

They walked to the van in silence, the girl lagging behind slightly. Nothing sexist about it. Just caution. With his back to her, she would have more time for a defensive move if he suddenly attacked. He knew that. He understood that. But he also knew that he was exposed with his back to her, so he kept his head turned, watching her more than the way ahead. Stalemate.

They got to the van without one of them dying.

She took the passenger seat. No sexism there, either. He would be unlikely to attack if he had to drive. He knew that. He understood that. But he also knew she wouldn't risk attacking him if he had control of a speeding vehicle. Stalemate.

They sat in silence. He watched her out of the corner of his eye. He knew she was doing the same. It was all very awkward, but understandable: they had been mortal enemies just minutes ago.

Are we still? he wondered. She had not asked him why he had been targeted, and he did not like that. She should have. People wanted him dead, and those people had killed her best friend, and it would be logical for her to assume that Nate knew them, or of them, or at least had some idea of why a bullseye was on his back.

So why hadn't she asked what he knew? Did she know more than she was letting on? He had to stamp down a blooming fear that she was playing him in some way, dead friend or not.

'Nate,' he said, holding out his hand. A test. They were not friends. He wouldn't have shaken her hand if proffered. *If it is a trick,* he thought, *she will probably shake my hand to keep up the deception.*

She looked at his outstretched hand and said, 'I think you have a bad memory.'

'Maybe I forgive easily.'

'What makes you think I share such a habit?'

He put his hand away. Anger could explain her unwillingness to shake hands – it didn't mean there was no trickery involved here. The silly experiment had achieved nothing, and so the paranoia remained.

He put the heaters on full blast to help dry them and started driving, peripheral vision all over her, so much so that he had to blink occasionally to focus his eyes on the road ahead. She said nothing further and the silence was fine with him. It was two minutes before curiosity got the better of her and she said, 'Where you going?'

'Shepherd's Bush.'

'What's in Shepherd's Bush?'

'In half an hour? Us.'

He said nothing further. He didn't want to outline his plan for her. She was here to help him, and he would give her information if and when she needed it in order to perform that help. She was going to be his public face, that was all. He was a wanted man and couldn't flash his own face around London. So if he needed information from someone, that was her job.

She said nothing, either.

Richmond Way, Shepherd's Bush, just after 1pm. A row of small shops on the ground floor of a four-storey building. Between two dry cleaners and a letting agency. There was a space a couple of shops down in the pay-and-display zone, and Nate pulled in. He did not pay or display. From this angle he couldn't see inside the big window. But he could see the sign: 'Palmer & Co.' Good.

He looked at her and found she was already watching him. Neither had spoken for the rest of the journey. And now it was really bothering him that she hadn't asked why he'd been targeted. But he ignored that for now, because they were here.

He pointed at the shop. 'Palmer & Co. Go in and ask for a man called Michael Senior. He's one of the owners. If his secretary tells you that he's unavailable, say you need to speak to his son. Say it's important. Get him on the phone if he's not there. Because it is important.'

'Why?'

'Why you? Because I'm a wanted man and they might have the news on.'

'No. Why?'

'Smarten yourself up a bit in the mirror first.'

'Give me money.'

She didn't wait for an answer, but delved into his jacket pocket and extracted his wallet.

'What's that for?'

She got out without answering. Nate waited and watched.

But she didn't go to the letting agency. Instead, she went across the road. He wound down his window and shouted to her. She ignored him, but others on the street didn't. He shut his window on their staring faces and sank low in his seat. Nobody screamed for the cops.

He watched her enter a charity shop. She was back in five minutes, carrying a loaded plastic bag. He wound down the window, but only waved frantically this time. Ignoring him again, she walked two doors down and vanished into a hairdressers.

Nate told himself to relax. Clothing and hair, that was all. A new look because she didn't want to run around London looking like a homeless car crash victim. Being practical, and maybe a bit vain. No problem. Calm down. He watched her flash money at the girls inside, then take a seat. He waited. When a traffic warden appeared and cruised along the parked cars like a hunting shark, Nate jumped and bought an hour. And then waited.

He didn't notice her return until the passenger door squealed open. Immediately he noticed her hair. Short shag with a ragged fringe to hide her forehead laceration and spikey portions on top where they'd had to cut away long sections ruined by glue. *A fantastic job,* Nate thought, and told himself not to stare even as he thought it.

She wasn't waiting for approval anyway. She climbed into the back. 'Me first, and don't look.'

Five minutes later, they were both done. She had selected only a new pair of jeans because her old ones had gotten ruined by the floor of the van and her blood. The pullover had dried, and her bomber jacket had wiped down easily with a wet napkin. She had bought Nate someone's old T-shirt and a black fleece, and jeans. And a knit cap, which he pulled right to his eyes. Now he felt blended in, and far more comfortable.

When he climbed back behind the wheel, she opened the door to get out again. 'Remember, don't tell him why you want to speak to his son, okay?'

'Okay, sir,' she said, scorn in her tone. She slammed the door before he could say another word.

This time, thankfully, she went straight to the letting agency. Nate prepared for another long wait, and half expected to see a stubborn Mr Senior burst headfirst through the window. But she was back in ninety seconds, and the window had stayed intact, and he thought she must have had no luck.

'His son should be at home,' she said as she entered the van. 'But if not then he's at the snooker club. Home is a few minutes in this direction.'

'He spoke to you okay? He didn't ask questions? He wasn't suspicious?'

'Why? Is my face all over the news, too?'

Unwilling to respond, Nate drove.

Six minutes after she got no answer at the home address

Michael Senior had given her, they arrived at the snooker club. It was beside a Co-op and had its front entrance at the back of the building, which was good because they could watch it from the tiny car park behind the superstore.

Nate pointed at a red Vauxhall Corsa with tinted windows and fiery flank stickers. 'He's here. That's his car.'

'Uh-huh,' she said, not even looking. In fact, she was studying her nails. An ex-girlfriend used to do that when he was boring her.

'He's a rude boy, deals drugs, mugs people. So you be careful when you go in there. He'll trust a woman, but a guy going in might spook him. He might think I'm someone he pissed off way back.'

'Okeydokey.'

'He might even remember me. I met him one time. And my face is in the news. So you have to go in. Okay?'

A glance up out of the window: 'Looks like it might rain.'

Uninterested. Mocking him. He could hold off no longer. 'I want to know why you haven't asked who this guy is or why we're here.'

'No need,' she said. 'This is obviously you following your theory that Achala Kaushal is the one behind all this.'

And there it was – why she hadn't asked that all-important question. She had heard the news report about Achala Kaushal, knew he suspected his ex-employee. And clearly thought his theory was full of shit.

'She has to be involved,' he said. 'It's obvious. She used to work for me and her family was pissed at me, and then she goes into hiding at the same time that people try to kill me and my brother. You think that's a coincidence? Culprit or not, she's involved, she knows something, and we need to find her. And the best way to do that is with the guy inside that snooker club. This idiot might just have the clout to pull off what's happened to me. He knows fools who'd commit crimes for pennies. Weirdos and druggies and the like. He's connected. And who is he? He's her boyfriend, or was four years ago when I knew her.'

'Ah, so that's your theory. Kaushal put him up to it, just before she went on the run – without him, strangely.' Delivered with a double-dose of scorn. She opened the door, started to get out.

'Yes. So in you go. This is what you do. Go inside and–'

She got out.

'–ask him where she is. If he's defensive, it means–'

He stopped as she slammed the door and started walking away. He got out. 'Hey. Wait. You don't even know what he looks–'

Two people at separate cars in the car park looked round at his shout. Suddenly fearful he'd be recognised, he got back inside, cursing.

He watched her go into the snooker club. She was back in seven minutes, grinning. He thought that meant she had something for him, until she got in and said, 'He dumped her three years ago. Said she was fucked in the head.'

'He answered your questions? Just like that? Was he suspicious? Did it sound like he–'

'Next, sir?' she interrupted. 'I am your loyal assistant. Where shall we go next to waste some time?'

'You think this is a waste of time? You have a better plan for finding Kaushal?'

'Forget Kaushal, okay? You're not thinking straight. She waits four years to come back at you, then goes into hiding and leaves her family scared and wondering, and the rude boy boyfriend who helped her set it all up goes about his business as usual?'

'Let's hear your better idea.'

'Even if he was involved, the way to go would be to follow him. If he's in contact with Kaushal, he'll eventually lead us to her. But going in and asking him where she is is just stupid. If you insist on this, then bon voyage, my friend. You go your way and I go mine.'

He knew she was right, but being told his plan was flawed did not sit well in his stomach. 'So we wait and follow him, is that what you want to do?'

'Is it hell. This is the wrong tree, barking dog.'

'How can you say that? She's missing and it has to be connected to me. Has to be.'

'Not impossible. But this isn't some little girl seeking payback for mental anguish. Too convoluted, too many people involved. This is bigger than that. And we need to be smarter in what we do. That means you need to step down as supreme commander of the mission and let me take over.'

He laughed at her, but he was angry. 'Fine. Take the reins, great one. I am your loyal servant now. What shall we do, O great one?'

'So, we do this my way now?'

'Whatever floats your boat. So, what's your genius plan?'

'Drive to Westminster.'

'What's in Westminster?'

'In half an hour? Us.'

His suspicions bubbled up again. The Westminster idea had been quick. Too quick to be improvised. She knew something after all. 'You know something you're not telling me. What it is?'

'I don't know anything. If I knew where the person who slit Damar's throat was, I'd go straight there. I don't. I just know we need to go to Westminster.'

'So what's there?'

'In half an hour? Us.'

He didn't ask again. Just drove. They both sat in silence. But soon it got to Nate. He didn't want silence. Silence allowed paranoid thoughts to creep in. Besides, talking would make him feel more comfortable around her, and they were going to be together for a while, and being comfortable beat feeling awkward, but it seemed as if she felt the opposite.

He tried an opening line: 'Fair enough, we'll do this in silence. Just remember that you tried to kill me first.'

She said nothing. He drove. Two minutes later, he held out his hand. Said his name again. She didn't even acknowledge him. He felt strange trying to make nice with someone who had helped smash in his teeth.

Silence. Two more miles. Nate's ruined fingertips were beginning to throb from all the driving and he reached for the glovebox, and she grabbed his wrist with the speed of a rattlesnake striking. A fingertip delved deep into a nerve, causing a shooting pain and then numbness to travel up his arm. Strangely, in the half second before he yanked his arm away, he had time to notice an indentation on her ring finger. So clear and deep that the ring could not have been removed more than a few days ago.

'What the hell was that for?' he moaned, rubbing his wrist.

She opened the glovebox. Inside were some painkillers.

'Calm down, doo-dah,' he said, taking the painkillers.

She looked at him. 'What did you call me?'

'Well, I don't know your name, do I, what's-your-face?'

She looked at him.

'We're not friends, like you said,' he said. 'Just give me a name to use so this isn't even more awkward.'

'It's Toni. Just Toni to you. Now please be quiet and drive. Drive to Westminster.'

'And what's in Westminster?'

She ignored him. He decided to ignore her back. So what if

she didn't speak again. Fuck her. They weren't sitting together because they were good buddies. As long as she helped him find out who had killed his brother, he would endure her company, silence and all, and soon they'd part and never see each other again. So he clammed up himself and drove.

A minute south of Tate Britain in Millbank, Westminster, they pulled up at the side of the road by an iron fence. Beyond it was a scrapyard. Battered cars were piled four high, like something a Lego-starved giant kid would build, or a crew of post-apocalyptic nomads to secure their camp. The gate was open. A guy was turning a flatbed truck in off the road, a Fiesta with a smashed front end strapped to the bed. Nate wondered if the owner was lying in an intensive care unit somewhere.

'So what's here?'

She had been silent for the remainder of the drive, and stayed silent now. Got out of the van, started walking towards the gate. Nate exited. She stepped between the gate and the truck, forcing the vehicle to stop so abruptly, the Fiesta rocked hard enough for the glass remnants in the busted side window to sprinkle out. The driver threw up his hands.

Right in his way, she stopped and turned, having heard Nate's door slam shut.

'You stay.'

'What's here?' he said.

She vanished inside the scrapyard. Nate leaned against the front of the van, but then became aware of the passing traffic, both vehicular and pedestrian. For a moment he'd forgotten about his fugitive status. He got back in the vehicle before someone could point and scream for the cops.

She was back in four minutes. Got in, said nothing. Nate just sat there until she looked at him.

'This isn't going to work if we don't talk.'

'What's to talk about?' she said.

'It also won't work if you don't tell me what you're doing. Remember, I'm not your bloody assistant here.'

'Maybe you want us to go our separate ways, then? See how far you get with all of London knowing your face and the cops kicking in doors looking for you.'

'Just tell me why we're here.'

'Lewisham next. It's over the Thames, so go south. Vauxhall Bridge.' She pointed behind them. South, apparently.

He didn't move. Didn't start the engine. She opened her door and swung a leg out, and for a moment he was going to be stubborn and let her go, but then he grabbed the key and started the engine, and she swung her leg back inside and shut the door.

Corner of the eye again, he watched her as he pulled the van away from the kerb. And was sure he saw a slight grin on her lips.

He calmed himself. Back to the task at hand. 'So, I'll beg again. Please? Please tell me what's in Lewisham.'

'When we get there.'

He unzipped his fleece and yanked the neck of his T-shirt, exposing the raw area on his shoulder. 'Remember when you did this? You remember the tattoo? You know what it was?'

'*Was* being the correct word, because it's now gone. I remember it. Some black men carrying a giant American football.'

He couldn't tell if that was a joke or not. The three 'black men' were – had been – silhouettes, and the so-called football they held raised over their heads had been–

Her phone was on the dashboard. She snatched it. He let her. She played with it. He focused on the road ahead. Tried to clear his mind by watching the pedestrians going about their inert business, but his mind turned on him. It told him that all those people on foot and in the cars knew his face, knew his story, believed he was a killer, would shop him to the cops in a second. It dredged up a story he'd read about as a teenager. The Night Stalker, a serial killer who had murdered a bunch of people in Los Angeles. The cops had put that guy's face and name in the news, just as they had with Nate's. The stalker hadn't been aware, though, until it was too late. Too late being when he was out and about in the busy daytime streets, like these ones. He'd been chased down and captured by normal members of the public, people no different from those Nate watched now. Thirty years later, the guy had died in prison, hated by the world.

His daydream cracked when he heard Toni say, 'Ah.' And giggle.

He snatched the phone. The screen showed a page of Google images, and one of them was a replica of his tattoo. He didn't know how she had found it, what she might have typed, because certainly 'football' wouldn't have pulled it up. But she had.

'So, now do I get a modicum of respect?' he said.

'For what? Having a job?'

'Piss off,' he snapped. She laughed. He concentrated on the road. He watched her put the phone to her ear and heard a tinny voice, but not loud enough to make anything out.

Two minutes later he felt her looking at him.

'What?'

'That scrapyard was where we got the van. I went there with Damar. He went to buy a van, then later, he told me that Lazar had arranged for it to be fixed up in a workshop. I never knew which workshop. That's what I went to the scrapyard for. I asked the guy which workshop. And he told me. That's where we're going now. The workshop. Maybe a guy at the workshop knows Lazar. That's the plan, and it's a better one than chasing your missing Indian woman.'

Something had changed in her tone. He snatched the phone again, or tried to. She was quicker, and his fingers got thin air. Then she propped the phone on the ledge where the dashboard clock was, and turned up the volume, and he saw a paused YouTube video. A newscaster behind a table, the words 'BBC London News' in one corner of the screen. But it was the caption across the bottom of the screen that sucked him in:

Suspect in house fire death is decorated soldier

She pressed play, and the memories came back.

'The man police wish to question about a fatal house fire in Wandsworth last night is a former soldier in the Corps of Royal Engineers.

'Nathan Barke, forty-two, is suspected of fleeing the scene of a fire at his home in Putney Village in which the body of an unidentified male was found. Barke served as a combat engineer with 33 Engineer Regiment, which specialises in bomb disposal. In March 2003, while on tour in Iraq, Barke's team was targeted by a suicide bomber. With what his superior officer called "self-less action and quick thinking", Sapper Barke detonated a grenade in the path of the suicide's vehicle, causing it to explode a safe distance away.

'Barke's bravery was rewarded with a Mention in Despatches, the oldest form of praise within the UK Armed Forces. This evening police are hunting the former soldier for–'

Nate stopped the video and looked at Toni, who only gave him a quick glance and said, 'What, no medal?'

'A Mention in–'

She waved a hand and he stopped. 'Oh, stop. You're trying to impress me. Survive the rest of today without getting your throat slit and I'll be impressed. Now, why don't you use that Internet to find us some relaxing music?'

'Piss off,' Nate said.

She giggled like a little girl. 'You're so easy to annoy, you know. It's all that carrying a big football while dressed in black.'

Now he laughed. Couldn't help it. He knew she knew that big football had been a bomb, the cartoon variety, with an oval body and tail fins. A tattoo he and his team had had done as raw recruits, long before suicide bombers in Iraq and before the fog of war had eroded the fun outlook they'd had at being part of a new team dedicated to saving lives.

She killed the moment when she said, 'Just don't get all high and mighty. Desert warfare is not the same as urban, and it was a long time ago that you were a soldier. Today, you're a wet businessman. Remember that and you might live through this.'

Lewisham.

She directed him into a car park outside a supermarket and he turned off the engine. He looked at the supermarket, wondering why they'd stopped here.

'Other way,' she said.

Across the road was a garage. It was a plain white building with a big blue shuttered door that was rolled up. 'Twentieth Century Fix' said a sign above the shutter. A couple of cars were parked outside, and inside they could see others in states of repair. Two guys in blue coveralls sat outside on plastic chairs, drinks on a small plastic table between them. Other guys roamed inside, repairing.

'This guy we need, he one of them?' he asked.

'No. So he should give up the info easily, if the van sale was just that, just a sale. Unless he's been told not to. I don't know his connection to them. Damar thought the guy was just a guy.'

'And what can he tell us?'

'If I knew that, he wouldn't need to tell us. Now, this should be a simple Q and A, but it might not be. We don't know what this guy knows, or who he knows. He might be in this deep, and trouble might be on the horizon. We need to be ready.'

'Don't worry about me.'

'I didn't mean you. I mean me. I'm no good with things like this. My shoulder's dislocated. It needs popping back in.'

He glared at her. He knew she wanted him to do it. 'That'll hurt.'

'It has to go in sometime.'

'So we go to the hospital. It's not a gunshot or stab wound. Nobody will call the police.'

'But I'll sit waiting while old ladies go in about their stuffy noses. Pop it.'

He grabbed her right arm and felt around.

'Swap seats.'

She looked puzzled, but didn't question his order. They got out, passed each other without a glance at the front of the van, and hopped back in. She held up her bad arm, which was now on the far side from him. 'So now what?' she said.

'It's popped out the back. Sit on my lap, facing me.'

She gave him a long look, like she suspected some trickery.

'Fine,' he said. 'Nearest hospital. Swap seats again.'

She didn't move. Continued to look at him. Five seconds, during which she was probably trying to work out if this was a game he was playing. And then she swung up her right leg, and climbed aboard him, knees either side, her ass on his upper thighs. She looked over his head, maybe unwilling to meet his eyes. He could smell diesel fumes on her clothing, maybe from the scrapyard. Which was good. Had it not masked the perfume remnants he'd inhaled earlier, he might have started to feel things he really didn't want to feel. Being sexually attracted to someone who'd tried to kill you might be right up some freaks' alleys, but not his.

'Arms around my neck, arms locked, and hold tight,' he said. He was aware that he tried to keep his lips close together as he spoke, so that his ragged teeth wouldn't show.

She lifted her arms, but they did not clamp around his neck. Instead, she grabbed his seat's headrest. Now her eyes fell and locked onto his, and they were full of mistrust. He raised his hands, as if to grab her breasts. She stiffened, but it wasn't wariness. Readiness. Preparation. The way a cat might get ready to pounce on a mouse. He knew if he grabbed those breasts, he was going to regret it about half a second later.

He placed his palms just above her chest, on her collar bones.

'If this is some game–' she began, and that was when he pushed, hard. He felt her right side move back two inches, and something shift under his fingers, and she grunted. She half climbed and half collapsed off him and back into the driver's seat, rubbing her right shoulder. When she looked at him again, there was a wry smile.

'If you had touched two inches lower, I would have crushed your nose on my forehead, you know.'

Oh, he knew all right. 'There might still be tissue damage, so no playing baseball for a while yet,' he said. 'And keep your ego in check. I need you whole in order to help me.'

'Where did you learn that trick?'

'I just made it up, based on a basic knowledge of physics that

any human would acquire after forty-odd years on this planet.'
He pointed at the garage. 'How do we do this?'

'We stroll in like a couple of customers, and we say to him, "Please tell us who asked you to fix up our van." That will be his one chance to get this done painlessly. After that, if he's stubborn, he'll be very unhappy that you fixed my shoulder.'

He didn't doubt it. 'So which guy? There might be ten in there.'

'A boss-type. Or we'll go for the first guy we get alone,' she said.

They opened their doors to get out, and that was when a guy exited the garage through a door near the shutter, probably from an office. He wore red coveralls, not blue. He was bald but had a big goatee, which from this distance made him look like his head was on upside down. He stood around while another guy wheeled a dirt bike out of the garage. He put on a helmet, both guys chatted and pointed at bits of the bike, and then the bald guy climbed on the machine and rode it onto a side street alongside the garage. Alone. Alone and looked like a boss-type...

'Follow him,' Nate said, even as Toni was already starting the engine.

The guy took some streets and the bike cut through the traffic easily, slipping between the lanes like a good queue jumper. But he kept his speed low, so they somehow managed to keep him in sight, or enter turns he took before he could vanish at the other end.

They drove in silence for a few miles, some ten minutes, and then Toni said,

'Hey, back in the van you looked horrified when I mentioned

your parents. What's the score there? They know what's happened?'

'Let's talk about your parents instead, eh?' he snapped. 'Where are they, Turkey? You're Turkish, right?'

'Okay, we'll talk about them. I don't have any parents. I never knew my dad and my mum kicked me out for my own good. But, yes, they're probably still over in Turkey. Good guess. There, done. Now you.'

Said with sincerity, not a joke. Nate looked at her and saw what might have been genuine concern on her face. It didn't sit well with the woman he knew. He didn't want to open up to her. But he felt he had to give her something. So all he said was, 'My dad's gone, too, when I was kid. It's just Mum, and I don't know how she's reacting to all this. My brother might be a charred body, so I imagine not well.'

'Shit,' she said, and he tensed, but then he saw she was looking ahead, and he looked ahead, too, and the biker was gone. Any sense of lost hope was smothered by gratitude that he could shift his mind away from his mother.

Then they passed a side street and she pointed. 'There.'

The guy was parked in a bus stop lay-by just past a school down that side street. There wasn't much traffic around, although the noise of children rioting in the playground was almost deafening.

Nate pulled into the side of the road a short way past the biker, parking between two cars outside a mini-mart. The biker was sixty metres back, just sitting on his bike.

Nate pulled out his knuckleduster. Toni put her hand on his and opened his fingers with hers, then slid the weapon off and dropped it into the footwell. 'This how soldiers do things, is it?' she said. 'Shoot first, then think, "Damn, maybe I should have asked a question"?'

She got out of the van and started walking back towards the

bike guy, who was now kneeling before the machine, seemingly checking out the front suspension.

Nate exited and rushed across the road. He had to assume this guy might know who he was, so he would use caution. He kept pace with Toni, but did not watch her or the biker. He kept his head down, pretending to fiddle with the zip on his fleece. He was also thinking about the other people around, any one of which might have his face fresh in their mind.

He saw the biker look up as Toni stopped by the bike and stroked the seat. He stood, and they faced each other over it. Nate crossed the road and stopped at the bus stop, four metres away. He was prepared for the guy to suddenly kick off.

He heard Toni say, '–if you can afford such things, sure. Hey, look, I'm a friend of the guy you fixed up a white van for.'

The guy stiffened, but didn't kick off. He didn't run, and he didn't pull a weapon. He simply said, 'Hey, that van was a sack of balls. Best I could do. If there's a problem–'

She held up a hand. 'It's okay, it's not a complaint. The van's fine. But the radio's locked. We just need the code.'

The guy scratched his head. And looked round, right at Nate. Their eyes met just long enough for Nate to realise he'd blown it. The guy had suspected she might have backup, and he'd searched for it, and Nate had been staring right at him. Nate started to approach, but slowly.

The guy turned back to Toni.

'I don't know the code, lady. I had the van three days. I fixed up all manner of faults with that thing, and I didn't touch the radio. That was the least of my worries. I specialise in bikes, you know? They don't have radios.'

Nate took a neutral position behind Toni, leaning against a wall. The guy ignored him. Up close, Nate could see he was quite well built, early thirties despite the bald head, and figured he was probably good with his fists. Nate hoped fists never played a part here.

'Would Lazar know the code?' Toni said.

'Who? I don't know any Lazar.'

'Didn't Lazar ask you to fix up the van for us?'

'I don't know this Lazar chap. It was a mate called Alfie. He told me there was a van he bought. I collected it from a junkyard. And I didn't bother checking the radio.'

'I think my friend mentioned an Alfie,' she lied. 'Would Alfie know the code?'

'Sod knows. I'd go see the junkyard people. Previous owner must have handed some paperwork over. Code might be in there.'

She took a breath, and Nate knew why. So far, just general chat, a few inane questions. But if she now asked where Alfie was, it could spook the guy. And if he didn't get suspicious, then he might simply want to protect Alfie's privacy. But they were not leaving this area without a new path to investigate.

'I'll go ask Alfie. Where is he now?'

But in the end, no worries. The guy said, 'Probably at work. The track in Joyce Green.'

'What track?'

In the end, sweetness and light. The guy had no suspicions at all. He gave up the address without concern. To keep him sweet, Toni asked if he had a card, in case she needed a bike fixing. He didn't, but reeled off his number and business name, and she mouthed the words back as if pretending to commit them to memory.

A minute later he was gone. Toni waved him away, and he blew his horn. She said nothing to Nate and headed back to the van. He followed like a loyal dog.

Inside, he said, 'Do you know this Alfie, then?'

'No. Never heard that name. But I don't know everyone Damar knows.'

'Knew,' Nate said, and regretted it half a second later.

But she didn't seem angered. 'Knew,' she whispered.

'So, we go talk to this guy?' Nate said quickly, wanting to get off the subject of Damar.

'Yes. But calm down. The last two guys haven't been in the loop, so they were just answering general questions. Alfie's higher up the ladder, and if he knows something, he might not be so willing to share information. So now you can have your toy back, because you might need it.'

She picked up his knuckleduster and dropped it into his lap.

'Remember, I'm trying to clear my name here. So if there's violence, it's to be a last resort. Right?'

She didn't look at him. 'I don't remember agreeing to that.'

It was called Spanner Farm, but it wasn't a farm. Go east, Dartford, border of Kent and Greater London, turn north off Bob Dunn Way at the Littlebrook Interchange. Keep left and you can't miss it. If you do, you'll end up in the Dartford Tunnel probably.

They did miss it at first, but didn't end up in the tunnel. They got the left, followed a curving road past some giant warehouse on their right. The farm was on the left, just past. They blew right past because the entrance, a farm gate in a hedge, looked like it led to cows and tractors. Strangely, the sign for the farm was fifty metres later, telling you it was back the way you'd just come.

Despite the fact that it was an old wooden gate, it opened automatically as they turned towards it. Beyond, a track between more hedges, which opened out onto a new car park beside an old building in stone and wood. Beyond the building was another, in stone, split into rented cottages. For the serious bikers. Nate couldn't see anything for the serious bikers' wives and girlfriends. Maybe bikers as serious as this didn't bother with them, or only hooked up with fellow enthusiasts.

The main building had a small extension of new brick, with a glass door and a bright sign made to look like graffiti: 'Big Air'. They could hear bike engines screaming.

A shuttered opening to one side of the extension allowed them to see inside. There was a large oval track that rose and dipped like dirt waves, and was lined with stacked tyres painted green and big bags of dirt. Bright spotlights in the rafters lit everything adequately. A few bikes were tearing round, getting Big Air, sliding round corners, throwing up dirt. Nate had to admit it looked like fun, even indoors.

A central area of flat dirt was host to a bunch of short people in yellow leathers and helmets, each standing next to a tiny dirt bike and watching a guy in red leathers with the top half hanging loose round his waist to expose a T-shirt. He was pacing before them, waving his hands, making gestures. Looked like he was lecturing kids.

'Think that's Alfie?' Nate said.

'Let's find out,' Toni said.

They got out.

Toni walked towards the glass door in the extension, and pushed through. Nate was two seconds behind.

It was a reception. A couple of chairs against a wall, a counter with a girl behind it. The counter held a till and some magazines for sale, and a rack of keyrings. The walls had biking posters, a large calendar with events printed on certain days, and some biker gear for sale. Nate's eyes scanned the walls. And locked onto a framed picture, centre stage on the wall behind the girl, perfectly placed to be unmissable.

The girl was young, had a nose ring and short spiky hair that didn't quite gel with her pretty face. Nate's immediate thought: just the sort of tomboy who'd make a good biker's partner, or liked to ride herself. She looked tough, like she'd take no shit, but her smile was all welcoming. Good at her job, or wholly respectful of anyone who shared her passion.

He stared at the picture behind her. Some guy back-grounded by a racetrack. Not this one. Outdoors, much bigger, with people in the stands. He was on a winners' podium with his bike, standing next to it. Full biker gear, helmet in one hand, a silver trophy in the other. Smiling.

'Can I help?' the tomboy said. Her accent was Welsh.

The rider's leathers were loaded with sponsor motifs.

'Yes,' said Toni.

On the bike's handguards: two evil-looking yellow dragon eyes. A fiery, forked tongue ran along the front mudguard.

'No,' said Nate. 'Let's go.'

He turned and left, just like that. Outside, he waited. As Toni exited, he heard the tomboy giggle. Some insult about him offloaded by Toni, he figured. Didn't care. Dragon eyes.

'What the hell was that all about?' Toni said. 'You know how rude you looked?'

He walked to the van, ignoring her.

She got in next to him. 'You want to explain?'

He didn't speak. He just handed her her phone.

'Now what?' she said.

'Hospitals. Only ones with A&E. Find them.'

This time she didn't doubt that he might have a valid idea about how to progress their hunt. Maybe it was his tone, or the look in his eyes. Whatever, she got down to Internet surfing and came up with a list – a long one. He took the phone back and she watched as he dialled a number. As he spoke:

'Hi, yes, I have a friend who was in a bike accident last night. Alfie.' He gave a location, and waited. 'I understand that, but...'

He hung up. Started dialling again. Toni snatched the phone from him and threw it in his lap. She looked annoyed. But without speaking, she left the van and went back inside the building. She was out in sixty seconds, back in the van within another twenty.

She gave him the name of a hospital. 'Alfie's the assistant manager. Should have been here today, but last night he was out somewhere and tried to jump two vans on his bike and the front wheel came off. Busted hip and right leg. He's got his own room on the Sunningdale Ward. If you wanted to search for Alfie, see how easy my way was?'

He understood. She must have simply engaged the receptionist in conversation. Maybe she had softly enquired about the guys running this place, or maybe she had outright asked where Alfie was. The tomboy had probably thought nothing of giving up the information. Not in the loop, not on the ladder.

'I was just being careful,' he said, but the excuse felt weak.

'Fine. Explain how you knew about the hospital.'

He mentioned the picture on the wall. 'That was Alfie. I recognised the bike.'

He recalled the dragon's eyes from the bike in the woods the other night. If that was Alfie on the wall, then Alfie was the guy who'd chased Nate on a bike and been bowled like a ball by a truck. He told her so. He did not mention that Damar had been part of the crew that had turned up.

'So no van jumping at all for this guy.'

'Ego. A pro biker getting hit by traffic doesn't have the same ring to it. Or he's been told to keep it all secret, which makes sense.'

'So, we go see this guy. I'll take back the reins now, if you don't mind. Your brain's not working very well. You're doing things the long way round. Probably the remnants of that drug.'

'Might you mean the one you injected into me?'

'See, the drug's making you forget that that part was done before I got on the scene.'

He didn't want an argument about that subject. Ever again. 'So what do you suggest, O great one? Go in and put an entire hospital under siege?'

'See? That's your brain working, not mine. We use two of these.'

She held up her phone.

Visiting hours started at four, and they got to the hospital ten minutes early. A slow stroll to Sunningdale via a Costa Coffee, where they bought hot drinks and chocolate muffins, put them outside the ward entrance bang on time, behind six or seven visitors already waiting. More joined the queue behind them before the staff unlocked the door.

Nate kept his head bowed and his cap pulled low until Toni told him that he looked like a guy up to no good. He walked upright after that, but rubbed around his eye constantly to cover his face. She found his concern funny.

Every other visitor knew exactly where to go and went there noisily, like holidaymakers, but Nate and Toni had to look around, and that just added to his anxiety. But they didn't get challenged. The patients were all responsible adults, not a known paedophile or Mafioso snitch amongst them, and budget cuts meant the nurses didn't have enough pause time to notice anything untoward.

The door to Alfie's room was ajar and a TV blared from within. They stood outside. Nate had a cheap pay-as-you-go phone, one of two they had bought half an hour earlier. He called a number and the phone in Toni's hand vibrated. They confirmed the line was open, then Toni put the phone in her jacket pocket and pushed open the door.

In the bed was a young man with shaved sides to his head and a curly mop on top. His leg and hip were smothered in plaster, a bandage wrapped his right shoulder, and cuts and bruises dotted his face. But he was awake and alert. He looked to be doing okay for a guy who, according to Nate, had been hit by a truck. He looked away from his phone, which was playing the TV noises, and up at her as she approached.

'Do you know me?' she said. She stood by the bed and grabbed the water jug on his overbed table and moved it a couple of inches. Just fiddling.

'I can get to know you all you want, if you like. What happened to your face?'

Her fingers roamed across the injury he referred to. 'I tried to jump two vans on my bike also. Front wheel fell off.'

He looked suspicious. 'You from the club? Liam's sister, you ain't her, are you?'

'No.' She approached and stroked his bedsheets. Looked up at a shelf above his head. 'I'm Damar's friend. I need to find him. Everything went wrong.'

Suspicion turned to shock, but he covered it by rubbing his face. 'I don't know any Damar, sorry. How did you find me and why? And who do you think I am?'

She fiddled with a vase on the shelf, standing over him. He was looking up with something close to concern, as if fearing an attack. She knew then that she had the right guy for sure, and that he knew more than he was letting on.

'If you hear anything about Damar, let me know. I'm hanging out in the canteen on floor four. It closes at five, but I'll be there until seven maximum. Then I'm gone.'

And with that, she left.

Outside, she and Nate scurried quickly from the corridor and into a disabled toilet. Nate held the burner phone between them. It was on speakerphone. They heard rustling noises, and TV noises. She had planted her own burner on the shelf in Alfie's room, behind the vase.

It took just thirty seconds. The TV noises went off and there was silence for a few seconds. Then: 'It's me,' they heard Alfie say. 'Forget your no-calls rule, man. I just had that girl in my hospital room. Walked right on in. Damar's bitch.'

Pause. Someone on the other end of Alfie's call speaking.

'No, dude, she didn't seem like she just escaped. The guy must have let her go.'

Pause.

'No idea about him. Didn't mention him. All she wanted was to know where Damar was. She just asked, didn't say anything else. But she did say where she's going to be hanging out.'

Pause.

'No idea. Listen, she's here in the hospital. Said she's gonna wait in the canteen on the fourth floor.'

Pause

'I'm in fucking plaster, I can't go anywhere. Fourth floor if you want her. You got until seven o'clock.'

Pause. Then nothing. The call had clearly ended and maybe Alfie was sitting back, thinking.

They gave it another two minutes, but he made no more calls, said nothing. Nate killed the call. He saw that Toni looked angry.

'Don't get any ideas about going back for that guy.' He put a hand around her arm, just in case she fled from the bathroom to get him. She shrugged it off.

'I have patience.'

'We need to tread carefully. This damn plan better work, because they're going to come for us.'

She looked at him, all steely-eyed. 'Good,' was her reply.

The canteen did indeed close at five, but the doors remained open because there was a vending machine. A big thing that you could order a hot pie from, if you didn't mind remortgaging your house in order to pay for it. The staff had put all the chairs upside down on the tables and turned off half the lights so you'd know you had to take your pie and eat it elsewhere. Long windows in the far wall looked down over a car park and outbuildings. It was night, so the glass reflected the room.

This was the postgraduate medical education floor, with no wards, just rooms bearing signs like 'Medical secretaries' and 'General management' and 'IT training', none of them emanating noise, and no groups of fresh-faced doctor-wannabes with clipboards following around a grizzled old veteran. Desolate.

Toni pronounced it perfect, with a smile on her face, while Nate worried that their bodies could lie in the canteen undiscovered until someone came to cook sausages the next morning. With little nooks and crannies and offshoots, the main corridor had plenty of hiding places close to the canteen. They chose a recessed doorway some twenty metres away. The lift and the stairs were on the other side of the canteen, so there was no chance of their guests coming along from this side of the corridor. Ten minutes after they slipped into the recessed doorway, the strips lights in the ceiling went out. Some feature designed to save money. The corridor was now dimly lit only by security lights.

'Perfect,' Toni said again.

Nate wished he could share her glee. He fidgeted and she saw him, and she said, 'The news said your brother was in the army, too. And he was older. Did you follow him?'

Nate nodded.

'Forced by your parents, I bet. Did they look up to him for it?'

'Pete never shut his face about how much fun the army was. He was big bro, so I looked up to him, and I chose to go and serve because I thought it would be great. He liked the brother-hood part of it. I just liked the never getting bored part.'

'And then, after that, you both started a security company? Must be doing well for you to have that big house.'

'Pete bought that house. He got mentioned in his partner's will. The guy died of–'

'Guy?'

'Yeah, Pete likes men. He was called Liam. I never realised how rich he was. He left Pete enough to buy the house, so we... anyway, what's with all the questions?'

'No reason. Small talk. Nothing happening here. Sorry to upset you.'

He wasn't upset, just emotional. Pete was back in his head. He had been trying to keep him out. The emotions such thoughts would stir would weaken him, even if the only one he felt was anger. Anger clouded the mind.

So he was thankful when, ninety seconds later, Toni's claim that nothing was happening here proved to be wrong.

They heard the lift doors open. Footsteps on the tiles. The lights flicked on down that end as whoever had come into the corridor activated a sensor. Using the reflective glass surface of a picture frame on the opposite wall some way down, Nate watched for movement.

Here came a skinny guy wearing denim and carrying a ruck-sack that looked as if it had been used to test wood chippers. He entered the canteen. Nate looked at Toni.

'No. Has to be two or more,' she said. 'They don't know if you're with me or not, and they can't risk having their guy go one-on-one anyway.'

Eighteen minutes in: giggling female voices. Nate peeked out just as two nurses, arm in arm like lovers, turned into the canteen. They nearly hit rucksack guy as he exited with a handful of chocolate bars. Nate looked at Toni.

'Possible, but I doubt it. Maybe a honey trap for you, but they expect me to be here and I don't go for girls.'

Twenty-seven minutes in, the lights down on their end of the corridor flickered on, which made Nate jump because they hadn't heard anyone approaching. Toni grabbed him in a hug as a young man in surgical greens, carrying a wad of papers, walked past.

'Get a room,' he said, a grin on his face. When he was past and gone, Toni pushed Nate roughly away as if he were a horny prom king overstepping the line.

Twenty-nine minutes: two yobbos in plastic jogging trousers and baseball caps sauntered past. They didn't even see the couple lurking in a doorway.

Thirty-two minutes down saw the nurses leave the canteen. One grabbed the ass of the other as they waddled away in the direction they'd come.

Forty-six minutes and two paramedics came out of the lift, pushing an empty wheelchair. Nate watched their reflections. Both were big guys, one stockier than the other. Shaved heads, one for style, one because he was going bald. Into the canteen they went. She got Nate's look again.

'No. The fat one I dated once – met him when I came here for a busted foot. They're legit paramedics.'

Sixty seconds later, she said, 'Hiding here like this isn't going to work. If they come and we don't recognise them as the bad guys, and I'm not in that canteen, they'll leave and we'll never know it. You'll have to go in and wait.'

Now his look was one of shock. 'Why me?'

'They'll know your face, but they're not expecting you, and that will throw them off enough for me to get the drop on them.'

'And what if you can't get the drop on them? What if they have guns, eh? Shall I go in naked and with my hands tied, just to make it easier for them?'

'We can't stay here, and we're sitting ducks if we both go inside. One has to distract so the other can jump them. If you really fancy trying to take them out, I'll go inside.'

She made to step out of the doorway but he grabbed her arm and she stepped back. He took a breath to compose himself, then walked to the canteen and quickly went inside before he could change his mind. A bad idea, but better than the alternative.

The two paramedics were still here, Toni's ex, the balding one, sat at a table while dialling on his phone. The other guy was at the vending machine.

'What do they call Cornish pasties in Cornwall?' the guy at the vending machine said.

They looked at Nate. He nodded and went to a seat near the serving counter, his back to it so he could watch the door. He hoped the paramedics would leave soon, even though he didn't like the idea of being here alone when their hunters arrived. He also hoped Toni was up to this. A killer attitude didn't guarantee killer skills.

A guy in green scrubs came in thirty seconds later, felt into a pocket on his chest, and huffed when he found it empty. Angry, he turned and left. Must have forgotten to bring money.

The paramedic at the vending machine was still trying to make up his mind about what to buy. Nate watched his face in the reflection on the glass front.

The other guy, the one Toni had dated, got up and put his phone away and walked past Nate, approaching the door. He stopped there, right in the doorway, looking at a menu on the wall beside the door. Nate hoped they'd both leave. Cornish Pasty moved away from the vending machine and past Nate, towards the serving counter. He was staring at a large menu on the wall behind the counter. Nate watched him in the vending machine's reflection.

His eyes jerked when he heard a thud. Toni's ex had shut the door. Nate's eyes immediately flicked back to the vending machine, and upon its glass front registered movement behind him. From Cornish Pasty. At the same time, the nerves fled from him. Here the human organism normally entered the flight or fight response, but immediate danger worked differently with Nate. Some error in the circuitry firing his sympathetic nervous system, he figured. The flight part never came into it. As if a switch had been thrown, he cranked instantly into fight mode.

He stood up quickly, hands on the chair, thrusting it backwards, helping with his knees as his legs straightened. The chair slid into the Toni's ex's knees, throwing him off balance. Nate turned and swung an arm. The guy was right behind him, within range of smacking Nate, and he could have beaten him to the punch – literally. But he wasted time slapping the chair aside. To Nate, the chair was a piece of ancient history. His own punch got the guy squarely in the throat.

He staggered back, and Nate turned to face Pasty, already aware of the running footsteps.

Pasty had a pistol, a strange looking one, half wood and half metal with two barrels, seemingly, one under the other. He fired as he ran, and Nate was sure he actually saw a yellow bullet streaming towards him a moment before he felt a sting in his shoulder. The impact wasn't as hard as he expected, and he didn't fall. A skim?

Then he started to stagger. Pasty ignored him for the moment and rushed to his pal. Nate felt wobbly and sat on the floor to avoid falling onto his face. By now Pasty was struggling to hold on to Toni's ex, who seemed to want to cave Nate's head in. Finally he got the guy calmed down somewhat and pushed him away. Toni's ex went to the vending machine to vent his anger by kicking it, since Nate's head was now off-limits.

Pasty squatted before Nate, still aiming that gun. 'Where's the girl?'

Nate opened his mouth to speak, but no words came. Pasty pulled a mobile and made a call. Nate heard him say: 'Bring the van. We got him. Down in five minutes.'

He felt the world going woozy around him, as if glimpsed through water. But he made out Toni's ex coming closer, pushing the wheelchair before him. He parked it by Nate.

His vision was blurring. The paramedic reached out and plucked something from Nate's shoulder. A dart. The shot hadn't missed at all. He'd been nailed with a tranquilliser dart. Drugged again.

Déjà vu, Nate thought, then the blackness came back.

PART II

He dreamed of being drowned, and woke into a nightmare far worse.

The drowning part was real, though. No breath came. His mouth was wet and he coughed. A great glob of phlegm fell over his chin, and suddenly he could breathe. That explained the dream.

His blurry eyes could see walls close by. A van. He was in the back of a van. Something bad had happened, and people with training in causing suffering had captured him, and that was a nightmare, wasn't it?

The walls of the van solidified into shelves of equipment and life-saving machinery. So not just some van at all. An ambulance. And then he remembered it all.

He was on a stretcher with a raised backrest, and night was flooding in through the open back doors. He could see a dirt road, trees on its right side, a chain-link fence on its left. Nobody out there digging his grave this time. Small mercies.

He wasn't naked or tied up, either. He sat upright. Some

strength back. And the nerves. When he was thrust into the deep shit of danger, when it was slammed right in his face, fright took a back seat. But now there seemed to be no immediate danger, and the anxiety was up front and driving.

So, on legs that shook – maybe because of the fear, or maybe because of the drug – he got off the stretcher and walked to the doors. Not wobbly, at least. Everything worked, and there was some strength, and a feeling that he had plenty more in reserve.

The dirt road sloped down and curved to the right out of sight. Some way ahead he could see and now hear traffic, bright white headlights and red tail lights. A motorway.

He jumped down and tried to run for the trees, but the moment he landed, his legs gave way and he fell to the ground. Then he saw one of the two paramedics by the fence, looking at him. Toni's ex.

Only he wasn't looking at Nate. He was sat with his back against a large chain-link gate, and his head was bowed towards his chest. And he was tied to the gate with what looked like bandages.

And a black liquid coated his chest and legs and the ground either side of his hips.

Nate stood up. He slowly approached the guy. Now he knew the black liquid was actually red. Blood. Lots of it. He stepped to the side and a gruesome gash in the guy's throat, hidden by his chin, revealed itself. Dead. Had whoever killed Damar killed him also? Same method. Loose ends?

A noise from the ambulance, behind him. He spun, wobbled, and raised an arm as if expecting a blow. But no blow came.

The other paramedic, the guy who liked Cornish pasties, was by the back wheel, sitting against it, head bowed. Blood on his head, but not that much. And none on his clothing. Alive, given the small moaning sounds and small movements he made.

But then, a realisation: he had no idea if this guy's mouth had touched either young Turkish women or baked half-circles of pastry. Because this guy had black hair. Someone new, albeit dressed as a paramedic also.

So, a third player.

But where was Pasty guy?

Another noise, this time from the trees. The other paramedic, returning. He must have put down his pair of comrades for some reason. Nate stiffened, knowing he was too wobbly to run. Strength in his body, but no cohesion between brain and muscles. He knew he was in no state to properly defend himself if an attack came.

But the person who stepped out of the trees wasn't a pasty-lover.

Toni.

His brain spun.

Almost without thinking, he stepped towards her and clutched her throat in a fist. She didn't even defend herself.

'What fucking trick is this? You set me up. You betrayed me.'

She even grinned. 'Let me go so I can speak,' she croaked.

He didn't.

She reached up and did that thing to his wrist again, same as she had in the van. Pain journeyed up his arm and he let go of her throat.

'You're not naked and not tied up. And you're not dead, but the guys who kidnapped you are. So how betrayed do you really feel, Nate?' Said with mirth, almost sarcasm.

He felt wobbly again, but knew this time it was shock, not whatever drug they'd administered. 'So where's the other guy?'

he said. 'And who's that?' He pointed at the new player. 'What the hell happened?'

She pulled a gun from her jacket. It was the gun he'd been shot with, that double-barrelled machine. She flicked a bolt and a portion opened up. She pulled out a bullet from the back, which wasn't a bullet at all. It had a needle point and an opaque glass tube filled with a dark liquid, and a yellow back end. The yellow flash he'd seen. Now he remembered: he'd been shot with a tranquilliser gun. She reinserted the strange bullet and worked the bolt mechanism again.

'They wanted you alive so they could kill you.'

Not a sentence that helped steady his vibrating mind.

'Where are we?'

'Dulwich,' she said, 'just off the A2199. A road for construction traffic. They're building a Toby Carvery. Maybe we should go for pie and chips sometime.' She pointed over the fence and he looked. A dark building taking shape, but just a skeleton so far, pie and chips a long way in the future. Heavy machinery parked around. A building site. Remote. Shut for the night. Eerie. He suddenly longed to be on a golden beach, surrounded by friends and drinks and drowning in comfort. If he could visit just one more beach one more time in his life, he'd die a happy man.

'What the hell's going on?' he said.

'Oh, Nate, how could you not realise that the guys who came for us would need to transport us out of that hospital? They need me buried to tie up loose ends, and they need you buried so that their little plan to frame you for your brother's murder works. So, there was going to be no shootout in a hospital canteen, was there?'

Maybe that thought had occurred. He couldn't remember, and right now, still drugged, it still didn't make much sense.

'It was why I chose the canteen, way up on the top floor. I knew if these guys were any good, they'd take no risks, and that would mean a disguise to fit the environment, and a legit reason to be taking an unconscious woman out of there. That meant men dressed as doctors or whatever. And then those two bozos turned up with a wheelchair. But here's the thing. Their disguise was good, and it fit right in, didn't it? Paramedics wheeling someone around a hospital, no big deal. But would it fit if the bozos wheeled me out of there and into a Ford Focus in the car park? Of course not. So they went the whole monty and got themselves an ambulance. An ambulance fits right in. But parking it right outside the hospital is risky. It could be called upon by hospital staff. So they needed a way to get that ambulance into position only after they had me safe and sound. Can you figure out how?'

He couldn't.

She indicated the new player. Nate was puzzled still. She pinched his cheek. 'A third man, Nate, a driver. Think.'

He tried to slap her hand away from his cheek, but she moved it and he hit nothing.

'This guy waited for a call and then brought the ambulance into position. By that time I was outside and waiting. I took him out and then waited for the other two to turn up and load you inside, and then I took them out, too. I know you're pissed at me for letting them take you, but we needed all three of them together, so you tell me your better idea of getting everyone, me and you included, into that ambulance without a fuss?'

He didn't have one, and didn't care to think of one. He was thinking only about the fact that there had been three guys, and he could see only two.

He reached up and felt his cheek where she had pinched him. It felt sticky. His fingers came away smeared in wet dirt.

'We didn't need all three. One guy could have given us the information we need.'

'Ever heard the fable of the six blind men and an elephant?'

Strangely, he was having trouble remembering portions of the last few hours, but he could recall that old fable where six blind men encounter an elephant and all come away with very different impressions. And he understood her point.

'We could have asked questions in the canteen, and forced the two to call the driver, and gotten all three that way.'

'Might have turned crazy. Bullets flying in a hospital. Nobody wanted that.'

'We could have headed outside and looked for an ambulance lurking around.'

'He could have waited half a mile away. Think of the number of streets in a half-mile radius of the hospital. Think of him driving away when his men report that the canteen was empty. And how would we have gotten them all together? This was the only way.'

'Bullshit. You wanted all three of them together, here, where it's nice and quiet.'

'Better for the interrogation.'

'Bullshit. Better for the torture and murder.'

She took a step to one side so she wasn't blocking the moonlight and could read his eyes. Drugged, he was sure, but still displaying his thoughts. His suspicions.

'We let them go,' she said, 'and they regroup and come back. Like warts if you don't clip the roots. That's what these people are. Warts. How many times do you want to capture the same people? How many times do you want the same bad guys shooting at us?'

He shook his head. 'Bullshit, Toni. I know what's going on. I picture you as an old lady in a nursing home many years from now. Vacant-eyed and unresponsive. The staff think it's dementia, but it isn't. Insanity. From knowing that no matter how many men you killed way back, you might have missed the *one*. That special *one* who actually drew the knife across Damar's throat. Insanity at knowing he might still be out there, laughing and fucking and sleeping and all fine in his life because he's not haunted at all by the memories of the guy he butchered so long ago.'

That got her. Her face turned angry and he saw her fists clench down by her sides. The cold wind and the silence and the dark all seemed to intensify, as if to try to remind him that he was out in the middle of nowhere with a killer who might still be his enemy. Who had planned to kill and bury *him* in the woods. He took a step back, and she saw it, and he knew she knew what he was thinking. That seemed to settle her. At least it helped her to leash the rage trying to burst out from within.

'They killed your brother,' she said. 'You want that to go unpunished?'

'Justice is perfectly fine in the form of a prison sentence.'

'Prison? That's punishment? Do you think these people are fraudulent bankers? People like this will thrive in prison. They'll make friends and have a laugh and plan new crimes for the day they get out. That's not happening. Walk away if you don't like it. You're wondering where the other man is, right?'

'Not anymore. I know he's dead and buried in these woods.' He tossed the wet dirt from his cheek against her jacket.

'That's right.' She jerked a thumb at the dead man against the fence. 'Guess this guy's future.'

He said nothing. Her finger jabbed at the guy slumped against the ambulance. 'Guess his.'

'And the next guy we meet on the ladder?'

'Dead. Buried. And the guy above, and the guy above him.

All of them, Nate. It's called revenge. I hope you clear your name, but that's not why I'm here, and I'm surprised you're not after the same thing. That was your brother, and they killed him. I picture you in that same nursing home, going insane because of a memory where you had your brother's murderer on his knees in front of you, and you let him go.'

'If I find the man who arranged Pete's murder and he's kneeling before me and I have a gun in my hand, I'll kill him without a thought. But that doesn't help me if I go to prison, does it? So, I'm going to try to clear my name. I don't fancy a life on the run. I guess I'm picky like that.'

She pulled another weapon from inside her jacket. The knife he'd stolen from the guest house. He took another step back, but she turned the knife and offered him the handle.

'So interrogate this guy,' she said. 'Take this, because I don't think the threat of a Chinese burn will make the guy talk.'

She approached Black Hair and lifted his head. His eyes were open but glazed. Maybe concussed. Certainly beaten. Nate saw puffy eyes, a split lip. She slapped his cheek to jolt him fully awake. 'You will answer this man's questions, okay?' To Nate: 'Go.'

Nate stood before the guy, but the knife stayed down by his side. He didn't know how to begin. He started with the ultimate question, in the hope this could all be resolved in two seconds: 'Who set all this up?'

'Set what up?' the guy croaked.

'Who hired you?'

The man said, 'Cube.'

'There you go,' Toni said. 'A job well done. You're a natural interrogator, Nate. *Cube.* Now you have a name to chase in your name-clearing quest.'

Nate didn't know what to say. So, he said, 'I don't know anyone called Cube.'

'Well, I doubt Cube's the name on his birth certificate, unless his parents are weirdos. Carry on. Milk the guy for all he's worth.'

She was playing with him, but he ignored her. Getting answers was the important thing here. He said to Black Hair, 'Lazar, you know that name?'

'Good question, Nate,' Toni said. 'I would never have thought of that.'

Good question, but it achieved nothing. The guy's groggy head took time to understand the question, before shaking.

Nate waved the knife now, and felt awkward doing it. He hoped the guy didn't call his bluff. 'Achala Kaushal. You must know that name. A young Indian woman.'

Something in his eyes. Recognition. Nate caught it before the guy looked at Toni, who was standing by like a security guard, arms folded. Nate understood. 'He's already answered these questions,' he said to her. 'You already know.'

She shrugged. 'You wanted to play a role. So now you've got an input.'

'I don't need an ego boost,' he snapped, turning away, striding away, towards the fence. He was within three feet of the dead guy against that fence before he realised it, and turned again to face the road through the trees. He heard Toni's footsteps come up behind him, but didn't turn around.

'You think I just parked here and started cutting people like a maniac, Nate? While you were dreaming of elves and treasure, I was asking questions. I want to know the truth, too. I had a long chat with him before you woke up, and I got what we need. He has no phone, no ID, no paperwork of any kind, but we needed information. You were dreaming of sheep and I'm good at getting information from people, so what was I to do? Next time I'll play solitaire until you wake up so you can do all the threats and torture to get what we need.'

'Piss off.'

She spun him to face Black Hair.

'So let me tell you what I learned. This man's a contract killer, Nate. Apparently good. Sounding off about himself before you woke up. Apparently he's going to kill my bloodline. I'm going to wish my great grandfather lost his testicles as a child. And I'm going to scream and beg to be killed. Strangely stopped all that hullabaloo when I cut his pal's throat right in front of him. Eager to talk after that.

'Lazar. He genuinely doesn't know that name. Cube, now he's some kind of gangster. I'm picturing gold teeth and tinted car windows. Cube hired this guy after you escaped from Damar and me. This hitman called a couple of lowlifes he keeps on speed-dial for snatch jobs and all three of them came for me at the hospital. The hospital aspect was a sweet bonus for them because these two just happen to be legitimate paramedics. So they came to interrogate me to find out where you are. Then to bury me, of course.' She gritted her teeth. 'At the Enfield warehouse, right next to Damar.'

Nate was still woozy. 'A hitman? That's... extreme.'

'Get James Bond films out of your head. It isn't as if you need a degree. Hitman is just a word for someone who's willing to kill people for money.'

'So what does he know? Does he know why all this is happening?'

'Says not, and I believe him. He was given a description of you and me, told he'd find me at the hospital, and told to take me to the warehouse in Enfield, and that was, according to him, all he needed or wanted. All he knows is Cube wants us dead, but not why. This guy was working for Cube on a couple of jobs and then he got the call for this little side mission. Side mission! Like taking out the trash.

'Nate, listen carefully. Of the two jobs this guy was hired for, one was a hit on some guy in America, and the other was to dispose of a body here. A body that turns your theory about all of this into dog poo. That body was your Achala Kaushal.'

Nate tried to let that sink in. It wouldn't.

'He did not know the name, but he recalls the body was that of a young Indian woman. He did not kill her. I believe him. He arranged for her body to be dumped in a lake up north some-where, but he doesn't know which one because his people didn't give him that information. Apparently he doesn't need all the details.'

Nate couldn't speak. This thing was getting too convoluted and his woozy brain was not yet up to the task.

'Understand, Nate? This is a breakthrough. Kaushal's not the enemy here: she's another victim.'

'Great. So we strike one name off the vast list of who it could be trying to fuck me over. That gets us no closer.'

'It gives us a clue, moron. Someone who used to work for you was also killed. So this might have something to do with your security company. That information puts us a step closer, even if you don't see it. And we have a name, Cube, even though that means nothing so far. So now you need to think of some reason why this Cube would want you and your brother, *and* this Kaushal, dead.'

He couldn't. After she left the job, Kaushal had not been part of Nate's life, or Pete's – as far as he knew. Four years. He hadn't seen her, or heard a thing about her, in all that time. Four years.

'I don't know. But what about this Cube and Lazar? How are they connected?'

'Well, I imagine Lazar's a henchman. Like the other goons. We don't concentrate on them. Cube's the boss. So we need to find Cube, whoever he is.'

'How can you be sure that this hitman isn't holding back? Or feeding us bullshit?'

She pulled something else from her pocket. A regular magician, this girl. It was a fob with a single key hanging from it. 'I have that covered. I know where the guy's staying. There must be more clues there. It's not exactly down the road, but I don't have any pressing plans. Do you? We'll go there after you've helped me kill this guy and bury him and the other one.'

'No way,' he said. *No damn way. No more killings.* 'I'm trying to clear my name for my brother's death. What the hell is the point of that if the cops just say, "Sure, yeah, wasn't you, but you're under arrest for being an accomplice in ten other murders"?'

She looked at him carefully. 'Remember what I said about warts? We leave this guy alive, he comes back at us. How many times do you want to keep capturing him and letting him go?'

'No more killings, dammit. You might be a psycho, but I'm not.'

'So make your damn decision, because I'm leaving in ten minutes.'

Nate cycled through his massive array of options – both of them. They could tie the hitman up, but come morning the guys building the Toby Carvery would release him back into the mix. Or they could take him prisoner, but that would bring about all sorts of problems. Of course, there was always that other option...

As if reading his mind, Toni reached into her magician's jacket again, and then held out the tranquilliser gun in one hand and cable ties in the other. As if giving him a choice. Like a toddler spotting a better toy, Nate dropped the knife in the dirt and ignored the cable ties and grabbed the gun.

Toni said, 'Fine. So he's luggage. Your luggage. So you take care of him.'

To pause would be to think, and that might allow his mind to freeze. So he stepped forward and aimed the gun and put a dart in Black Hair's shoulder, and watched as he fell limp and slid over onto his face.

'Now you need to manhandle him into the van.'

She clearly wasn't going to help. It took three minutes and the guy slipped from his grasp twice as Nate was feeding him into the ambulance, and hit the dirt again. Eventually the guy was on the stretcher. Nate tied him with bandages. Toni watched from the back of the vehicle, offering no help.

But she expected help of her own once Nate had finished. 'Now the other guy. We bury him, or do you want to carry him along, too?'

'He's your luggage,' he said, like a petulant kid.

He thought it was a smart comment, but it elicited only a grin. 'He manhandled you, Nate. DNA. You're not going to clear your name if the cops find his body. Best hope for you, he's the last to die and his body's never found.'

He knew she was right. The guy was already dead, and now posed a problem to be solved. Abhorrent, but the only way. They had to bury him.

'Look on the bright side,' she said, 'at least I already dug the hole.'

When it was done, they got in the van. Nate took the passenger seat and rubbed his face. He had performed the burial service quite well, he thought. Meaning he hadn't vomited or thrown a seizure due to shock. But that didn't mean he would erase the memories anytime within the rest of his life. Actually, he thought he might recall them during sweaty, screaming nights over the next fifty years.

He had the knife in his hand, resting in his lap but pointing at her. She couldn't miss it.

'Hey, I'm sorry for lying when I said I'd dated one of them. But I needed to convince you they were real paramedics. So you'd relax. It was to help you, that was all.'

He said nothing.

'No more trust?'

'You just stay away from me, okay? There's something badly wrong with your head. You're a bomb, and I don't want you going off in my face.'

She seemed hurt. 'Get the hell out and go your own way, then. Go.'

He didn't move.

'Exactly. You need me, remember. Now put that away.'

He slid the knife out of sight, but kept it in his hand. 'Let's just get where we're going quick. The sooner this is over, the better.'

She drove. In silence. He calmed down, seeing her normal like this. He reminded himself that she'd lost her good friend. Not that it excused her behaviour. Her violence. Ten minutes later, he was staring out the window, at the road rushing by, trying to think of nothing. But all he could think about was, not his brother, or Lazar, or contract killers, but her. That he was sitting beside a vicious killer and she seemed so normal. This was the world he'd entered. Peopled by monsters in human skin. He–

'Penny for the thoughts?' she said, cutting into those thoughts.

He continued to stare at the night road. 'I was just thinking,

"Congratulations. It's been a couple of hours since you last threatened my life".'

'Out loud,' she said, and winked. He caught it out of the corner of his eye, which meant she knew he could see her peripherally.

'And I'm thinking you seem very robotic. Not jerky movements, of course. More the lack of human compassion in any way. You sit there humming like we're actually going on holiday. You were born in Turkey, right? I'm thinking the woods. Brought up by wolves until you were about eighteen. Do you laugh when children trip and hurt themselves?'

She laughed now. But said nothing. Continued to drive through the night.

He put his head back and closed his eyes.

His eyes jerked open as the van hit a bump. Shockingly, the dashboard clock said nineteen minutes had passed. Toni was still driving, but had her phone in her hand. She saw him looking.

'I thought I'd check you out online. Seems there's no bigger news story today.'

She tossed the phone into his lap. He picked it up and saw an image. Saw his own face. His passport photo, which made him look like a fugitive. It was a still from a news video. He could see the news program's logo in the corner of the screen.

And a ticker along the bottom that said:

Missing fugitive was investigated for robbery murder

And there it was. The HyperX thing, back to bite him on the ass. 'Christ,' he muttered, allowing his head to drop back. 'This is all looking so much worse now.'

'Play it, bad boy.'

He did. The video was just a series of still pictures, with a voiceover: 'Nathan Barke, the man wanted by police in relation to an arson attack on his home that claimed the life of his brother, Peter Barke, was questioned by police about a garage robbery in which one of the perpetrators–'

He paused the video. It was a story he knew well, of course. 'That's nothing,' he said. But she didn't look convinced. A grin. She reached over and pressed play.

The reporter went on, his tinny voice filling the van. Now he was talking about how he'd failed to get a response on the robbery thing from the cops, but through his own brilliance had learned that two of the three-strong team of Acorn Security guards had all served time for violent offences and robberies...

The third member being Achala Kaushal, Nate thought. 'Violent' criminal was an unfair description of Carl Webber, who had made one mistake years earlier and whose conviction was spent by the time Nate hired him. Jon Agar was a vastly different animal. Kaushal, however, had been squeaky clean. Hired as a trainee accountant, she had expressed a willingness to dive into the deep end, get her hands dirty, do some hard graft. And here came her name again. Missing. Now presumed to be in danger. But the police were still unsure as to why this girl might pose a problem to Nate Barke. A hint that her lack of a criminal past could be a reason. Nate wondered about that. Did the cops assume that Acorn Security, with its complement of ex-cons, was up to no good and that the law-abiding young Indian woman had threatened to expose something, which had prompted Nate to... do something to her?

Sure they did. It was all part of the effort to frame him. The cops believed Nate had hurt Kaushal, and he was getting the feeling that her body, when found, was going to scream evidence that Nate was the culprit. Set-up for two killings now. An insurmountable wall to climb. He could only hope that the hitman had been lying for some reason, or that the woman he'd buried in a lake wasn't Kaushal. He needed her to be found alive and well so the police would realise they'd been wrong about him, because maybe that would help him convince them they'd been wrong about his involvement in the house fire and the death of...

He shut that thought down. He didn't want Pete in his head. It was hard to think of him without picturing a burned corpse.

Nate became aware of Toni looking at him. Staring.

'I'm not going to survive this thing, am I?' he said.

'Don't think like that. We don't know what evidence is out there that you're innocent. That's why we're looking.'

'That headline is bad. That, plus the house fire... no way I survive this.'

'Is it true, though? The cops investigated you for murder and robbery?'

A sudden image of a nation in uproar, of crowds baying for blood. 'Yes, but it's not as bad as it sounds.' He didn't know why he felt the need to defend himself to a woman who had just killed two men.

'Tell me your version.'

He tried to ignore her choice of words. Not 'Tell me *what happened*', but 'Tell me *your version*'. Did she have doubts? Understandable, because nobody did the things they'd done to Nate for no reason. Did she think that Nate was a bad man who was now dying by the sword?

Putting aside that worry, he explained. HyperX Customs had been a high-end car restoration and customisation joint that did private work, and also sold cars they'd overhauled. It had two branches, one here and one in Dubai. The Dubai side was larger, catering to rich people who wanted their flash rides to stand out amongst the serious and expensive vehicles in that country. But sometimes blinging out a Ferrari or Lamborghini wasn't enough, and that was where the London branch came in. Here a Vauxhall Corsa wasn't exclusive, but roll around in a diamond-studded one over there, you turned heads. In London the guys would customise run-of-the-mill rides and ship them to Dubai, and the beauty of the deal was that tycoons bored of their gold-plated Rolls-Royces would, here and there, do a straight swap – a car worth £10,000 for a car worth fifty times as much. These luxury cars would head overseas and be sold in London for tidy sums.

That fateful night, the London branch of HyperX had three Rolls-Royce Wraiths in the workshop, and Acorn Security had been hired to watch the place. Some guys had broken in, but since the cars couldn't be started without the keys, and the keys were off-site with the boss, none had been stolen. Instead of arranging a tow, the angry robbers had taken the cars to pieces and stolen various expensive parts.

Nate's team of three had tried to defend the place, and things had gone badly wrong. Nate and his brother and two of the three guards had been pulled in for questioning, but nothing had come of it. The cops had let them go after a few interviews. No big deal. He didn't know why it was even being brought up. It had no bearing on what had happened at his house. But it didn't make him look good.

'Maybe I could get a reward for handing you in.'

'They just want to make me look like a fucking maniac who's running around out there.'

'On a serious note, Nate, you're going to have a hard time convincing the cops that you did nothing wrong this time. Not with that little secret in your past. We might have to get more extreme. Hurt some people.'

'A dream come true for you. Which gives me an idea. I'm going back to sleep. Maybe this is all a bad dream and I'll wake in bed two days ago.'

At least the remnants of the drug were letting him drift off quickly. She started laughing, and he was gone before she had finished.

Fifty-seven minutes later, the ambulance was in Kent, running northeast through the Hoo Peninsula after leaving the M2 south of where the River Thames became the Thames Estuary.

He had woken after another sleep, exactly nineteen minutes later. She was checking the phone, probably the route. When she saw him awake, she said nothing, but she tossed the phone into his lap. She went back to watching the road ahead.

Now, after over half an hour of ignoring each other, he heard her rooting in the driver's door pocket. Seconds later, a penny landed in his lap. He understood. He'd spent the first ten minutes of that half hour on Google, and the rest staring out the side window.

'Monoamine oxidase A mutation,' he said. And caught her perplexed look. 'It's a problem with the prefrontal cortex part of the brain. That's what you have, maybe. Brunner Syndrome. Might explain your violent brain and lack of empathy.'

Perplexity became mirth. She said, 'And you have cyber-chondria.'

He looked that up on Google, too. Anxiety over one's health brought on by searching medical websites. Now he understood what she found so funny. He tossed the phone into her lap and put his forehead back against the side window.

The A228 took them past Upper Stoke, then it was a north-wards run through Lower Stoke, strangely higher than Upper Stoke on the map. Eventually they were at the end of a typical residential street when ahead they saw a large blue sign.

As Toni pulled up at the kerb, Nate studied the key in his hand. The key Toni had taken from the hitman. The emblem on the fob matched the picture on the sign: a grassy expanse with the sun above and a mobile home, and 'Sunny Dream Leisure Park' floating in a blue sky. On the back was the number 47.

The phone landed in his lap. Playing the game, he looked at the screen and saw a website about something called 'The Warrior gene'.

'Maybe that's what I have,' Toni said with a grin. 'A guy got it successfully used in a murder case to defend his actions a few years ago. So, I may escape prison because my genes are at fault. Thanks for that.'

'Sounds like cyberchondria to me.'

She turned to face him, a little angry suddenly. 'If I must explain my whimsical attitude, it was for you. Because you're a little girl, so I was trying to lighten the mood so you don't piss in your pants and wake screaming at night. You've still got the walk-away option. Go right now if you like and I'll finish this myself.'

'I'm staying,' Nate snapped back. 'This isn't your show. It's mine. And we're not killing anyone else unless we have to. Understand?'

'Maybe I have to. Read some more about my genes, since you know them so well, doctor.'

He glared at her. 'Jokes aside now. We need to talk about something serious.'

She looked at him, saw on his face that all the humour was gone. She turned off the engine and looked at him.

He said, 'You were part of the group that killed my brother and tried to kill me. And I was fully prepared to kill you. You think I might want to do that again when this is over and I don't need your help.'

She glared back and he knew he had hit the spot.

'I have no plans to try to kill you, Toni. You did not kill my brother. I do not hold you responsible.'

Her silence told him she didn't believe that.

'When this is over, I plan to walk away. I will not try to hurt you.'

Now her eyes couldn't meet his. They fell over his shoulder, out his window and across the planet, seeing nothing.

'If I had not escaped from you, Damar would still be alive. It's my fault in a way. You kind of said that earlier. So, I know you will either want to kill me for that, or you will want to kill me because you think I will kill you. You don't trust anyone, that much I know about you.'

She started the engine. 'Time is ticking,' she said. 'Let's get this done.'

'Believe me or don't, Toni, and I hope you do for both our sakes, but if you don't, then let's have an agreement. Nothing out of the blue. No cheap shot. When this is over, we agree that it is so and work it from there. Because if you try to pull a fast one and sink a blade into me, Toni, I will react. I will react. Understand?'

She ignored the question and pointed out the windscreen, at the leisure park. Said, 'We can't take an ambulance inside.'

She was right. Too much attention. People would stare, wondering who might have died.

They drove the streets, seeking another vehicle. They didn't find one, but they did happen across a row of lock-up garages with a battered abandoned car parked in the scrubland between two buildings. Toni got out and removed the wheelchair, then Nate parked the ambulance on the hidden side of the last garage, where it just fit between that building and a wooden fence. There was no-one around. Toni parked the wheelchair by the open back doors.

The hitman was stirring. He had come round halfway here and Nate had had to blast him with the gun again. There was one dart left, and he used it now to put the guy back to sleep.

'Turn his jacket inside out so this doesn't look suspicious,' Toni said.

Nate understood. Civilians wheeling a paramedic in a wheelchair – dodgy. He did as asked, and of course, she didn't help.

She helped him get the guy out of the vehicle and into the wheelchair, though. Not to be helpful, he knew. But because they couldn't prolong their exposure out here. Toni threw the blanket over him, tucked it in, covering all but his head. Now he just looked like some disabled guy having a kip.

They started walking.

Twenty minutes later they were back at the entrance to the caravan park. The map showed a C-shaped main road with icons plastered all over it, as if a kid had been given a bunch of stickers. An insert showed a larger view of the 'entertainment complex', and seeing this reminded Nate of when he'd been to such places as a kid. He instantly started to feel better. These were anonymous places. Places where you forgot about the outside world and its news of fugitive fratricides. He pulled off his cap, determined to try to relax a little while here. He had been wired now for twenty-four hours and would probably burst something vital in his brain if he didn't calm the hell down.

There was a guardhouse and a barrier, but the barrier was up and nobody was home. Cars came and went without a care. They passed through and walked along the pavement. Other side of the road, two other people in wheelchairs sat near a bench upon which their carers rested. That made Nate and Toni feel better. They knew they wouldn't stand out here.

The main road was lined on both sides with pavements and shoulder-height hedges that broke for roads leading into the caravan sites. Five minutes of walking and they found the sign for 'Seagull Wings'. A sea of pale brown static caravans stretched before them on both sides of a road and along a series of side roads. The grass was bright green and mowed, and benches where scattered everywhere. All very quaint and quiet. A few people scattered around, some just chatting, some headed somewhere or back from somewhere. Nobody gave them a second look, never mind a suspicious one. Nate felt the tension dribble away, as if he were leaving it as a stain with each footstep. To bolster his resolve, he even waved at an old couple who were playing chess at a table outside their caravan.

Number 47, enchantingly called Starfish, was at the back near a berm representing the boundary between this site and the next. The caravans beyond the berm were a weak yellow colour, as if they'd sat under the sun for a thousand years.

The caravan next to theirs had a people carrier parked alongside and a kid sitting on the grass playing with toys. No parents in view, but the caravan's door was wide open and light and TV noise oozed out. The kid ignored them as they turned in. Far more interested in seeing if Peppa Pig could outwrestle a *T. rex* half her size.

Toni went cautiously to the door and peered in the window, then unlocked it. She glanced at their neighbour's open door, then waved him on. Nate wheeled the chair up to the steps and turned it around.

Together they tipped the chair over backwards and dragged the guy out and inside. The door delivered them into the kitchenette, with the living room to their left and a door on the right that led to the bedrooms. They dropped him on the linoleum and Toni flicked on the light as Nate stepped out. He started to collapse the wheelchair, but froze as a handsome young man appeared at the door twenty feet away. The guy was topless, carrying a can of lager in one hand and a shirt on a hanger in the other. Nate nodded at him. The guy nodded back and vanished. Nate slid the collapsed wheelchair under the caravan and darted back inside.

The hitman was on his back and was slowly coming round. Toni had a foot placed heavily on a forearm and was staring down at him, patiently waiting for his revival. Nate put his own foot on the free arm, pinning him there.

His eyes finally opened. They watched confusion turn to understanding, then morph into shock. He started to struggle, but the drug wasn't yet ready to return his strength to him.

'I'm still not wishing death to my great grandfather's balls,' Toni said. 'Get a move on.'

The guy's throat got up to full power quickly. He started to yell for help. Nate pulled out the dart gun, but before he could take a shot, Toni bent down and applied a choke from the front. The guy grabbed her hair, but his hands fell limp in just seconds. Back to sleep.

'The gun's empty,' she said. Nate suddenly remembered that. 'You let him live, so you tie him up. I'll look around.'

Since they'd cut away the bandages in order to move the guy from the ambulance and hadn't brought others, Nate had to improvise. Cables from the TV for his wrists and ankles. Nate sat him on a wooden chair in the kitchenette, facing a knife block just so the guy would know, when he woke, that his cosy home was not a safe place for him. Then he joined Toni in searching the Starfish.

Toni found a laptop computer under a pile of magazines on the coffee table and immediately immersed herself in it. Nate thought she was wasting her time: surely a professional hitman wouldn't be silly enough to leave clues and evidence on a computer. So he searched for physical things in invisible spots.

So intent was he upon awkward nooks and crannies that he didn't notice the item atop the TV until he sat down on the sofa to think.

A metal briefcase.

And it was unlocked. Inside it was lined with foam that had shapes cut out to accommodate a few scary items. A pair of small binoculars rested in their home, as well as a small knife. There were two empty spaces for guns, one of which looked like the home for the tranquilliser pistol. A small metal box contained more darts for that pistol. And there were two spaces for syringes, one still in place. He plucked this out and held it up. A plastic medical syringe, short and fat, the needle capped. It contained a strange, bright green liquid, like molten Kryptonite. Like magic dragon's blood from a fantasy film.

Toni saw it and stopped playing on the laptop.

'Damar was given a syringe like that. Same green fluid. It was what we were told to inject you with.'

Her tone said she was thinking the same thing as him: the hitman's involvement in this was deeper than he'd claimed. And that was a good thing, sure, of course, but Nate couldn't bring himself to be pleased while imagining this nasty green shit flooding through his veins.

'Damar said it had Rohypnol in it,' she said. 'Date rape drug.' A ghost of a smile on her face, as if she thought this was funny – a *guy* being knocked out with a date rape drug.

'Why the hell is it green?'

'Like I'd know,' she said. She looked at the clock above the cooker.

'It has additions to make it quicker acting,' said the hitman. His accent was thick Scottish.

Nate whirled round.

The hitman was awake, head turned so he could watch them. 'Rohypnol is one ingredient. There are others that confuse

the mind even long after the sleep effects are gone. I don't know
the full arrangement. The bright green colour is a scare tactic to
aid in the collection of information.'

Nate got that part fully. If some guy threatened to jab this
shit into his neck, he'd admit he was the guy on the grassy knoll
in Dallas's Dealey Plaza in 1963. He was angry.

'So you supplied this drug, yet you said you were hired
recently to capture us in the hospital. Bullshit. You've been in
this from the start. You need to start telling us what you know.
Start with why my brother was killed, and why they're trying to
kill me.'

The hitman shook his head. 'I don't have those answers. I
wasn't involved in that. I was hired four days ago and I told my
employer what I needed and who I knew in London could
supply it. The tasks I was given did not involve you or the lady. I
only learned of your existence earlier today when he called me
with a side mission. I was told only that there was a young
woman who had to be detained, and used to locate a man. I
know nothing about you, my friend. This is the first time I've
seen you.'

Nate waved the syringe. 'No, we've met, dickhead. Remember, this fucks with your brain.'

'If you let me go, I will give you my employer's name. He's–'

'Cube,' Nate said. The hitman looked surprised, then embarrassed. 'You told us. You told us a lot. Like you told us you killed
a young Indian woman–'

'No,' the hitman snapped. 'Cube only tasked me with one
hit, and that was a fellow way off in another country. I only kill
abroad. That's what I'm good at. Here at home I deal only in
paving the way for others if they require someone dead.'

Nate had tried to trick the hitman into admitting he'd termi-
nated Kaushal. Now he believed the guy was telling the truth.
Which meant Kaushal had already been dead by the time the

hitman had gotten involved. Which meant someone else had killed her.

'So who killed her?'

'I don't know. I didn't need to know. I don't ever need to know. I never want to know.'

Something in the man's tone, or his eyes? Something, though. Something about him that said he wasn't a liar. A killer for money, but not a liar. And deeply offended to be called such. Again, Nate believed him. So this guy had gotten involved only after Toni had visited the biker called Alfie in hospital.

As if he knew Nate was in a trusting – maybe even forgiving – mood, the hitman said, 'I have a wife and son in Scotland and I run a small business in Edinburgh that helps local charities. I am not a snitch. I am a man with a family and employees who rely on me. I will not make them suffer in order to protect a London gangster. I will tell you what you need to know in order to get back to my family. I will not lie to you about anything. Cube, my employer on this job, is a man no doubt used to comebacks, and I'm sure he is prepared to deal with the one you threaten him with. The computer.'

Nate and Toni looked at the laptop.

'A hidden file,' the hitman said and explained how to find it. 'I met Cube in a public place and only for thirty seconds while an employee of his gave me the file on a flash drive. I cannot direct you to this man or give you any other information about him. But I will give you the file he gave me. Maybe there will be information within that you can use. I will do that. It is all I have, which means my giving it to you is testament to helping you to the best of my abilities. Maybe it will be enough for you to be swayed into letting me live.'

'Don't bet the house,' Toni said as she hit the computer again. She quickly found the file. Nate stood by her and looked.

It was a Word document with embedded photos. Thirty-seven pages, according to the status bar at the bottom. Toni scrolled quickly, zipping by text and pictures of street maps and landscapes and buildings and people–

Nate slapped her hand away from the page-down button, causing the document to cease scrolling. He jabbed his finger at the page-up button, and the document scrolled the other way, and onto the screen slipped a photograph of a man with wiry ginger hair and beard and freckles, mid-thirties.

'I know him,' Nate said. 'Jesus. I know what this is about.'

HyperX Customs was an old brick building made to look new with wood panelling. It was a squat block with three entrances. One was a single glass door behind which was a reception, neat and shiny with plants and computers and a TV and a fish tank and, during business hours, a sweet girl in a black suit behind a desk. You got to use one of the other two entrances after talking to this girl. Tell her you had a car that needed fixing up or customising, and she'd send you round back, where a corrugated iron shutter delivered vehicles into a grimy workshop. Say you wanted to buy an exotic ride, and she'd escort you round to the side of the building, where folding glass doors led to a showroom.

Five other people worked here. Two mechanics, both guys in their fifties, over thirty years' experience between them; two bodykit experts, both brash young egos on legs, and an electrician, whose speciality was mammoth stereo systems and insane gadgetry. The old-school veterans and the tattooed players had left for the evening, but the electrician had hung around to meet the three people who arrived at eight that night. He showed them the coffee machine, the TV, various switches, asked them not to go in the showroom, warned them to stay out of the work-shop, and then left.

Even though the building often boasted expensive vehicles, this was the first time HyperX had ever hired security to watch the place overnight, and the three guards knew it, and so the first thing they did was go to see the reason why, and that meant ignoring the electrician's warning.

The workshop was a long, high space that was surprisingly neat and clean. The three security guards stood in the doorway and stared at what they were here to protect: three Rolls-Royce Wraiths, guests for one night only. Shiny and white, already sold to the British elite and awaiting collection, they were wrapped in what looked like thick cling film. The three guards looked, and then they left to go do other things.

At almost midnight, the guards were killing time. Eight hours to go. Carl Webber was in the reception, watching sci-fi on TV, and he planned to be there all night. On the desk, where his feet rested, was a retractable truncheon. With ironic timing, or a trick of his senses, the sound of a spaceship exploding occurred at exactly the same time that the reception door burst open, and that threw him off. So much so that the four masked men who rushed in had him surrounded even before he fully realised what was going on. £29.99 spent on the truncheon, and every penny wasted.

Achala Kaushal was at the showroom doors, which she'd opened to let her cigarette smoke out. She leaned against the frame and stared at the high dark buildings across the way, and listened to Nina Simone through her headphones. Again, noise was to blame. When she saw Webber stumbling towards her in the black-ness, flapping his hands, working his mouth wide and fast, she did not hear his words and didn't know he was trying to warn her. Only when four masked men materialised out of the dark behind him, one holding Webber's upper arm, did simple curiosity advance into suspicion on its journey towards panic and terror. By then, too late. £8.49 for a 40ml bottle of Farb Gel self-defence spray – wasted.

Jon Agar was in the workshop, where he shouldn't have been. He had sliced the plastic wrapping around the driver's door of one of the Wraiths and had been sitting behind the wheel, pretending he was affluent. And doing so in silence, which meant he heard the commotion from another room. Shouting. He heard his pals, and he heard gruff voices he didn't know. That gave him plenty of time to whip out his weapon, which hadn't cost him a penny.

He exited the car, aware that if the voices he heard belonged to robbers, then these cars were their target. So he got out of there. But with the roller shutter that led outside locked, the door into the main building was the only way out – or in. He managed to get himself under a table with a long plastic cloth moments before the door was kicked open.

Kneeling, face pressed to the pitted concrete so he could see out of a thin gap between floor and tablecloth, he watched in horror as his two colleagues stumbled into the workshop, followed by blurry black forms that shimmered in the glass as they moved. Just black shapes, but he could tell them apart by flashes of colour on the ends of their arms. Four men in black jeans and tight black pullovers and black balaclavas, but each wearing gloves of a different colour. Blue, white, green, red.

He heard them shouting for his colleagues to sit against the wall, 'Don't move! Do fucking nothing!'

Then he heard one say, 'Where's the other guy?' and saw a red glove waving something at them. A long blade. A damn machete. So, they had come prepared, because they knew there were meant to be three guards here.

The black shapes moved. They swarmed over and inside the three Wraiths. They used tools to take the vehicle apart, quickly, like a piranha stripping a carcass. Agar froze in fear, gripping his weapon and hoping the raiders would take their booty and vanish.

Time dragged. Agar controlled his breathing lest ragged puffs gave him away, and his colleagues sat with their heads in their hands, wishing this nightmare away. But eventually the men moved away from the Wraiths. Car parts from the engine bay and the interior, even the three drivers' seats and the steering wheels, had been scattered across the floor. Two men carried armfuls of loot out of the workshop, returning a few minutes later for another batch. In four trips, everything stripped from the Rolls-Royces was gone, probably in the back of a van outside. And then, beautifully, the four masked men looked ready to leave.

This knowledge put a loosening in Agar's muscles, and he suddenly felt terrible pain in his knees. He got a hand under him, to raise his chest from the cold floor and relieve the pressure, but that hand held his weapon and it made a soft clack against the concrete. Impossible for the men to have heard it at such a distance, above their own noise, but Agar saw a head flick around, eyes alighting immediately upon the table. If there was a gesture from him to the others, Agar missed it. But he watched all four move towards him, spreading out, planning to circle the table. The pain in his knees sank away once more. With no good escape scenario to promote, his whirling mind settled for praying that the men would somehow overlook the table as they searched the sparse workshop. But he heard their boots from all sides as they encircled the table.

He expected the tablecloth to be whipped off, but instead the entire wooden table flipped away at a kick, and he was exposed like a magician's rabbit. Four men, staring down at him. The one in front of him, Green Gloves, lifted his machete and grinned. 'Enjoy the show, did you?' he said. 'Up you get.'

An order he wouldn't dream of disobeying, of course, but Red Gloves wasn't convinced and instantly lurched forward. When the man took a handful of hair and jerked him upright on his knees, Agar was aware of the weight of the gun in his own hand. But not the arm attached to that hand.

Not until Red Gloves jerked backwards did Agar realise he'd fired. The other three robbers backed away and raised their weapons, yelling. But Red Gloves, some kind of Terminator, this guy, snarled and rushed forward again. This time Agar saw his own outstretched arm, and felt his finger crush the trigger.

Bullet number two made the balaclava flutter as it entered Red Gloves' face. He staggered back again, and once more made a snarling noise, but there the replay ended. He collapsed as if suddenly boneless, and a pool matching the colour of his gloves started to spread out around his head.

Blue, Green and White ran.

'His name is Jon Agar. He'd been in prison for firearms offences and a Post Office robbery when he was young. He was a big guy, mean-looking with wiry ginger hair and a ginger beard and tattoos on his neck and the backs of his hands, and I thought he just looked like he'd be good at security. I gave him a job. And he was good at it. Polite to customers, always eager for overtime. He had the patience to sit and watch a place all night alone, or to stand around in a supermarket and smile at old ladies and look mean at groups of teenaged hoodies.'

They had moved to the back of the caravan and were standing close together so the hitman couldn't overhear as Nate recounted the story of HyperX. Toni was watching his eyes, but Nate was looking over her shoulder, trying to stare out the large window. But it was night and the interior light was on, and that meant he could only see his own paled face. He knew that he would be visible to anyone outside, but at the moment didn't care about that.

'The robbers had lethal weapons, and they attacked first, so maybe Jon Agar would have avoided prison for killing the guy. I think he would have, even firing twice. But Agar obviously thought otherwise, what with his record, and the fact that he was not Security Industry Authority licensed. And he wasn't about to hang around and learn the hard way. So he ran. Ten seconds after he shot the guy, he was out the door and running. And that was the last anyone saw of him. He didn't even go home to pack. His girlfriend never saw him again. The rumour was that he knew people in America, so he'd gone into hiding over there.'

Nate reached past Toni and pulled the curtains shut, sick now of seeing yet more fear and distress on his own face. He moved back to the sofa and sat before the laptop. Toni sat silently beside him, but with space between them. Nate stared at Agar's face on the laptop. A face he hadn't seen in four years, had never expected to see again, yet knew he could never forget. Ten feet away, the hitman was no longer watching, his head turned towards the knife block again, his back to them, maybe pretending to be invisible in the hope they'd forget he existed.

'That was the big problem. He ran. By running, he was admitting he knew he'd done wrong. A man with prison time for gun offences had now shot and killed a man with an illegal gun. While undertaking duties he wasn't licensed for. The police ignored that last part until they'd completed their murder investigation, then they came back at us. Pete was listed as company director, so he took the blow. Three-and-a-half grand fine, banned from acting as a director for nine months. I got nothing. Because Agar was not around to answer questions, we used his short time with us, just two months, to claim he had insisted he was licensed and we'd just been lazy in not checking this out and not disclosing information to the SIA. So we were saying he was a liar, and his past criminal convictions bore this out. The fact that our other eight employees were properly licensed probably helped our cause. It could have been worse. It could have been jail time.

'But shit sticks, Toni. My company might be legit now, but four years ago I employed a known criminal who committed murder and went on the run, and now I'm on the run for murder. You can't not think that's suspicious. Nobody's going to be on my side.'

She kicked his shin, which made him hiss and face her. 'Get your head in gear. Forget what the public might gossip about over garden fences. Worry about proving to the police that you didn't kill your brother. And instead of wishing that you'd never hired this Jon Agar, try thinking about why he's connected to this thing.'

She was right. But he'd already racked his brain on that score, and had come up short. He shook his head. 'I don't know.'

'You were on the right track all along, Nate. This whole thing is all about HyperX. Five people were involved that night. Your brother is dead, Kaushal is dead, you should be dead, and they want Agar dead. That leaves one person. Carl Webber. So we need to know about him. Could he be behind this?'

Nate shrugged.

Toni said, 'Either he's a bad guy, or he's a dead guy. Whichever, it's all about HyperX. Why? HyperX, Nate. Think. Connect the dots.'

He shrugged again, like a docile and petulant child.

Rising with a grunt of anger, Toni approached the hitman.

He heard her footsteps and turned his head and watched her come with wide eyes. She took a knife from a drawer. Not from the knife block. Not a big carving knife. Because anyone could jab one of those bad boys and cause damage. A butter knife. If you could cause pain and bleeding with one of those, there was something a bit wild in your brain. Watching, Nate thought this was the idea she wanted to present. And it worked. Or maybe the hitman was just remembering what she had already done to him and his colleagues. Either way, he started talking, unprompted.

'That man in the file, Cube wants him dead, that's all I know. That's all I want to know. He hired me to kill him.'

She didn't crowd his space, didn't wave the knife in a threatening manner. Didn't even look at him. She just used the blunt blade to scrape dirt from under a fingernail. Like she was keeping to herself, ignoring the world, whittling time. But the threat was there, like an aura, or the electric buzz around a pylon. Nate watched intently. She was off to the hitman's side, so he had to turn his head ninety degrees to watch her, and Nate watched his profile. The guy licked his lips a lot. Nervous dehydration.

The hitman finally got the clue. She wasn't going to ask questions. The guy just needed to talk.

He said, 'Jon Agar is in Williamsport, Pennsylvania. In jail, awaiting trial for delivery of a controlled substance and criminal conspiracy. This is really all I know.'

Now she looked at him. 'So, this wasn't to be a slit throat in a dark alleyway behind his local pub. You were going to kill this guy in a prison thousands of miles away? That seems like mission impossible.'

The hitman shrugged. He didn't seem as scared now. Nate watched the corner of his lip pull back. A smile. 'Stepping stones are in place. Cube is a powerful man.'

Powerful man. Nate tasted that line in his mind, and something seemed to click into place. He pulled the laptop onto his knees.

'So Agar was clearly not Cube's business rival or cheating boyfriend. He *must* have told you why?' she said. A wink: *come on, spill the beans.*

'No,' the hitman said. He didn't need to know such things. Not relevant to the job.

Nate started typing.

'And when he told you there was the body of a young Indian woman to get rid of, you didn't ask why she'd been killed, either?'

The hitman hadn't. No need, not relevant.

Nate hit page-down, searching.

'How about simple nosiness, then? I'd be mad with curiosity to know what connects a criminal in America with a nice young woman in London. You asked, didn't you? You had to know, didn't you?' That wink again.

No. Safer for his employers if he didn't know such information. He was a professional.

Nate stopped scrolling and tapped the mousepad. He got up. Toni and the hitman watched him approach. He held the laptop so she could see the screen, and she looked. The hitman couldn't see it, but he clearly worried about what Nate had found on his personal machine.

An online newspaper displaying a page. A London newspaper. Dated six years ago. She quickly scanned it. A story called 'Money magnets', about lottery winners who had already been rich before their moment of good fortune. It listed five London-based businessmen, each with a photo and a mini-biography. A scathing damnation of an unfair society that rewarded the wealthy, rather than a feel-good piece.

But she was puzzled. 'What's this?'

He tapped the screen near the bottom. Spawney git number three. He was a handsome white man, maybe forty-five years old. Big teeth, a wide smile, in a suit jacket and jeans, holding a glass of bubbly in one hand and cosying up to a woman in a sparkly dress. An elegant party in the background. The name was James Ryback. The bio said he was a businessman involved in imports and exports. Current net worth: £3,220,000. Two years ago he had won nearly £15,000 on a scratch card.

'Repeat: what is this, Nate? Is the lottery something to do with this?'

'No. This is just the only online photo I know of this man. This is James Ryback. He owned HyperX.'

She still looked puzzled. Nate bloated the picture in the screen, and turned the laptop to the hitman. 'Who is this?'

The hitman looked surprised at what he saw on the screen. He leaned back, seemed to think, maybe wondering how much trouble his answer might get him into. 'That's Cube.'

Nate said, 'James Ryback lost a lot of money when those Rolls-Royces were taken apart and had their parts stolen at HyperX. Acorn Security took responsibility for their safety that night, so this–'

Toni cut in with: 'So this is all about revenge. This is a rich businessman with a daft nickname getting back at you and your brother and the rest of your team.'

The phone rang for a long time, and Toni was about to hang up, but Nate shook his head.

'There's no answer, Nate. So– Hello?'

Answered. Toni and Nate stared at each other as she said, 'I'm trying to find Carl Webber. Is he there?' She looked at the clock.

Nate could hear the crackle of a raised voice on the other end of the phone. Toni's shocked face told the rest. Then she looked at the phone, and Nate knew whoever had answered it had hung up.

'She thought I was one of his girlfriends,' she said. 'Apparently he's a lying, cheating scumbag and I can keep him. End quote. He didn't come home from playing football last night and his phone's turned off.'

Nate rubbed his face hard.

'Maybe he really is shacked up with his bit on the side,' Toni said, but didn't sound convinced herself. 'Bad guy or dead guy? You know the guy, so what do you think?'

'Carl was always a ladies' man, but he went home to his wife every night. Every time, as far as I know. But the guy left the company two years ago, so I have no idea what's going on in his life. But my gut says... dead man.'

'Why now? It's been four years since Ryback's place got smashed up. Why wait so long for revenge?'

Nate already had a theory on that one. 'Agar. Maybe Ryback wanted to take us all down at the same time, make sure nobody escaped. But Agar was missing. Until recently, when he got arrested in America and suddenly his name surfaced. Now Ryback knew where all five of us were, and he let his dogs off the leash.'

There was a noise outside. Toni's eyes jerked to the door. But then someone laughed outside and she relaxed.

'We can't stay here,' she said. 'We have to go soon, Nate.'

'But where?'

'Ryback. We've got Ryback now.' She looked at the clock. 'We need to steal a car. Now.'

'Where from?'

She looked at him as if he had said something stupid. 'This is a holiday place. People will be at the restaurants and bars and things. Their cars won't be. They'll be parked outside empty caravans, in the dark.'

'We can't drag this guy around out there.'

'No, you stay here with him. I'll go steal a car and bring it back here.'

He shook his head. 'I'll go.'

She looked surprised by this. And suspicious. 'Can you hot-wire a car?'

'No. But I can't fight like you, so if I stay here and this guy gets free...' Nate considered himself pretty tasty with his fists. He'd done mixed martial arts in the army. He'd been in fights at college. He didn't fear the hitman, not after all he'd been through in the past two days. He trusted himself to handle the guy if he broke his bonds. But what he didn't trust was Toni to come back for him. She was not here as his friend or helper. She was driven by revenge and now she had a name to chase, and he thought she might abandon him and push on alone if she got a car.

What she said next surprised him. 'You're not going to just drive away when you get one, right? We're in this together. You need me.' Said as a statement, but her tone said she feared this fact might be no such thing any longer. It said she needed him.

'I'll come back, Toni. Partners.'

She came close and put a hand on his shoulder. 'Nate, I won't trick you again. I promise. That was the last time.'

He searched her eyes. They showed genuine remorse – but for what?

'This place is just a hideaway,' she said. 'I knew that the moment I saw the key. This guy needed a place that he could return to if something went wrong, like a base of operations. Where Ryback's men could get hold of him. When he didn't turn up at the warehouse in Enfield, they would want to find him. That means coming here.'

Realisation swept in. He slapped her arm away. He was shocked. She had played her own game again, and again had suckered him into unwittingly going along with it. It explained all the clock-watching. 'You didn't come here for clues, did you? You came here to wait for these people to turn up? Led me into the lion's den, basically?'

'Yes, and I'm sorry. I was fully prepared to end it here. But now we have Ryback's name. He's top of the ladder so won't be coming here, but we can go to him. But we don't have long. Ryback's men would wait until they know their hitman's not coming, then they'll probably come here. I figured we might have five hours in total since we snatched him. That time will soon be up. We need that car now.'

Strangely, he was not angry this time. Last time her trickery had resulted in his being been drugged and kidnapped and fearing for his life, so rage had been a quite normal response. All he felt now was a sense of discomfiture because he hadn't been smart enough to work out a plan of his own. A sense of busted pride because he knew that none of the breakthroughs they'd had had been his doing. He was a sheep to her shepherd. Without her, he'd either be shitting his pants in a police cell or starving to death in a sewer. If alive at all.

He put a hand on her shoulder. 'I'll kick your ass later,' he joked.

That wiped the worry from her face, even found a smile. She tossed him the key to the caravan. 'Get a pen and I'll show you how to steal a car without hot-wiring it. Oh, and a coin.'

Most people here are from all over Britain and their own cities will have their own headlines.

He hid his face at first, by keeping to the shadows and

yawning and scratching his nose and pretending to spot something on the ground or in the night sky. But trying to stay invisible would prove impossible once he got to the entertainment complex. Bright lights, dozens of people.

Most people here have been cooped up here for days and won't have seen the news. News is bad and they're here for good times.

So he gave up the deception and walked with his head held high and a confident stride, like he belonged here. Like a regular holidaymaker out to sample the nightlife.

This is Kent, not London. My story is of little interest to those outside London.

His internal sermon seemed to work. Or was the simple fact that he'd bumped shoulders with dozens of people so far and nobody had yelled for the cops? Whatever. The fear flaked away like dead skin.

In the centre of the complex was a semi-circle of buildings that included a restaurant bar called Lagoon Surf, which had a seating deck and a long garden that sloped down to a boating lake adorned with small trees bearing coloured lanterns. He aimed there.

Inside, it was bustling. Nate entered and went to the bar. To avoid seeming out of place he ordered a drink. A cool glass of beer would have comforted him like a good friend, but would become an enemy if things turned bad and he needed sharp reflexes. So, a coke. There was a TV above the bar, and he expected it at any moment to flash up his face, and for the barman to dive over the counter and wrestle him to the ground. But the TV stayed on a football game. The barman stayed behind the counter and took his cash.

He swivelled his bar stool so he could watch the room, and looked for a suitable victim.

The hitman said, 'Let me go now and I'll make sure you don't get hurt.'

'Thank you.'

'Be wise, girl. My people know where I am. I should have called in when I had you. I didn't, and that was a long time ago. They won't just forget about me.'

She was on the sofa, watching the TV, but with the sound off so she could hear the slightest sounds – namely those of a guy trying to break his bonds. 'Shut up. You're killing the quiet mood.'

'I don't know how many will come to rescue me, but you can't take them all down. Not even a superwoman like you. Last chance.'

She looked at him. At the back of his head. He no longer strained to turn his head to watch her. That and his tone suggested he no longer feared her. At first she assumed this was because Nate had gone and he was now alone with a woman. But that couldn't be – it was this very woman, not Nate, who had taken him down and caused him pain. Something else...

She got up. He heard the floor creak as she approached, but still he didn't turn his head.

She reached over his shoulder, past his face, hoping to scare him. But he didn't flinch. Not even when she picked up the butter knife that she'd laid on the counter two feet in front of his face. She brought it slowly backward, and to his throat, and put the blade there just lightly enough to let him feel the cold metal.

'If they kick in the door in the next five seconds, you might have a chance,' she said. 'If they bring a needle and thread and a blood pack, and the nearest hospital's in their satnav. Shall we count down?'

Now he lost it, his breathing suddenly becoming loud and ragged. But over the noise of his lungs sucking in air, they both heard the sound of a car pulling up outside, opposite side to the door.

'Maybe that's them now,' she said, seeing the clock, noting that Nate had used up his hour and three extra minutes. She fought the urge to slice the guy's throat. 'Five, four...'

'It's them,' the hitman said. 'Last chance. Untie me before they come in, and I'll see that you don't get hurt.'

She heard a car door click quietly shut. She gripped the knife hard, and now the urge to open him up was so uncontrollable that she knew she had to kill him, just had to. Some void would remain in her being forever if she didn't. The rotten part of her brain could not be denied.

She dropped the knife into his lap and clamped her hand over his mouth, cutting away his air. He started to buck and thrash, but the hand stayed solidly in place, and there was no air to find. The rotten part of her brain could not be denied.

Footsteps now behind her, beyond the door, on the steps outside. The hand squeezed tighter. The rotten part of her brain could not be denied, but it could be obstructed. She knew that Nate would be inside and wrestling her away from the hitman long before the point where his oxygen-starved brain suffered irreversible damage.

The door opened. Sensing a lost cause, the rotten part of her threw her free hand around the hitman's neck in a desperate attempt to end this in the next few seconds. And knowing it was a lost cause, she let out a long yell of rage as all her strength was redirected into her vice-like hands.

Fourth vodka gone, Dutch courage coursing through his veins, Nate spotted the clock again. One hour and ten minutes gone! He turned away from the bar and the barman he'd been chatting to about football. Time to do this. He surveyed the room. Couples and families and singles and groups of young men and women, all having a great time because they had closed off their world to the bad news and bad people out there. His eyes settled on a pair of young women eating ice cream in a booth. At least they wouldn't punch in his head if they realised what he was doing.

He stopped by their table, holding out his key fob.

'Hi, sorry, but either of you girls know what this Q is?'

He showed them the fob, and they both leaned close to look. On the paper inside the glass fob there was a big letter Q. One girl shook her head, but looked at her friend. Who pulled her own key out from her handbag. Her key had no Q written on it. He thanked them and left. No good. He had caught sight of a train timetable inside one girl's bag.

A drunken guy on his own came next, but Nate stopped himself halfway through his question. Nobody came to a caravan park alone, but he was in the bar alone, which probably meant a partner back at the caravan. Dud.

A pair of young men pulled their key out a minute later, and from the set dangled car keys. No good.

Nate went out into the garden, fearful that he was becoming suspicious by approaching so many people. He was thinking about giving up when he spotted a pair of middle-aged couples at a table garden table.

The two men and two women looked up as he approached, his head down, staring at his key fob. He stopped by them and said, 'Anyone know what this Q is?'

The two men regarded him with a touch of hostility, as if fearful of all strangers, or annoyed that he was intruding on their quiet time. But the two women, in charge of the keys, pulled theirs out. Both scrutinised them and announced that they didn't know, because theirs didn't have a Q. One set of keys was vast, containing maybe every key the couple needed, including car keys. The other was simply like Nate's: just the key for a caravan.

Nate leaned close to both sets. The single key's fob said 'Sunrise 88' on it. Neither had a Q, of course. Toni had written the one on Nate's.

'Just mine then. I'll ask the staff.'

They forgot him and he moved on. Eight minutes later he was outside a caravan parked near a fenced zone housing large wheeled bins. Next to the caravan was a Ford Kuga. He broke the flimsy door lock of number 88, Sunrise zone, and rushed inside. Using the screen light from Toni's phone, he began his search. It was over in seconds. A set of keys sat on the worktop, right near the sink. He snatched them up and left the caravan and unlocked the Kuga. And felt a buzz. His first stolen car, and he'd done it as a middle-aged man.

She woke to see a handsome blond man in denim standing in front of her, arms crossed, like he'd been waiting for her to wake up. She was on the sofa, hands tied behind her back, feet tied together. Behind the blond man was a bigger white guy with a Hitler moustache and a bald head. A guy employed for his mean look as much as his power. And the hitman was untied. He was lounging on the chair he'd been tied in, using a handheld mirror to check out the damage Toni had done to his face.

Her head hurt at the back. She knew she'd been whacked from behind. She cursed her foolishness. Keeping her back to the door as it opened! 'What's this?' she said to the blond man. 'I told you I escaped from…'

She stopped, aware that the hitman could expose her lie. Probably already had. Foolish girl.

'We know you're with Nate,' the blond guy said. 'What I want to know is how? You were supposed to kill him, and now you're on his side. I love a good story. Tell me.'

The way he took centre stage filled in the gaps. She felt her anger rising. 'You're Lazar.'

'That's me. So, why are you suddenly bosom buddies?'

He unfolded his arms and she noticed a knuckleduster on his right hand. But he didn't need to threaten her for this answer. She *wanted* to give it. 'Damar.'

Realisation on his face. 'Ah. You found him. You went back to the warehouse. Right. Like a little lost puppy returning home. Well, Damar, he fucked up, didn't he? Both of you. You especially, by siding with a guy who should be dead.'

'And he got his throat cut just for that? Did you do it?'

'That's black ops stuff. I'm management.' He almost looked upset by the idea that she thought of him as a simple thug.

'I don't care if it was you who cut his throat. I'm still going to cut yours.'

'If only you knew.' He stepped closer and squatted in front of her. 'Do it. Do it right now.'

A macho show for his colleagues. Or maybe he simply liked to taunt the defenceless. But he was careful to keep the distance between them a good three feet. Out of her instant range. Maybe he had heard from Damar all about her vicious streak. Maybe he was just the very cautious type. To get to him, she would have to stand and launch herself because her feet were tied. She could propel herself head first into his face, shattering his nose. But the three feet gap would give him half a second or so to avoid whatever came his way. She took a sliver of comfort from knowing that his caution highlighted his understanding that she should not be underestimated.

'I can't. I'm tied up, and there's three of you. Later. Definitely later.'

His caution, or machismo, jumped on this chance for a break, and he stood and backed away. 'Can't wait. Now, Nathan was supposed to be gone no more than an hour. He's half an hour late already. We'll wait, of course, in case he stopped for a burger. But in case he's gone elsewhere, where would that be?'

So, he knew about their plan. The hitman, who had overheard enough of their chatter to connect some dots and work out their plan. And blabbed it like a schoolboy grass. She must have been out a while. Long enough for the hitman and Lazar to have a nice chinwag.

And his question was a good one. Where the hell was Nate? She worried that he had decided to leave her here. Better than killing her, she supposed. She knew he still carried extreme resentment towards her – his brother was dead and he himself wearing physical reminders of her attempt to kill him. That resentment would bubble to the surface once the mental adrenaline of this nightmare had dissipated. So, it was quite likely that he had found a car and run out on her to hunt down Ryback alone. She couldn't expect loyalty.

'The police, maybe,' she said.

Just then, Lazar's mobile rang. He answered with, 'Tell me good news.'

So, it wasn't just Lazar and the bald guy who'd come. There was at least one guy outside somewhere, watching. Which was the right tactic. Bad to have all your guys in one place.

'There's a car coming,' she heard a tinny male voice say on speakerphone. The Hitler guy pulled out a roll of gaffer tape.

Lazar smiled. 'I guess Nathan's finished his burger.'

Nate had driven the car onto the road and stopped to check the glovebox. Paperwork, a half-empty box of tampons, a pair of earphones, and, wrapped in a plastic supermarket bag, a mobile phone. It was a cheap Nokia, twenty quid tops, with big rubber keys. The battery was held against the screen by an elastic band. He slotted the battery home, let the phone power up, and had a quick look to make sure it had credit. It did: a nice, neat £5. It had just three numbers in the phonebook: mobile number of a guy called Dan, a home number beginning in 0161, and a place called Fettlers Autos. And no calls or texts sent or received. An emergency phone, Nate guessed. Probably unused, saved for occasions when the owner found herself broken down and without the use of her main mobile. Which, apparently, had never happened.

So, the phone could not be traced and would never be linked to him. Handy.

Nate returned to Seagull Wings and worked his way to the back, and slowly towards Starfish. His eyes were everywhere, looking for something untoward. But nothing leaped out. Everything seemed normal. He approached the caravan. As he drew alongside, he flicked a glance out of the passenger window. The curtains were closed over the big back window still, and they were too thick to allow him to see movement beyond. The door of the neighbours' caravan was shut now, kid gone, nothing happening. All quiet and peaceful, just what you'd want from a place like this. Nothing that should have spooked him. But he drove past and took a turn and increased speed, and got the hell out of there. His heart was racing. Because the coin was on the step.

Following her instructions, he had left the caravan, shut the door and jammed the two-pence piece into the side of the door-frame a foot from the base. It had been quite visible because it was brown metal against white plastic.

'If the door opens, the coin falls,' Toni had told him before he left. 'Only against a sincere attempt by me to prevent it will that door open before you get back.'

'Gone past,' said the voice on the phone. 'Not him.'

Toni felt relief, and fear. She didn't think Nate would have stood a chance of taking out these guys – the relief. But he had been gone a long time now – the fear. Maybe he'd fled after all, now that he had a new car and a name to chase. But at least these bozos didn't have him.

Lazar and his henchman had been waiting by the door, one either side. The hitman had put his hands behind his back, pretending to be all tied up and full of fear again. Now that guy relaxed and Lazar and Hitler came back into the living room. Lazar looked annoyed. He yanked the gaffer tape off her mouth.

'Where is he?'

'I don't believe he'll be back,' said the hitman.

'Maybe he got fries with his burger,' Toni said. Hitler laughed and Lazar gave him a hard look, which shut him up.

Lazar sat on the sofa and swung up his legs and put them on her lap. Dropped them hard enough to make her grunt. He leaned back and got nice and comfortable.

'So we wait.'

'I think that's a bad idea,' the hitman said.

'We wait.'

A road marked 'Deliveries only' curved around the back of the semi-circular entertainment complex and Nate followed it to a secluded staff car park bookended by a thin river and a walled yard for bins. He parked and locked the car – there might be thieves around – and walked back the way he'd come. If there were watchers, he didn't want them to see the same car lurking around again.

He entered Shadows, the caravan plot next to his own, and made his way towards the berm that separated it from Seagull Wings. He found a spot that allowed him to see Starfish and a portion of the plot. There was a map on a board so he pretended to study it while surveying his surroundings. He was looking for people who seemed out of place. People with seemingly nothing to do but be where they were.

He waited.

Half an hour. Nothing. Lazar was getting impatient. He didn't speak, but he paced a lot, and snorted a lot. Like an angry bull locked in a cage. Hitler and the hitman seemed to get annoyed by his constant noise and movement within such a small space. But they said nothing. And Toni said nothing. She didn't want to draw attention to herself. Nobody had even acknowledged her existence in the last ten minutes or so.

Eventually Lazar stopped pacing and got on his phone and made a call. He went into the corridor to the bedrooms and shut the door. It was an important call, Toni could tell. Lazar listened more than he spoke. Lazar's voice easily came through the thin door, but all he uttered was the odd affirmative. Whoever he was talking to, it seemed to be a superior. She heard him bid goodbye to whoever was on the phone, but the door did not open. Seconds later, he was talking again. Another call. He was more in charge with this call, and Toni figured he was talking to his watcher outside. But this time his voice was quieter and his words were distorted.

Then he was back, and his face said things had changed.

Toni's suspicions climbed a level. He approached Hitler and whispered in his ear.

'What's happening?' the hitman said.

Lazar faced Toni. 'Change of plan,' Lazar said. 'We're out of here in one minute.'

'This place is compromised,' the hitman said. 'We need to sterilise it.'

'No,' Lazar said. Hitler went to the knife block and extracted a long blade. Lazar stood before Toni and grinned at her. 'This place is a crime scene. We're leaving a dead body behind.'

To be certain, Nate approached the exit. He stopped by a tree and pretended to be interested in how the bark would flake under a fingernail. But what he was really interested in was the car parked on the main road.

It was fifty metres away from his position, in a lay-by on the far side of the main road. Mid-way between this plot and his own. *Not proof of anything,* he told himself.

Nate exited the plot and ran across the road and stopped. Here the curve of the road put the car out of sight behind the hedge, but that meant he was out of sight, too. He made sure no-one was watching then ungracefully clambered over the hedge and into Leafy Oak. There was a scattering of people on their doorsteps and walking the roads and hanging about, but nobody seemed to have watched his strange entrance, or those who had didn't give a shit.

He followed a path that hugged the hedge some ten metres out, all the while watching the main road through the foliage. When the grey of tarmac was suddenly interrupted, he stopped and focused his sight and knew that the blockage was a car.

He approached the hedge slowly. The car rose into view slowly above the hedge.

A skinny guy with a buzz cut sat in the driver's seat, far side. Just sitting there, but with his head turned so he could stare out the window. Above and beyond the car was Seagull Wings. Nate looked carefully and spotted Starfish. *Not proof of anything,* he told himself again.

A car came up the road. Its headlights briefly washed the parked car. Then it was gone. But the light had lit up the dashboard of the parked car and allowed Nate to see what rested there.

A pair of binoculars.

Proof. His heart started thumping.

Making sure no-one was watching, Nate pulled out the syringe he'd pocketed and approached the hedge. Another glance around, and then he hopped on top and rolled and came to his feet on the other side, then he ducked and approached the car and squatted by the rear passenger-side door, all in one, fluid motion. The plastic tube that had capped the syringe's needle slipped from his fingers.

Something his army comrades had said about him: he could be nervous as hell about the prospect of danger, until it was in his face. Then, he forgot his reservations and dove right in. He was in that zone right now. There was no fear. And none of it was down to the vodka he'd consumed. He knew what he had to do and all that remained was to do it.

He peeked through the window. As he did, something lit up on the dashboard. A phone. A call, although he couldn't hear a ringtone. Buzzcut snatched it up and stuck it against his head. Ten seconds later the call was done and the phone was back on the dashboard, but the binoculars weren't.

Buzzcut was using them to watch Starfish, which was over a hundred metres away. Nate risked standing up so he could look over the roof. Just for one second, a quick up-and-down. Just that single one-second glance, and the dark and the distance hindered him, but he registered three things, each worse than the last.

First, the lights in Starfish were off. Second, there was a vehicle parked outside – not the neighbours' car, because this vehicle was on the other side of the caravan. Third, he saw human activity in the vicinity of both vehicles – three people moving from one to the other.

Undeniable, then. The kill crew had come for them, just as Toni had thought. One guy to watch from a distance and a number of others to enter the caravan.

Where Toni was. Which meant they had her.

He knew if he waited too long, he might feel the danger passing, and back would come the nerves. So he dove right in while the momentum of action was still within him. He yanked open the front passenger door and dove inside, a hand raised, thrust forward. The syringe's needle had been aimed at the back of Buzzcut's neck, but he managed to turn his head from the window and Nate felt it jab the jawbone. But it skidded off and angled down and sank into his throat. The door's opening had kicked on the interior light and Nate saw everything in great detail.

Buzzcut swiped at Nate's arm, knocking it away. The syringe stayed in the side of his throat, aimed upwards like a clock hand at 2 o'clock. Nate backed out of the car. The guy stared at him, then reached for the syringe, horror all over his face, as if he might believe a knife protruded from his flesh.

He yanked the syringe free and stared at it. The horror

heightened within him. This guy, Nate knew, was well aware of what that green shit in the tube was all about.

'Shit,' Buzzcut said. He looked around, into the back seat, as if for a weapon, or an antidote. Then he gave it up, perhaps realising that one did not exist and the other would not help. He looked at Nate. 'You got it wrong, pal,' he said, and already his eyes were closing and his voice wavering. 'Shit. Don't fuck me up, mate. I'm only here to...' He knew what was coming and tried to fight it. He pinched his own face, hard, like someone trying to stay awake. His eyes, just before they closed, turned puzzled, as if the English language had deserted his failing brain.

'Only here to what?' Nate said. He got in the passenger seat and slapped the guy's cheek. Conversely to his intention, the blow seemed to knock the last fragments of consciousness away. Or was it just comical timing? Either way, one second post-slap, the guy's chin fell onto his chest and he was gone.

Nate shut the door to kill the interior light. Alternative light took its place as another car came up the road. Then all was dark again. His brain raced. Who was this guy? On the back seat was a jacket, which he searched. The inside pocket contained a snub-nosed revolver, fully loaded. Probably what the guy had been thinking about grabbing before he'd realised it might be safer for him to fall unconscious without letting Nate know there was a lethal weapon he could freely take. Nate freely took it. He was surprised at how alien it felt in his hand. Once upon a time, he'd carried firearms daily. And used them.

The gun proved nothing, but another pocket contained a clear indication that this guy had come here for Nate. A photo of Nate printed on thin paper. The image was a selfie Nate had taken on his phone for his LinkedIn profile. Maybe Buzzcut was a new addition to the kill crew and the photo was so he'd know his target. Maybe the photo was for showing to people at the caravan park – *Looking for my brother. Got some bad news for him about our dad. Ya seen this guy around?*

But the photo didn't seem to fit with what the guy had said: *You got it wrong... I'm only here to...* What did that mean? That he hadn't been sent to capture Nate? Then what was he here for?

Nate slipped low in the seat as the car that had been by his caravan slipped into the road some fifty metres away and turned away from him, towards the exit. Both indicators flashed – clearly a signal. Nate reached for the stalk with the controls for the lights and flashed them on and back off once, hoping that he was adequately responding to nothing more than a *see ya later* signal. The car sped away, so maybe he'd gotten away with it.

Nate now couldn't doubt that the car contained a kill crew. And they had been to the caravan, where they would have found Toni.

The question was, what had they done to her?

He would have to return to the caravan to find out.

Nate dragged Buzzcut out of the passenger seat and into a fireman's lift. The gate barring the walled area housing the bins was thankfully unlocked. He dumped the guy in a bin.

The revolver went into a pocket. He'd also found a clamshell mobile phone in the glove box and now sat and scrutinised it. Like Damar's, and Toni's, it was a burner bought just for a single mission. No text messages, no contacts in the phone book, no stored music or e-mail account or person-alised home screen. There was one number in the call history, but it was incomplete. The first seven digits of a mobile number. A faulty input, or maybe Buzzcut had the final four digits memorised. No use to Nate. The clamshell design made the device easy to snap. He left the pieces in the passenger footwell. The sim card got bent into a chevron and tossed into the darkness.

Because he wasn't sure if others in the kill crew had been left behind, and because the woman who used Fettlers Autos might have reported her car missing by now, Nate decided not to use a vehicle to return to Starfish. So he walked.

His neighbours were outside, and they had brought friends. At least eight people were grouped outside the caravan. Drinking from cans of alcohol, standing around chatting to each other. The door was open and loud music drifted out. A regular alfresco party. A girl was handing out slices of pizza. A guy was waving a video camera around. Nate wondered if the kid was crying in bed because he couldn't sleep.

He had no idea if there were other baddies awaiting him inside the caravan, but he was sure that eight or nine witnesses fifteen feet away had made them reassess their plans. They certainly made him change his. He had intended to creep up to the caravan nice and slow and peek in the window, but now he strolled right up to the door and knocked.

No bullets tore through the door and into him. He heard no commotion from within.

'No-one in, mate,' shouted a voice, and he turned to see a guy looking at him.

'It's mine,' Nate said, and opened the door. Black as an abyssal plain inside. A dangerous moment. The kill crew's plan to blame Nate for all this shit wouldn't work if his body was found in a leisure park, but maybe they were beyond all that now. Maybe they just wanted him dead any old how. A nuisance fly that you couldn't coerce out the window eventually got swatted against the glass.

So, he opened the door fully and pretended to have a problem hooking it to the latch on the wall, and he called out a fake girl's name, asking if she was asleep in order to explain the darkness and silence within. Behind him, a quick glance proved that the partiers had forgotten him already.

No sounds of movement, at least not any loud enough to hear above the racket behind him. So he steeled himself and stepped inside, and immediately saw a body.

The hitman. With the door fully open, ambient light from next door's caravan reflected off the blood all over the guy's uniform. He was still in the chair, but now it was in the centre of the living room. His head lay back at an unnatural angle, allowed to do so by the lack of tension given by a taut throat since his had been sliced. Like Damar's. This seemed to be their MO. He shut out a thought of Pete with his throat sliced.

He shut the door and turned on the light. Someone told him he was alone here. At least, he was the only living thing.

With the revolver now in his hand and leading the way, Nate searched the rest of the caravan. Each empty room accentuated his fear. When he was certain the place was empty, his anxiety reached full throttle. No bad guys present, but no Toni, either. They had taken her. She had been one of the three he'd seen leaving. But where had they taken her?

And why?

You got it wrong, pal... I'm only here to...

Buzzcut had vanished.

Shit. It seemed that the modified drug was unreliable. It had put Nate and the hitman out for quite a while, but Buzzcut had succumbed only for a few minutes. Or it was the dosage? Nate had retrieved the syringe and only half the green shit had gone into the guy's system.

The car driver's door was wide open. Nate looked inside and saw the busted phone. No longer in the footwell, but on the dashboard. Both pieces lay close together, as if Buzzcut, disoriented still by the drug, had tried to slot them together like a little jigsaw. Hoodwinked by his enemy and unable to move his car, he had then decided he really needed to make a call. So what would he do when he was foiled in that, too?

Go for another phone.

Nate ran for the entertainment complex. The goods stores, the swimming pool, the bowling alley, and the Krazee Golf were closed, but the bar was still open and next to it something called FunUniverse oozed light from its windows. He remembered that the bar had no payphone. The only phone was the joint's private landline, which was behind the bar. Buzzcut would have to ask the barman for permission to make a call on that phone, and Nate didn't think Buzzcut was going to do such a thing.

That left FunUniverse, which, with a name like that, could only be an amusement arcade. Nate entered into a world of noise and heat. Despite the late hour, it was rammed with kids and adults. Ahead of him three teenaged girls stamped on pads that flashed different colours as they tried to emulate the dance of an animated disco diva on a big computer screen. A beefy lad egged on by his two mates was gearing up to crack his radius on a punchbag. A middle-aged lady was being laughed at by her partner because she couldn't dunk a mini-basketball into a mini-basket. Adults spun reels on fruit machines in search of jackpot pay-outs and kids twisted steering wheels to avoid smashing computer-generated race cars into computer-generated trees. And everybody seemed oblivious to everyone else. Except for one guy, who was in a black uniform and wearing rolls of tickets around his neck and shoulder like an ammunition belt. He approached Nate, but before he could utter a word from his sales pitch, Nate asked him if there was a payphone. A finger pointed the way.

A quiet corner, near a fire exit and a vending machine,

between a light gun shooter where you blasted big game with a big rifle, and a twin cockpit driving game that was black and dead. No-one was at either working machine or the phone. And that included Buzzcut. He wondered if he was too late. He wondered what was happening in the car carrying Toni – was she bound and gagged in the boot and headed somewhere, or had her captors dumped her dead body as soon as they'd found a remote spot outside the caravan park?

Nate turned to leave, and froze.

Buzzcut was ten metres away.

He hadn't seen Nate, though. It was clear that the drug still had a grip on him. He was staggering through the jubilant crowd like a guy suffering from diabetic shock, tapping people on the shoulder, saying something to each of them. Some ignored him and went about the business of fun. Some clearly gave him an earful. A woman pushed him aside. He seemed to be asking for something. He was blatantly obvious to Nate, like a shining beacon, but the general population seemed to be oblivious to him. Maybe they thought he was just one more drunk guy amongst myriad inebriated holidaymakers.

He watched Buzzcut approach a child of about five, who offered him what looked like a handful of coins. Buzzcut grabbed a couple, spilling others onto the floor in the process.

Then he came Nate's way.

Nate turned away, heart racing. He stepped up to the light gun shooter and picked up the rifle, and aimed it at an elephant running behind INSERT COIN(S) on the screen. He waited for a shout of alarm, or, worse, a blow to the back of the head. Instead, amazingly, Buzzcut appeared ten feet beside him, at the phone. His desperate call had been delayed because he had no money.

Nate slipped the revolver out of his jacket.

Buzzcut dropped a coin and bent slowly to pick it up. He was as stiff and cautious as someone twice his age.

Nate put the revolver alongside the plastic rifle, finger through both triggers.

Buzzcut picked up the receiver, dropped it, and grabbed it again by sliding his hand along the cable.

Nate turned the plastic gun towards Buzzcut. A peculiar sight for anyone witnessing this, he knew. 'Hello again,' he shouted above the noise.

Receiver in one hand, raised coin in the other, all ready to go, Buzzcut stopped dead like a paused video. Then his head turned. There was a faint red stain on the guy's jaw, where he had probably wiped away a trickle of blood from the needle puncture wound. His irises were big and black, something Nate recalled from his own romance with the drug.

Nate watched those demon eyes slowly trying to take him in like an old camera with a dodgy autofocus. Clarity soon came, but not recognition. Nate tilted the rifle so that both guns were visible, but only to Buzzcut, of course.

'Put the phone down,' Nate said, but the guy didn't move. Except to sway like a skyscraper in a high wind. 'You really want to call your boss and tell him the guy you were supposed to watch got away and nicked your gun?'

Then, in those zombie eyes, recognition at last. Realisation. He dropped the phone. And dropped his eyes to the real gun that hugged the fake one. His own gun, liberated from him.

'Into the driving game, now.'

Buzzcut turned and looked at the item in question. Then back at Nate. Then he staggered over to the driving game and fell into one of the seats. Keeping the revolver against his waist, aimed at the guy still, Nate took the other seat. He put one hand on the steering wheel and jammed the gun in his armpit, short barrel just poking out and at Buzzcut.

'I guess I got it wrong, pal,' Nate said. 'You're only here to...?'

The guy didn't get the hint. His brain was still mushy. Nate had to ask him outright: what was he doing here?

'I should have called in five minutes ago,' the guy said. Surprisingly, his voice was shipshape and a stark contrast to his dozy eyes and jelly body.

'Why don't you give me the number you were going to call?'

A quick glance down at the gun and then he recited the number. The area code was 01923.

'So, tell me how I got it wrong?'

It wasn't a quick process, but Nate steered the guy's messed-up brain and got what he wanted. He got it along with a whole bucketload of shock.

Buzzcut's orders had not been to apprehend or hurt Nate, but only to deliver a message. He showed Nate a pen scrawl on his forearm. A number and a postcode. Cube wanted to meet. Cube wanted to do a trade. Cube wanted to swap the girl for Nate.

It was a trap, of course. No way they'd let Toni go. But it changed nothing. He could not abandon Toni. So, trap or no, he had to go. Into the lion's den.

The guy got another dose of green nectar right there in the driving seat of an F1 car. This time it took him seven minutes to go under, despite already having some in his system. Nate had to sit and wait as he rocked and grumbled like an old man on the verge of falling asleep, until he was finally out. Then Nate went for the exit.

Despite the hubbub of excited people, he knew something was wrong. Then he noticed that a larger-than-typical crowd was milled by the exit. He went over and pushed slowly through the crowd with a *sorry* and an *excuse me*. And then heard a terrible word over the chatter of a dozen people: Police.

Outside, more people had gathered, and they were all facing the same way. Nate looked in the same direction, and a lump formed in his throat.

In the distance, above the roofs of caravans, he saw a pulsing blue aura.

Police. And he knew, just knew, they were at his caravan. The cops had found the dead hitman.

The throng started to move in that direction, already voicing claims of *murder*. Nate stepped out of the moving sea of people, but froze when a cop car with a flashing light but no siren turned into the car park out front of the entertainment complex.

Quickly, he forced his way into the moving mass of excited people and fought against the current and reached the door and pulled himself back inside FunUniverse. Other people were headed for the exit, having sensed some excitement occurring outside, but most were still at their electronic fun. He side-stepped bodies coming at him like cannonballs and quickly got back to the quiet corner with the racing game and the unconscious Buzzcut. He kicked open the fire exit. An alarm blared. Two seconds later he was outside, on a path running between the rear of the building and dark woods. He looked left, looked right, decided that cops could come from either direction if they assumed that a dead guy in a paramedic's outfit and a fire alarm were connected, and bolted into the trees.

He had time only to wonder if running into dark, unknown woods was a good idea, and then he emerged into open land again. Beyond a wooden fence at the treeline was sloping scrubland and then a beach. A black sea lapped at it. No sunbathers at this time of night, of course, but he saw a number of loving couples strolling with clasped hands and people walking dogs.

The trees stretched off to his right, but to his left gave over to a housing estate some hundred or so metres away. He could see a wooden pier cutting through the sand and assumed it was accessible from the housing estate. Which meant a way out.

The pier led into a small car park with a locked gate, and beyond that ran a road between two rows of semi-detached real estate. The way out. A car sat before the gate, bright headlights washing the tarmac. Nate came at the gate from the side to avoid being lit up like an exhibit. As he vaulted the gate and rushed into the road, the car started to reverse and turn. Cars clogged both sides of the road at this end, most doubtless owned by visitors who were determined not to let a locked gate stall their sex-on-the-beach fantasies, and this driver was trying to back into a space.

Nate could hear sirens some way off. The cops might have sneaked into the caravan park, but there was no treading softly now they'd found a body with its throat slit. They'd cordon off the park, but they'd also throw out a wider net, and Nate had to get a move on if he wanted to avoid being caught in it.

The driver had his head turned so he could watch the reverse. Some old guy, his old wife in the passenger seat, a dog in the back. Amazingly, it was another Ford Kuga.

He yanked the driver's door open, which caused the old guy to jerk in shock and jam the accelerator. The Kuga leaped backwards and hit the car behind. Nate wondered if he was going to be undone by a trail of alarms like musical breadcrumbs. The shaken dog started to bark.

'Out,' Nate hissed. Actually hissed, just for effect. Showed them his teeth, too. Like a cat trying to look dangerous.

The guy got out, and the woman got out, and Nate got in. He twisted the wheel and slipped the Kuga neatly out of the space. Then stopped. The old couple were in the street, just staring. Nate dropped his window.

'Get your dog,' he snapped.

The old lady rushed to the back, lifted the hatch. The dog jumped out, and all three scampered away. Nate had to jump out to shut the hatch.

Ten feet ahead was the locked gate and there was no room to turn in the road because of the parked cars. Lights came on in bedrooms, and in lit living rooms curtains twitched, and at doorways bold owners appeared. They watched a car racing quickly in reverse down their street.

A car turned into the road. There might just be room for two to pass, but Nate wasn't going to waste time slowing down to attempt such a tricky manoeuvre in reverse. He kept going. The other driver seemed to realise Nate wasn't going to stop. So he stopped. Nate kept coming. Soon, in a scene that was surely comical to witnesses, two cars were reversing quickly down the road.

Towards the other end of the road the parked cars thinned. Nate found his way clear as the other driver curved into the side of the road and laid on his horn to show his annoyance.

This time of night, the main road bore little traffic, and Nate slipped backwards into it without problem. He turned, stopped, got first gear, and was away. He drove well over the speed limit until he couldn't hear the sirens anymore. But even after that, he could not relax.

And then Toni's phone rang.

Unknown number, of course. But he recognised the first seven digits. The number that Buzzcut guy had part-stored in his phone.

He answered the call, but didn't speak.

'You got to another of my men, then,' said a voice he recognised. It seemed like a lifetime ago that he'd heard it. But it was one he'd never forget. The guy on the bike. The blond guy who had tried to kill him. The guy whose presence had made Nate realise he was in much deeper shit than he'd thought. The guy possibly behind everything.

Lazar.

A flicker of fear ran up his spine, which he immediately felt embarrassed about. The guy was on the phone, not right in front of him with a gun. Nate clutched the phone hard to his ear, more out of anger at himself than at the man who might have killed his brother. After all he'd been through, and here he was getting scared by a phone call.

'I'll get to them one by one, until they're all gone,' Nate said. 'How did you get this number?'

He already knew. Toni. And the guy confirmed it a second later. Said she had willingly given it up because she knew what was best. And she had self-preservation. 'And she knows how good I can be at inflicting pain, too.'

Immediately he had a tactic. Do not show he cared about her. And how could he, really, since she had started out as one of the enemy? Pretend she was nothing to him, and force Lazar to abandon her as a bargaining chip. 'She got away from me, so well done. You saved her life – for now. She's one more that will end up in the ground when I'm finished.'

Laughter. Real, not an effect. Nate knew his trick hadn't worked. 'Don't play games, Nathan. She's got a pretty face, and a nice thing three feet below it that can get us men all weird inside. Weird enough to suddenly care about them, even though the night before they might have been ready to chop us up and bury us. You want to help her live?'

No use denying things now. Besides, if he somehow did convince this guy that she meant nothing, they'd have no use for her and she'd end up in the ground anyway.

'What do you want, Lazar?'

A pause. He could almost hear Lazar wondering how Nate knew his name. Wondering what else Nate might know, and how damaging might this information be.

'Come on in and we'll sort this problem of ours out. Maybe you'll get a chance to punch me in the face. I'm sure you've dreamed of that. I'm guessing you found the postcode if you took down my man.'

'Maybe. Maybe I'll come and bring the police with me. I'm sure they'd love to know that I didn't get on a plane at Heathrow after all.'

Another pause. Nate knew he had to be careful. If he showed that he had too much information, it might make these guys do something wild, or even slip underground and out of reach.

'You'll come alone, Nate, because the police are not on your side. Trust me on that.'

'Will you feel so confident after they hear my story?'

Lazar laughed. 'You'll be alone, trust me. Be there at midday tomorrow.'

He hung up.

Thirty-five minutes later, the phone rang again. No, not that phone. The new, unused one found in the car he stole. The one nobody should have the number to except a few people in the 0161 area code.

He answered without speaking. A voice said, 'Who is this, please?'

Nate said nothing.

'My name is Detective Sergeant Alan Wright, with Kent police. You need to talk to me. I need to know how you got hold of this phone.' He sounded urgent.

Nate hung up. So much for a clean phone. He broke it apart, sim card also. Out the window the pieces went. The owner must have given the number to the cops after she found her car missing, knowing it could be a way to trace the thief. But what didn't make sense was why a simple car theft would have gotten the cops so worked up so quickly.

Worry sat in his gut like a bad meal.

Considerate traffic let him make good time and he got back to London at close to one in the morning. He found a side street and parked between two RAC vans, then climbed in the back and put his jacket over himself. If any sleep at all came, he would think himself lucky. Because, for sure, Toni would be getting none. Unless she was already in eternal sleep. He wanted to convince himself that she deserved it. Live by the sword and die by the sword, and all that crap. But he couldn't help thinking that her life was not one she'd willingly chosen. Besides, he'd started to like her a little bit.

While he lay there, he used Toni's phone. It died as soon as he lit the screen up, so he ripped the new battery off the back and was soon back in business. First, he typed in the 01923 number that Buzzcut had given him, and was shocked to find it belonged to a police station in Watford.

Buzzcut had tried to call the cops? What the hell? And Watford had been the home of HyperX. A connection? Sure. Had to be. But how?

He turned his attention to himself. Nathan Barke. A search on the name brought up more new stories and he read them voraciously.

The 'dangerous fugitive' was now believed to be out of the country, despite a police claim that no CCTV footage had shown him sneaking on board a plane at Heathrow wearing a fake beard. They were still seeking camera shots of his BMW's journey that night, but no joy yet. *Understandable,* Nate thought. Heathrow was west of his home, so their eyes would be on a sliver of the country that included Feltham and Twickenham and Hounslow and Richmond and Isleworth. But the car hadn't gone west from Putney Village; it had gone north to the warehouse in Enfield. Maybe somewhere in Parsons Green or South Kensington or Regent's Park or Camden Town there was a camera that had caught a clear image of a woman and a man who wasn't Nate in his car. He could help the police with a little phone call. But he didn't want to do that. It might muddy the waters some, but he didn't think it would help his cause.

He got back to the news stories. There was a feature in a Wandsworth paper on his life, as told by some people who knew him. Two neighbours, and the guy who ran the local pet shop, where Nate sometimes dropped by to pet the rabbits – his answer to how to have a pet without spending a penny or cleaning up a single piece of shit. All three people were shocked that such a thing could have happened in their community. It was almost a feel-good piece, as if he were a recently departed charity worker instead of a suspected killer.

One of the neighbours, though: not *that* shocked. Never trusted his eyes, she said. He figured he knew who she might be, even though no names were published. Bitch.

He flicked through others. Rehashed theory and ground already covered. He almost yearned for a terrorist attack just so people would focus on something else. Nothing caught his eye, and then something did: the word 'mum'.

It was a link under 'more on this story'. He jabbed the link so hard he nearly knocked the phone from his hand.

Fugitive's mum begs for son to give himself up

He couldn't believe what he was reading. Some asshole parasite with a microphone had tracked down his mother, and even though she lived in Scotland, the bloodsucking dick had hopped in a car and gone to visit her. She had declined to comment, thankfully, except to say she hoped her son would return alive and well. The reporter had obviously performed a kind of small-world experiment with a thesaurus to determine that she had actually meant 'surrender' when she said 'return'. If a reporter had been to visit her, Nate had to assume the cops had, too. First port of call for a killer on the run, of course: mummy's apron strings.

Nate's heart sank. He hadn't considered his mother even nearly enough since this nightmare had hit the headlines. He hoped she was doing well. He wanted to call her, give her his version of events, but knew he could not do that. A call might help her to know he was okay, but maybe it would instead increase her worry. He didn't know, but he couldn't risk it.

Nate no longer wanted to read about his supposed exploits. He just wanted to sleep. There was still a chance he could wake up to find that the last few days had been a bad dream. Hell, he'd happily wake as a snotty-nosed toddler who'd dreamed the last forty years if it would make his problems go away.

'Note to future self: stay in the damn army or pick up a McDonald's application form the day you leave school,' he said to the empty car, and closed his eyes.

Given time to think on ways his life could get worse, he probably would have chosen disease: *Police have reported an update in the Nathan Barke manhunt. His GP has released files that prove Barke is terminally ill with AIDS, and admits he withheld this information from his fugitive patient.*

Next might have been the revelation that Nate found himself faced with when he turned on the car radio after waking the next morning: 'In an explosive new twist to the manhunt following the discovery of a body in a house fire in Wandsworth two days ago, police have announced that the fugitive Nathan Barke is wanted in connection with a separate incident that occurred in Kent...'

Kent. His heart sank. He knew what was coming. The police had been called to Sunny Dream Leisure Park, where they had found the body of a man in a caravan, with his throat cut.

'An investigation is underway into the circumstances of exactly what has happened but I'd appeal to anybody staying at the caravan park or who lives in the immediate vicinity, anyone who heard a commotion or witnessed anything untoward, to contact the police...'

That soundbite from a Detective Superintendent Jones from Kent's major crime unit. Vague, though, and nothing about how they had connected him to the murder. The station DJ returned with more information, and directed listeners to the station's website, where Nate clicked on a video link and found himself watching... himself.

He had tried to shield his face, of course, but that hadn't worked. The camera held by the partying neighbour from the caravan next door to Starfish had captured a fine shot of Nate's mug as he stood outside the door of the crime scene. Maybe a bloody knife in his hand might have looked worse, but not by much.

Another video, taken from someone's shaking mobile phone, showed the entrance to the park. The gate was down, and there was a cop car blocking the road, sideways on. The cop car backed up to allow an ambulance through. There was excited chatter from off-screen as the phone's owner gossiped with someone.

A voiceover quoted words from the Met Police, who were still searching for Barke. They now suspected he could be armed and dangerous. Call in any sightings, any information at all, the cops said, but do not approach the man.

Wow, not just dangerous, but *armed* and dangerous. Nate shook his head.

The voiceover had an opinion: Barke had fled the country, but had now come back because he had unfinished killing business. And it was possible he was driving a Ford Kuga, because one had been stolen from the leisure park last night, around the time of the brutal murder.

That explained the call the night before. A detective thinking he might actually have the killer on the phone, and treading carefully because of it.

The voiceover continued, 'Police are looking into possible reasons that Barke had been at the leisure park, and hope that the dead man's identity, which they have yet to establish, might shed some light. They haven't yet determined a motive for the murder. The post-mortem is scheduled for later today.'

Nate's head swam. He tried to focus on positive things: the police would scrutinise the hitman's laptop and find out about his killer-for-hire hobby; they might find DNA other than Nate's on the body; they might unearth another Zapruder who had, by some fantastic fluke, accidentally filmed Lazar killing the hitman and then boasted about how he'd set-up an innocent man for everything.

But he couldn't be sure of anything. And he was now no longer sure that he could do anything to help his cause. Clearing his name was beginning to seem like a pipe dream. Mission impossible. There was only one path open to him now: trying to save Toni. It was the most pressing thing in his life right now. Maybe the only thing of importance that would ever enter the rest of his life. At least if he could do–

He stopped dead. And listened as the voiceover reported that police had arrived on the scene following a tip-off. So, the body hadn't been discovered by nosy neighbours or some member of the park's staff. No, no, no. Someone had phoned the cops and said they suspected a dead man was in the caravan. Nate couldn't believe his ears, but then he could... He so could. Because that made perfect sense.

Lazar and Ryback.

When Buzzcut didn't call in, Lazar, knowing Nate had escaped again, killed the hitman and fled the scene with his remaining henchman and Toni. And then, damned well knowing that CCTV somewhere in the park would have Nate's face (the holidaymaker with the camera must have felt like a surprise windfall), he called the bloody cops. Plan B: make sure that Nate was truly doomed if he got arrested.

Of course, he gave Nate enough time to clear the park before they arrived, because giving him to the cops was not their primary objective. Plan A: bury Nate's diced corpse in a shallow grave.

But that didn't explain why Buzzcut had tried to call a police station in Watford. That was the anomaly here. It cut into Nate's mind like a knife. He needed more answers. There was more to this.

The answers lay with Lazar, and Ryback, and maybe others. They didn't just have answers, they had Toni, too. It was time to go get them.

Screaming woke him.

He jerked into a sitting position, full panic, but started to calm immediately. The two RAC vans had gone and the way ahead was clear, and it was daytime, and he could see loud mothers and their raucous children all over the place. The school run. Christ, he must have slept for about seven hours, which was a surprise.

He quickly climbed into the driver's seat because he knew it looked more suspicious for a lone guy to be sitting in the back seat of a car. He kept his head down and a hand on his forehead as he pulled Toni's phone and typed a street in Watford into the Traveller app. Not excessive caution, yet he felt silly doing it. What, some four-year-old still trying to learn his own name was going to point and say, *Mummy, there's that missing vehicle that the constabulary seeks to apprehend*?

The street in Watford was eleven miles away. The route would put him on the M1 for a time, which was good. No traffic lights, no jams, no cops on foot. Much less chance of getting his face spotted. The car, though? He must have still been suffering the effects of the drug last night, because taking a second stolen Kuga had been a terrible idea. Sure, the registration and the colour were different, but the public wouldn't have that in their minds this morning. They'd just know that a suspected double-killer was using a Ford Kuga, and they'd wonder about each one they saw. But he'd been lucky to steal a car at all. He didn't fancy his chances of doing so again, so he would have to stick by the Kuga.

Forty minutes later, the Kuga turned onto a street a few hundred metres east of West Hertfordshire Sports Ground. Tall, white houses on one side and tiny shops in a terrace facing them across the road. Neighbouring the terrace was an old hotel, a gap of seven feet between them. Nate drew up near the alleyway. It was the only way into the centre of a big square created by four connected streets. Four years ago, the walls of the alleyway had been lined with rubber foam to a height of six feet because vehicles often scraped their flanks along the brickwork, creating more work for the body shop they were headed for. Now, the foam was gone and the gouges beneath had been smothered by new paintwork. The cobblestone road had been transformed into shiny new tarmac. A wooden gate with 'HyperX Customs' graffitied upon it was now a wrought-iron affair with a security camera and no clue as to what lay beyond. He got the feeling HyperX was gone. Vanished. History. Erased like a stain on the land.

He turned in the road, not wanting to seem as if he were lingering, and studied the gate as he performed the manoeuvre. There were no bolts or handles, but there was a quarter-moon track in the tarmac, so he guessed the gate was automatic. He couldn't see much beyond because the alleyway curved slightly out of sight behind the terrace. But the gate looked like the sort an affluent homeowner might buy, so maybe the land in the centre of the square had become some rich soul's house and garden. Nate wondered if the lethal history of the building that had once stood there would have knocked the price up or down.

Nate parked a short distance down the road and selected a newsagents. He needed answers.

Behind the counter, a middle-aged man in a crisp blue shirt, black trousers and a large white turban. He had a thick beard and healthy eyes, and teeth just as shiny. Genuine smile, maybe because he owned the place and wasn't paid hourly for his customer service.

Four years ago HyperX had been a fairly big local news story and maybe this guy, if he'd been manning the counter back then, had had to deal with reporters and morbid crime fans popping into his shop to ask questions. Nate hoped that meant the guy wouldn't be suspicious if Nate asked a few now. But as he stepped into the shop, he was confronted by a rack of newspapers, and at least four of them, including one national, had his mug right on the front page. Images of the Night Stalker hit him like shots of adrenaline. His legs nearly gave out.

A blitz of bad words jumped out at him, including 'killer,

fugitive, dangerous'. Here it came, any second now: a scream from the shopkeeper and a frenzied chase through the streets of Watford, then violent capture by angry vigilantes, then a prison cell for the next–

'Can I help you, sir?' the guy said. He was staring right at Nate, but his demeanour didn't suggest that he thought Nate was a dangerous, fugitive killer. Nate relaxed a jot, telling himself that nobody expected some wild madman they'd seen in the papers to confront them. That always happened to someone else. He stepped up, but couldn't meet the guy's eyes, and he rubbed his nose as he spoke, just to cover his face.

'I was looking to get my car fixed up. Apparently there's a customs place round here?'

He pulled some cash out and picked up a chocolate bar, just to soften the guy a bit.

'It's gone, sir,' the guy said as he rang in the chocolate bar. 'It was back behind us, but it closed a few years ago. It's been turned into a private house now. There was a robbery, and the owners just closed it down afterwards. I think there's a place about a mile away that way.'

Nate pocketed his change and the confectionary. And then feigned shock. 'A robbery? Someone stealing old cars? What's that all about?'

'Not sure. I didn't really follow the story. My father was ill at the time. The police knocked on our doors, but they didn't tell us much. Someone was shot and he died, I do know that. But it was three or four years ago and crime hasn't exactly been on the wane around here since.'

'Wow? What else do you know about it?'

'That's it, really.'

Nate didn't think a guy seeking a body shop would push the questions. 'Let me be honest with you, sir. I'm a reporter doing a follow-up story. I need to know as much as possible about what happened that day, and if there's anyone around here showing an interest in that story.'

The shopkeeper rubbed his beard as he thought. Nate unwrapped the chocolate, just to give his clammy hands something to do and to put his eyes elsewhere. He heard a scrape and looked up to see the guy rooting in a drawer under the counter. Out came a dog-eared wallet, bloated almost into a cylinder with cards and receipts. Nate chewed chocolate and wafer. The guy rifled through the cards. Nate swallowed caramel. The guy handed him a card.

'The police handed these out. You could call this gentleman. I don't know anything else, I'm afraid.'

Nate thanked the man and left quickly. He didn't look at the business card until he was safely ensconced in the Kuga.

It was a card for a Detective Inspector David Jubbs, with an office number and a mobile number. This guy had probably been the senior investigating officer on the HyperX case. He didn't recognise the name. His interview had been conducted in Wandsworth, by Wandsworth detectives seconded to the case. Nate's eyes locked onto the landline.

The same number Buzzcut had given him.

Had Buzzcut been about to call DI Jubbs? Was the HyperX investigation still active? What was going on?

Then he spotted something else, and it all became clear. Below the DI's name, in smaller print, was another. The guy's right-hand man, a detective sergeant.

Detective Sergeant Richard Lazar.

He took a detour. Not far northeast of the Olympic Stadium, Stratford, he parked down a residential street where three guys were working on a souped-up Vauxhall Corsa in a garden.

They looked up because he was blocking the gate. One guy waved him away. Nate got out and held up the keys.

'Five-year-old Ford Kuga, guys. Worth ten grand. Yours for half an hour's work.'

They looked at him like he was funny in the head. One guy approached. Looked like he had the Kuga's worth in ink on his arms and neck. The guy stood at the gate and eyed the car.

'You want me to suck your dick for half an hour?'

Said in jest. But Nate wondered. He told the guy what he wanted. And then he drove northeast to Westfield Stratford City shopping centre. Nate's choice to pick the London town statistically noted as the crime hotspot of England had clearly been a good one.

Thirty-four minutes after lying up in car park B, recipient of a Park Mark Safer Parking Award, the three guys drew up next to the stolen Kuga in a stolen 1995 Ford Mondeo with a smashed front bumper and a bonnet that was a different shade of green to the rest of the vehicle.

He swapped the Kuga's keys for the Mondeo's. And he kept his hand on the revolver in his jacket in case the bozos tried something cheeky. They didn't. It was a very professional illegal deal. Maybe they were just as wary of Nate as he was of them.

For the second time, one of the guys asked him why he wanted to get rid of his car. Nate gave the same answer as before: wife shagged my best mate in the back. And told the guy he'd find the logbook and other documents in the back. He knew the guy wouldn't make a hasty check to make sure it was all in order. The car would be in pieces and spread far and wide within the day.

'If this car comes back to bite me on the ass, I'll have yours,' said the guy two seconds before all three tore away in their new vehicle. A strange thing to say, given that he'd just stolen a car to swap for it.

'It'll come swallow you whole, dickhead,' Nate said as he waved the Kuga away.

He sat in his new car and pulled out DI Jubbs's business card. He stared at Lazar's name.

Buzzcut, in drug-fuelled confusion and without his phone, and thus without the first seven digits of the mobile number he was meant to call, must have opted to try to contact Lazar the only way he knew how: by calling the Watford station where he worked.

Detective Richard Lazar, who had worked on the HyperX case.

Things were falling into place, finally. Nobody had been punished for the HyperX fiasco, and at least two people felt the sting of that quite badly. Had a businessman who lost money and a cop who couldn't catch a bad guy, joined forces and decided that, in the absence of the real culprits, they would seek revenge against the security team that failed so badly and thus, in their opinion, caused it all?

Their mission of vengeance was almost complete. Pete and Kaushal, and probably Webber – dead. Agar – a sitting duck for the next hitman. And Nate himself – drawn finally into their net. He had an hour to go until the twelve o'clock appointment and couldn't shake the feeling that this would all be over very soon. Clearing his name, of course, would mean a new investigation once the police had the truth, and that would be a lengthy process – so why did he have the entrenched belief that things were spiralling ever faster to a conclusion?

Because he was no longer in this to clear his name. Like Toni, he was under the control of an irresistible force.

This was now all about revenge for him, too.

Half an hour later he found a parking space – at least, he found a spot the car would fit into, and dumped it. It was hot, and he wouldn't ever see it again. But at least when the cops found it, they wouldn't connect it to Nate, at least not until they had spoken to the three idiots now driving around in a Ford that homicide detectives dearly wished to trace, if the old couple had reported it stolen. He left the keys in the ignition and the door open, hoping someone would steal it and take it a hundred miles away. Better if there was no evidence that he had been here.

Here was St George's Wharf in Nine Elms, which was an area undergoing a massive commercial and residential facelift with nearly two dozen interlinked redevelopment schemes bubbling away, as evidenced by swathes of open land teeming with heavy machinery and tall cranes that poked high into the sky, and unfinished skyscrapers wrapped like presents, as if they'd been delivered whole by gods. Almost thirty-five thousand new homes were planned and Pete had often said he would love one, primarily in Vauxhall Tower or overlooking the Thames. He'd shown Nate artists' impressions on the Internet of how the finished project would look, utterly impressed by the way London was breathing new life into derelict industrial land... reinventing itself... looking to the future – blah, blah, blah. Nate had never cared and didn't now as he passed the Vauxhall Tower, inaugural nominee for the Carbuncle Cup and twice voted worst building in the world by *Architects' Journal* – Nate recalled using these facts, sucked from the Internet also, to try to shut Pete up. Pete was shut up forever now. Nate kept his head down while others looked up and walked on.

A couple of minutes later he was on Riverside Walk, a walled pathway running alongside the Thames. He walked quickly and stared at the river and tried to keep Pete out of his mind.

At some point he became aware that he had passed out of

Lambeth and into Wandsworth. Home. Home? Not really. If anything, it was now the most hostile place on earth, because if he was going to be recognised by anyone, it would probably be here, even in such an anonymous city as London.

And immediately, as if Wandsworth itself wanted to remind him that he was unwelcome here, it happened.

A woman in a dress suit, dragging a suitcase on wheels, watched him walk towards her, and he couldn't help but watch her, because something in her look told him what was coming.

'You're that guy,' she said. She stopped, but he didn't. He gave a wry shake of the head, hoping the gesture might look like that of a man now getting a bit annoyed by people constantly likening him to someone else. Then he was past, and he didn't look back. He didn't know if his act had persuaded her she was wrong, that she'd made the same mistake others had, but he heard no shout from her. Thirty seconds later he looked behind, half expecting her to be talking to a growing crowd and pointing at him. Those damned images of the Night Stalker chased by vigilantes again. He was ready to leap into the Thames and swim if that happened. But it didn't. The woman had her back to him and was walking on. Maybe *that guy* had been a busker who'd impressed her with street theatre.

Toni's phone said it was ten past twelve. He didn't worry. It wasn't a job interview. What were they going to do if he was late? Ask him to phone their secretary and reschedule?

Nate had expected the postcode Buzzcut had given him to belong to an empty building under construction, given the area. He had imagined the setting for this final showdown, and it had been something right out of an action film: an empty top floor, unfinished walls, cement dust on the floor, builders' tools scattered everywhere, windowless frames letting in cold air, bullets flying as everyone ran around a maze created by pallets of bricks and giant coils of rubber piping and stacks of two-by-four.

But Google had corrected him. Eight Oaks, Nine Elms Lane, was a luxury riverside residential block with apartments selling around the £800,000 mark. And up ahead, there it was: three conjoined brown-brick towers of different heights, the centre one the tallest, making the building look like a giant winner's podium. And then shock piled upon amazement when further Google interrogation coughed up the name of one of the apartments' owners.

James Ryback.

Getting in seemed easy. Too easy. Suspiciously easy.

A steel fire exit of switchback stairs rose up a bare brick central section of the middle building, and at each floor a concrete balcony with a frameless glass balustrade ran the length of the building, with gates to provide apartment boundaries. Google had also given Nate a floor plan, so he knew that Ryback's apartment was on the fourth floor, and he now stared at an open window beside a solid door on that level. No other window was open as wide as that one. Obviously Ryback's. Clearly an invitation: come on in. Clearly a damn trap, too.

He was being led like a lamb to the chopping block and he knew it, yet here he was climbing the back wall of the block, now crossing a neat lawn with garden benches and coloured rockeries. Now mounting the stairs. Climbing. *Baa.*

He pulled Buzzcut's snub-nosed pistol. He'd googled it and learned that it was a five-shot Ruger SP101.

He exited onto the balcony on floor four, passed through the first gate, ducked below the window of the apartment next to Ryback's, and opened the next gate. Now he was just three feet from the window. No glass at all in the PVC door, so he put his ear to it, but heard nothing from within.

He gripped the Ruger, finger on the trigger. It was double-action, which meant a single pull of the trigger to fire, but more power would be needed, and that would affect accuracy. At least he probably wouldn't shoot by accident if a noise startled him. He found this concern strange, given his time handling much more deadly weapons in the army. But, as Toni had said, these days he was a wet businessman. He certainly felt like one now.

Back to the window. Double-casement, only the farthest half open. Reaching it would mean exposing himself in front of the closed section, and that just wouldn't do. However, he noticed that the open section was angled perfectly to allow him to see the room beyond reflected. No guys aiming guns at the open window as far as he could tell. So he did the exposure thing. And had a funny thought: *if I get shot, try not to fall over the wall. Three bullets in the head is bad enough without a fifty-metre fall to boot.*

No bullets. No Icarus impression. He climbed into a large living room with bamboo furniture, all of it. Table, chairs, sofa, although it had soft cushions. Tribal masks and paintings on the wall. A massive flat screen TV. Other items, some expensive, some just cheap trinkets to fill space. Just the kind of living room he'd expect in any house. But all of it was busted, as if a tornado had slipped in through the window. Everything breakable had suffered. Even the wallpaper had been torn.

Kitchen, the same. The vandals had even gone to the trouble of yanking off the oven and fridge doors.

Bedrooms, no different. The mattresses were slashed.

Complete destruction. Nate couldn't put down a foot without crunching glass or bits of wood. Not a robbery. Someone had turned the place over, but not looking for something. Unless it was the size of a thimble. Unless they had gotten very angry at not being able to find it. Which he doubted. Too much carnage. No-one stayed that angry for that long. Any thirst for violence would have long dissipated before the place looked even as half as bad as it did. This destruction was to make a statement.

Nate got the impression that the chaos was meant to look like his work.

He went to the kitchen window, stepping over and around busted items. Across the road, past bushy trees lining the pavement, was New Covent Garden Market. He took in the London skyline beyond for a few seconds and then looked down, past a small balcony outside Ryback's door, and onto Nine Elms Lane. Traffic moving slowly both ways. People going about their lives. He thought about his mother. He thought about Pete. Being this high, watching the tiny world moving, often made him think of his place in that world. He thought about all the exotic places, all the lives that were so vastly different from his own. He often envied people who never had to deal with the normal city things that people like him went through. Barmen on beaches in Hawaii. Builders in the forests of China. People who'd never heard of the term 'rat race'.

Now, though, he envied every rat below him. The businessman rushing to the office. The postman finishing up his deliveries. The cops racing south – even the robber they might be chasing.

Double-take on the cop car. Lights flashing but no siren wailing, it was blasting southeast along Nine Elms Lane, headed this way. Not just this way, Nate knew. Here. He knew that even before it pulled in directly below him. The cops were coming for him, but he did not move.

Just like at the leisure park, someone had set-up a crime scene and then called the police to frame him, but he did not move.

Not until he saw the black van. A hundred metres behind the cop car. Now slowing as it neared its destination. Cops got out of the patrol car, but they didn't rush anywhere. Instead, they watched the black van make a sharp turn and zip down the side of the Eight Oaks.

Nate rushed to the living room window and stuck his head out. The van had parked alongside the garden wall, right by a gate. The side door opened and men in black exploded out. Armed cops. They opened the gate and stormed through and split up. One rushed for the fire exit. There was always a chance that there was another dangerous fugitive in the building and that they were here for him. But taking that long-shot bet could win Nate twenty years in a cell if he was wrong. It wasn't a bet he was willing to take.

Back to the kitchen window. The boys in blue had gone, no doubt now inside the building. Blue and black, all coming up for him. They would cover the lifts and the stairs, of course, which now meant no way out.

He opened the door that led onto the balcony. Unlike at the building's rear, here each resident got their own little outdoor space, a balcony barely longer than a man. The neighbour's was ten feet away. It had a bamboo privacy screen, a deck chair, a potted plant, a small table with a book under a paperweight, and a scuffed rug. A personal place where a person could sit and be left alone while feeling out in the world. Being left alone would have thrilled Nate no end right now.

He closed the door and leaned over the iron railing, trying to see the balcony below. He could see that people on the street had stopped to watch the action. They knew something was kicking off, but he couldn't tell if anyone was looking at him. No pointing fingers at least.

He climbed over the railing and paused on the insane side. Heels over thin air, just ten little fingers keeping the ambulance crews at bay.

'In what world is this a good idea, Nate?' he said aloud.

He lowered himself into a squat and slid his hands down the bars. No screams from below. His fingers started to hurt from clutching the bars so tightly. But he didn't move. He wasn't at the point of no return yet. No way he was going to risk what he was risking unless he had absolutely no choice. The cops might yet kick in another door and arrest someone else.

'Hurry the fuck up,' he hissed.

A minute that felt like years later, he heard the front door go. 'Go' as in bashed open.

'We're coming for you, Barke,' he heard someone shout. There it was, then: they were here for him. Then they were inside and everyone was shouting. In a roundabout way, the cops were suggesting that he should show himself with his hands up because they were armed police and they would shoot if he had a weapon.

Now, the point of no return. He tried to kick his feet off the balcony, but they wouldn't move. He pictured himself frozen here as the cops opened the balcony door. Maybe they'd pause and try to talk him back to the sane side of the railing, or maybe they'd kick his fingers and tell their bosses he jumped.

Neither appealed. The shouting got closer, too close, seconds-from-being-caught-or-kicked-close. His feet slipped away from the concrete lip. The awkward horizontal grip he had on the bars wrenched his wrists as his arms were pulled vertical by his weight.

He swung forward and his wrists actually creaked like old hinges as they were torqued. His index fingers were tugged free, and the others didn't have the strength to stay in place after that. A moment of sheer panic unlike any he'd ever felt before as his touch upon the world and everything in it was gone.

And then the panic was replaced with pain, a sharp blow across his buttocks. For a second he was balanced perfectly in a sitting position on the balcony railing below, his ass out over the dangerous side. But before he could wonder which way this pendulum would swing, he was toppling forward. He hit the deck hard, and the pain in his knees was glorious because it was there, because it beat eternal oblivion.

There was no time for enjoying his extended life, though. He heard the door on the balcony above open.

Nate got up and tried the balcony door of the flat under Ryback's. Locked. He looked through the window and saw an old man in a dressing gown over pyjamas. They locked stares.

Nate could think of nothing else to do but wave. The guy was sitting at the kitchen table, but he got up, started a slow shuffle towards the door. Nate tensed, even held his breath in case the cops heard it. Above, the shouting had stopped. Having determined that no-one was going to jump out at them with a gun, the cops were probably doing a slow search to see if Nate had stuffed himself in a drawer. He could hear the murmur of the odd remark. He wondered if they'd assume they'd missed him.

'What you doing? Maybe he flew, that it?' he heard someone say just a few feet above him. Someone had stepped out onto the balcony.

The old guy appeared at the window in the upper half of the door, a puzzled look on his face. He reached for the handle. Behind Nate, he heard a scrape and saw the back half of a foot appear on the ledge. A guy climbing onto the insane side of the railing just as Nate had, he realised.

'What you doing?' the same cop said.

'Piss off back inside and check under the bed, why doncha?' came the reply.

Now two feet were on the balcony. Surely the cop wasn't about to copy Nate's lunatic move? He wondered if he could bring himself to push a guy sitting on the railing, if it was a choice between that and prison. Nate looked at the old guy, who seemed to have forgotten how the hell to open a door.

A black ass came into view behind the feet. Amazingly, the cop was squatting, just as Nate had.

The old guy opened the door. Nate pushed past him, moving him back. The guy said nothing. Didn't look scared, as if his slow brain hadn't yet determined a threat.

Nate shut the door quietly and bent down below the window and pulled the guy with him. Just in time. He saw an arm, then a shoulder, then a head, sideways on. Some daredevil cop leaning out, squatting, then bending to the side to create the angle to see the balcony below. Nate waited for a shout, because he had seen the cop's head, and that meant the cop might have seen his. He gave it ten seconds, certain that the cop would not stay insane-side for that long. And when he poked his head up again, the guy had gone.

He stood and grabbed the old guy's arm and led him into the living room. The old guy stared at him as they marched.

'You locked out?' he said.

The guy was surely eighty, thin, wrinkled like an old shirt left balled up in a bag for six months. Not all there in the brain department.

'Yes,' Nate said. He softly pushed the guy down into an armchair. 'I live above. Couldn't get out of the front door.'

The living room was modern, much smaller than Ryback's,

and there was an Xbox on a shelf near the flat screen TV, and a number of pictures on the wall that showed a young couple with a baby, all of which made Nate think the guy was someone's visiting father. Maybe the old guy had gotten too senile for his own good and his son or daughter had invited him to stay. A quilt rumpled on the sofa gave this theory credence.

A noise from another room. A gruff male voice laughing.

Nate rushed for the front door, checked the peephole and then opened it slowly. A corridor, empty. Doors down both sides. That explained the size of the apartment. Top floor for the richer people. Four big apartments taking up the entire floor, while here there were twice as many. But that meant he had no access to the fire exit on the other side of the building.

Nate headed out and started walking fast along the corridor.

At the end, he froze at the door to the stairs as he heard footsteps. He ducked aside as he saw legs run into view, coming down.

He rushed back, his plan to knock on the guy's door again. But as he passed the door before that one, he heard it start to unlock, and he stopped. It started to open and he helped with a slamming forearm. He heard a feminine yelp as the door crashed into someone behind it.

He rushed into a hallway just in time to see a black woman vanish through another door. He closed the front door and followed her.

He entered a living room with two occupants. The black woman was at a computer table, a phone already in her hand. There was a white woman sitting on a sofa, staring at her mumbling friend in shock. Before her on the coffee table was a purse with a bunch of keys hanging off the zip. Seeing him, the white woman jumped up and backed away to the big front window.

'Put the phone down,' he ordered. He heard footsteps go running past outside. The cops, deciding to check the downstairs flat, maybe. Or all of them, starting with that one.

But the black woman didn't put the phone down. She jabbed numbers into it instead, while her awestruck friend just watched. He rushed over and grabbed the handset, and she screamed and backed away. A second later both women had their backs against the window, and they were shaking with fear.

'Just shut up and you'll be fine,' he snapped. 'You won't get hurt.' He looked around for something, anything, that could help him here. No Santa Claus disguise or invisibility spray. No zip line from the window to the ground or fireman's pole descending through the flats below. The living room and kitchen were side by side and he was near enough to the doorway to consider going in for a knife. But he had a knife. And he didn't want to let the women out of his sight.

'Please,' the black woman said. 'She has a safe with jewels across the hall. Please. I have nothing.'

Her friend looked at her in shock.

Nate grabbed the purse off the coffee table and ran for the door.

He checked the peephole, saw no-one, and opened the door. And that was when he saw the cops just feet away.

Normal cops. Blue, not black. Unarmed, not carrying deadly machine guns. No way they'd checked the first two floors already, so the entire team was concentrating on the upper floors.

One cop was at the old man's door, waiting. He must have

knocked. The other was at the far end of the hallway, where there was an open utilities cupboard that he was peering into. Nate crossed the hall and held up the purse and stuck a key from the dangling bunch into the Yale lock.

'Hey,' said a voice. Nate rubbed his face as he turned that way. The cop at the door, staring at him. 'You see anyone else here? You live here?'

Nate pushed open the door and held up the keys and waggled them. 'Does it look like I just broke into this flat? Anyone else like who?'

The cop stared, and then the door he waited at was opened. He turned to the old man, and Nate quickly rushed inside the flat.

'Hey, stop there!' the cop called out. Nate shut the door. He heard hard knocking just seconds later. 'Open this door, please. I need to speak to you about an urgent matter. Hey.'

He heard the guy get on his radio. Calling for a check on the flat owner, maybe. At least the cop hadn't recognised him.

Nate moved through a living room he barely looked at, towards the window at the back.

He opened the window and peered out. The black van was still there at the gateway to the back garden, but now two armed cops stood by it. Their rifles hung limp from shoulder straps and they were chatting to the driver. Just killing time, seemingly unconcerned that their colleagues were inside and hunting a dangerous fugitive killer. He was thankful that the area wasn't swarming with armed men. Maybe that was because they hadn't yet received confirmation that Nate was here.

A scuffling sound from above. Movement. There was a cop on the upper balcony, eight feet above Nate. No other sounds. Just that one cop, then. Maybe he was too fat to get through the window, or had chosen to enjoy the view north of the river while his colleagues searched Ryback's apartment for a guy hiding in a drawer.

Tense, expecting the cops to look up at any moment, Nate exited onto the balcony. He cursed the glass balustrade, but thankfully no-one looked up. He slowly walked towards the fire exit, fearing that fast movement would be more likely to register in the ground cops' peripheral vision. He got there without being spotted.

Worse was to come, he knew. The stairs extended outwards, which meant descending them would put him far enough from the building to be exposed to the balcony cop as well as the crew below. But his choices were limited. Down he went.

Balcony cop slid into view. He had his back to the world. Nate relaxed. He took the inward-facing stairs quickly, because they hid him from view of the ground cops. He paused on the next landing, his back against the cold wall. He had to do it all over again.

This time, balcony cop turned around when Nate was preparing to make the turn onto the inward stairs. The guy hawked phlegm into the air, watched it land far below, then turned away. Nate moved on, heart thudding.

On the second floor, he didn't pause this time. He wanted this hell over with.

He got to the first floor without incident and exited onto the balcony. No way the cop above could hear or see him now. The ground cops, though, were much closer. Twenty metres away to Nate's left, twenty feet below. The wall hid the bottom half of the van and all but the cops' heads and shoulders, but they would see movement from his position easily.

But he got a break, finally: here the glass balustrade had blue protective film over its entire length, giving it a translucency that would shield Nate from view. Maybe the sheets of glass were new. Maybe the film had been left in place to accord the residents some privacy. Maybe someone had figured there would come a day when a wanted man needed to crawl along the balcony without being seen.

At the end of the building, he risked poking up his head for a glance at the ground cops. At this angle, the wall hid them, and only the front of the van and one guy's right leg and right arm were visible through the gate.

Nate slapped the concrete and grunted in triumph. Then checked himself. He wasn't safe yet.

He climbed over the end of the balcony and dropped fifteen feet into the garden, close to the wall. He was over that in five seconds.

A pedestrianised road ran between the wall and the next building, which was a large clothing store with cars parked outside it. To his right, the way out onto Nine Elms Lane, but he didn't know if other police vehicles had turned up and that put the main road out of the running.

To his left, the road ended at bollards blocking vehicular access to the river walkway, although there was a guy on a bike parked there.

Pedestrians everywhere, headed this way and that, busy being rats. No-one seemed to have cared that he'd just jumped off a wall. They had ignored his arrival and now ignored his presence.

Except a guy in one of the cars parked outside the clothing store. Who stared straight at him and lifted a phone to his mouth, and spoke loud enough for Nate to hear even though the window: 'Christ, he's right here.'

Ryback's kill crew were back in the show, it seemed.

Fifteen feet. Nate got across the distance before the guy could fully exit the car, which was his downfall. Shouldn't have even tried. He was half out when Nate launched himself at the door like a long jumper. He hit the door right next to the handle, slamming the window into the guy's head. He was knocked back into the vehicle. Still moving forward, Nate twisted and put his shoulder into the window, cracking it as the door's movement was checked by the pair of legs caught between it and the sill.

The guy screamed in pain, and a number of pedestrians looked over.

To his left, he heard the bike engine roar. The guy flipped up the front wheel, pivoted, and came racing this way.

He waited until the guy was close, and pulling something from his jacket, and then yanked open the door, using it as a shield. The biker swerved. By then his gun was out of his jacket, but he was past and needed to turn in order to take a shot.

Car guy sat upright and leaned forward, reaching for Nate. Nate slammed the door again. A window right in the face again. Already cracked, the glass burst upon contact with his nose, spraying glass all over him. Without the glass to check its movement, the door once again cut into the guy's shins, eliciting another scream.

That woke up the rats. Realising that violence had entered their world, they started yelling. Some froze on the spot, but others darted for cover. One woman ran into biker's path as he was cutting a sharp turn and fell over his front wheel, which caused him to stop suddenly and plant his feet to avoid toppling. Beyond the guy, Nate saw two men running his way. That made four enemies now.

Nate ran. Behind him, the bike roared and the woman screamed – Nate figured the guy had ridden right over her rather than waste time going around. Now he'd be in a good position to make a shot, but Nate wasn't sure he'd risk it with people flying about like debris in a crosswind.

He ran to the end of the road, between the bollards, onto Riverside Walk. Left, no good – that went back towards the cops. Right, no good – it was some way to the end of the building, and people were scarce, and the biker would get off a shot before Nate could find an exit.

So, instead, he put his hands on the mossy top of the low retaining wall and leaped over.

He landed hard on the foreshore, rolling to lessen the impact. Good theory, bad application. His back fell on a sharp rock, and his ankle thudded down onto another one. He got up, limping, and ran across the stony mud to his right, parallel to the river. St George's Wharf Tower was some way ahead, and beyond it the pier with a river bus pulling up, and beyond that Vauxhall Bridge. He thought about taking the river bus, and he thought about climbing up onto the bridge, and then he discarded both ideas because the distance was too much for a bad ankle on stony ground.

So he angled towards the river, past a man whose dog tried to nip him, and a guy at the water's edge with a metal detector. He waded in, taking big, comical steps as the water reached his knees and then his waist. He threw a look back and saw the biker at the walk wall, aiming his gun. But he didn't fire, probably because he'd realised the same thing Nate had: handgun, that distance, no way. He soon sped off down the walkway, towards the bridge, maybe hoping to get across, get round to the north bank before Nate did.

Metal detector guy called out to him: 'Hey, you got Port Authority permission?'

'Charity swim,' Nate shouted back.

Then the cold water was up to his neck. His breath came in gasps and he swore. That was the cold shock response, and he made sure his feet could still touch the riverbed. People died from this when they took an involuntary breath with the head submerged, or fainted due to hyperventilation, or the heart gave up because of the increased effort involved in pumping blood through narrowed arteries.

'People also die when they get shot in the back of the head, dickhead,' he chided himself, and started swimming.

He put his eyes on one of five white cube-like buildings dead ahead. Getting to those buildings was the only important thing in his life at the minute. Distance: two hundred and fifty, maybe three hundred metres. Three minutes, he figured. Three little minutes of cold and exertion, and it would be all over. In his university days, he'd had drunken outdoor sex in February winds that had been colder and harder – and the same length of time! Easy.

Three minutes in the water, another minute to cross the foreshore and scale the flood wall, and then he'd be able to lose himself in the maze of buildings on the north bank. *Buildings, Nate, get to the buildings.*

But he began to worry when the buildings started to shift to his left. The current, dragging him east. Now Vauxhall Bridge was getting closer, too. He tried not to imagine his head cracking open against one of its concrete piers.

'Then swim fucking faster,' he shouted at himself.

Halfway across now, and the feeling had started to go in his hands and feet. Exactly bloody halfway to the inch, probably. A natural bodily reaction to the cold: blood routed away from his extremities and into his torso to keep the vital organs warm as his temperature dropped. But his brain's attempt to help him survive the cold would kill him if his arms and legs stopped working.

He risked a look around, but saw no-one in the water behind him, no-one on the foreshore aiming a gun. Made sense. If they were smart, they'd be gunning it for Vauxhall Bridge, left at the Panoramic and then down Grosvenor Road to cut him off. Or, if he was dragged too far east, they could wait atop the bridge and drop bricks onto his nose when he drifted below them. If undertows created by the bridge and the uneven riverbed didn't drag him under and keep him as a house guest for two days.

'Shut the fuck up!' he screamed aloud at his own mind. And pushed on.

When he hit the far foreshore, he had drifted so far downriver that his original plan to scale the slimy green flood wall was cast aside for another option. Vauxhall Bridge was only a short distance to his right. It was close enough that he could see the detail in Pomeroy's *Agriculture*, one of four large statues on the bridge's piers. The foreshore was piled high at the bridge's abutment, making the wall climb appear easy, and once on solid ground there were steps leading onto the bridge. Hopefully the kill crew had already picked their ambush positions way to the west on Grosvenor Road.

His ankle felt strong again and he moved quickly, despite water-laden clothing, but as he reached the archway at the top of the steps, a guy turned into his path, fast, head down, hand in his jacket. They collided. Nate, travelling faster even though uphill, and carrying extra weight in his soaked clothing, stopped dead, while the guy staggered back from the impact and dropped onto his ass. And on the ground between them, a hammer clattered. Both men stared at it for a second, and then both men made a grab for it.

Having scrambled onto his knees to lunge forward, the guy was perfectly placed for a knee in the face. Back onto his ass he went, and Nate snatched the hammer and raised it high.

Halfway to his feet again, the guy realised he'd lost this battle and turned his head away, and put his hands up. But Nate didn't want to spill blood in the middle of London, so instead he stamped hard on the guy's ankle to hobble him. A convenient car horn from some annoyed driver on the bridge smothered the guy's scream of pain.

Nate exited onto the bridge and immediately saw a bike parked by the bus stop. The helmeted biker, not the guy from the south bank episode, was at the balustrade, fifteen feet away, staring down at the steps. He must have missed seeing Nate on the steps by a second or two.

The bike's engine was still running.

Nate ran for the bike, but as he got within feet, a blue van slipped out of traffic and into the red bus lane, drawing in fast behind the bike. The horn blared, making the biker jump. Nate stopped, but the van didn't. The bike was between them both and the van struck it without slowing, knocking it like a cannonball towards him. With no time for any reaction but fear, he froze and put his hands across his face and heard the crash, then waited for the searing pain of 250lbs. of sharp metal to tear into him. But he felt only the wind as the bike blasted past him. He heard it bouncing along the road behind him and turned to see it smash into the back of a car waiting at the junction.

Nate ran between two lanes of stationary cars, out into the junction. Traffic came at him from left and right, which he dodged easily, not even a horn sounding.

Across the road he saw trees. He knew the place. Crown

Estate property called Bessborough Gardens. A van couldn't get in through the thin gateway.

He turned in, nearly knocking over a young black lady with a double pram. Twin paths created a large X in the garden, but he ran alongside the shrubbery and trees by the fence, and knew immediately it was a bad idea because the van drew alongside him on Vauxhall Bridge Road, slowing down, matching his pace. In the passenger seat, a bearded guy looked at him and held up a gun, and Nate could see him smiling.

On the other side of the garden, tall white stucco houses bordered two sides in an L-shape. His only way out of the garden was another gate at the end of the fence. But the van would be right there as he exited, and this time he didn't think the presence of pedestrians would prevent the bad guys from shooting at him.

He turned, running across the grass and towards the houses. Rear entrances, by the looks of them. In the corner were three arched gateways, each blocked by a wrought-iron fence. He was over in three seconds and found himself in a covered walkway. More gates ahead at the end, but these were open. Beyond, a square with parking and little seating areas with benches, and a small white hut of glass and more stucco sitting by a road leading out through a swing-arm gate.

Nate ran onto the road. A guy in a security uniform came out of the hut and put a hand up. His other held a radio.

Nate slowed as he approached the guard, and jabbed a thumb back at the building. He opened his mouth and, as planned, the guard looked, expecting to hear a complaint of some ilk, and that was when Nate elbowed him aside and increased speed. He ducked the gate and was out onto a public highway.

Behind him, the guard was shouting, possibly into the radio for backup. 'Intruders, intruders!'

Ahead, all around, tall residential properties. It looked like a dead end to the left, but there was a gap between two buildings that almost met at right angles. The way right led to Vauxhall Bridge Road, and going back there was not an option.

As he paused, the van came into view, from the right, turning onto the road. He turned left. The gap. Safety. The van couldn't make the squeeze.

Too late, the significance of the guard's shout registered. Intruders. Intruders with an S, as in plural. He turned his head, and there was a guy behind him. The biker, minus his helmet but carrying it in his hand. Unable to use his broken bike, he had run in pursuit, and through it all Nate had not realised the guy was pounding concrete just behind him.

He was just metres away. With no time to turn and run, knowing he'd never get up to speed in time, Nate reached into his jacket for the gun. The biker swung his arm and launched the helmet. It missed by such a distance that Nate didn't even flinch.

But behind the helmet was a gun, hidden in the helmet while the guy ran through the streets. By the time he'd registered it, he'd already been hit. Pain that was sharp but light, a pain he knew well by now.

He aimed his revolver. The dart was sticking straight up from his elbow. The biker stopped and put his hands up. Behind Nate, the van screeched to a halt a few metres away.

He felt the world wobbling. Nobody got out of the van. He looked and saw two Turkish-looking guys in the front, staring at him. Waiting, because they knew it wouldn't take long. He stepped closer to the biker, angry. The guy dropped to his knees.

'We got you and if you shoot me it'll just mean you wake up with no balls,' he said.

Nate looked around. The alleyway was too far. There were a few people about, and he could shout for help, but already they were making themselves scarce. Even the guard was staying clear now that guns had entered this picture.

His legs started to weaken, vision starting to blur. They had him indeed, no doubt about that. He remembered the panic in Buzzcut's face when he realised that the drug was going to take him down and there was nothing he could do about it. So, did Nate want to keep his balls or not?

Everyone seemed to be waiting for the inevitable. Nate sat down on the pavement, then lay on his back, knowing he'd end up there eventually. Less painful this way. He heard the van's doors open and feet hit the ground. He put the gun in his pocket, hoping these bozos were half-witted enough to miss it.

The biker's tall frame appeared next to him, blocking the meagre sunlight.

'Shit. Don't fuck me up, mate. I'm only here to...' Nate said, quoting Buzzcut, as if it were some magical formula.

'How about I decide on those balls after I see what damage you did to my bike?' the biker said, and raised his foot as if to stomp on Nate's face. He prayed for the tranquilliser to suck him under before the blow landed.

PART III

He dreamed of being crushed, and woke into a nightmare far worse.

The crushing part was real, though. His head felt like a vice was having a real good go at popping it. Surely the reason for the dream.

His blurry eyes could see walls close by. A vehicle. A van. He was in the back of a van. An ambulance, maybe? Some hazy memory of an ambulance was there–

No. Even before the walls of the van lost their blurriness, he knew it all, because this time he was woozy due to being cracked on the head, not drugged. Or both. Whatever: he remembered everything.

Not naked this time, but tied again. Feet tightly together, hands behind his back. He lay between two rows of seats, and right by him were a pair of feet. He looked up. A guy in jeans and a T-shirt sat there, towering high above him and staring down, watching him like he was some captivating TV show. He had the skin tone of Damar and Toni, and Nate had never seen him before. Were these bastards growing on trees or something?

'Weird, eh?' the guy said. He rocked this way and that as the van bounced over uneven ground. 'My ass is killing me, and I'm starving and can't wait to get there, but since you don't know what's coming, you probably want this trip to last forever. Weird, eh?'

He seemed to actually be awaiting an answer. Nate grinned at him. 'Yeah, weird.' He didn't feel that scared. And he could feel his balls trapped between his legs, so the biker had obviously determined that his bike was salvageable. But what he couldn't feel was the weight of a gun in his pocket. Not half-witted bozos after all.

The van stopped and the side door rasped open almost immediately. Another Turkish guy got in and they both bent and grabbed Nate. One jammed a canvas bag over his head as they lifted him. He took the presence of the bag as good news, figuring it meant they didn't want him to see where he was, and that was an unnecessary tactic if you planned to kill your prisoner.

'Can't have you describing our faces to the police when we let you go, can we?' said one guy. But a hint of mirth in his tone set Nate's fear bubbling. They were just fucking with his head, maybe just getting his hopes up, or trying to make sure he didn't fight like a rat backed into a corner.

They eased out of the van, carrying him carefully between them, face-down, as if he were a prized possession. Which he was, actually. These people had been hunting high and low for him. They needed him captured for their plan to work. And now they had him.

He felt the wind on him. Heard no sounds other than the men walking. He wasn't in London, he was sure of that.

A doorway, and then some creaky wooden stairs going down.

They laid him down on a cold but carpeted floor and he heard them going back up. He waited for a minute after they'd gone, and then scraped his head against the floor until he'd shifted the bag enough to uncover one eye.

He was in a dim room, lying next to a wooden chair. It was the only piece of furniture. The ceiling was low, the wall to his right bare house brick, the wall to his left lined with wine racks, easily half of them occupied. A wine cellar, some eight feet wide, twenty feet long.

And at the far wall was Toni.

She was sitting with her back against a rusty cast iron pipe as thick as his upper arm that ran from under the floor, up the wall and across the concrete ceiling, and disappeared through a ragged hole in the back wall. Her hands were above her head, tied by rope just above a split clamp.

She was grimy all over and naked from the neck down. He could see a dark patch under each arm, a few days' worth of hair growth. Her head, though, was covered by a black mask. It seemed too big for her, making her head look larger than it was. He tried not to look at her female parts.

Nate called her name but got no response. He got to his knees and made a slow effort of walking on them, more like a shuffle, until he was right in front of her. He called again. Nothing. But her head did not hang forward, so he didn't think she was dead. And he could see her chest rise and fall.

As he moved closer, his knee touched her foot and she gave a gasp and a jerk, and tried to shrink back from him.

'It's me,' he said. Nothing. She was shaking. He knew someone had hurt her, and not just because she was covered in dirt.

He leaned forward and grasped her hood in his teeth, and pulled it free. She jerked and blinked, and turned her head away. She wore large ear defenders, which explained why she had not heard his shout. She had been left in the dark and the silence, not knowing who or how many might be in the room with her, unaware of when the torment would end, when the next strike might come.

And then she saw him.

Immediately she broke into tears, and he felt for her. Tough, but still weak in ways. Her arms jerked the pipe as if trying to embrace him. The pipe rattled against its split clamps. Rust flakes rained down into their hair from a flanged elbow joint that connected the vertical and horizontal sections of pipe. The look in her eyes was something he didn't understand. Not relief that she might now be saved, but something else.

Her head dropped. He sensed that the other emotion she felt was embarrassment, maybe because of her nakedness. Her chest started to rise and fall faster, harder, and when she finally looked up again, her face was all rage and hate.

She shook her head and the ear defenders slipped off. 'How did they catch you?' she said.

He quickly explained: cops at the leisure park, Lazar on the phone, cops again at Ryback's apartment block, and tranquilliser guns in the hands of Ryback's kill crew. 'Did they bring you straight here? Have you been here all night?'

'They came into the caravan,' she said, ignoring the question. 'Lazar and another man. I watched the other man slit the hitman's neck wide. They got me while I was unprepared.'

That explained the embarrassment: not her naked body, but the fact that she'd been caught. No damage done to her ego, then. Her nakedness bothered him more than it did her, it seemed.

'It's okay,' he said. 'They got me, too, and there's bloody loads of them.'

'I'm sorry about your brother. He had some problem with his foot. They identified him.'

He was puzzled. She explained. Before they'd put the ear defenders on her, she had overheard a conversation. One of their captors had taken a phone call and announced the news to his cronies: the post-mortem had confirmed that the dead man in the fire was Pete Barke. But not through DNA. Something to do with an old surgery on one of his feet. This had made the kidnappers raucous with joy.

'They must have someone in the know somehow,' she said. 'Because it's not official yet. I heard them say that. Who do we think that could be?'

Nate had never doubted it was his brother's body, but hearing it confirmed like that knocked the wind out of him. So much so that he barely registered that it might have been his phone call to the police that made it happen. It was a few seconds before he composed himself. Knowing he was suffering, Toni patiently waited.

'Maybe a police officer,' Nate said. 'Lazar, he's a police officer. He was involved in the investigation into the robbery at HyperX.'

'I know. One of his men took great pride in telling me that, when my body was found, you'd be blamed for it. Lazar would influence the investigation somehow and cover the truth. He's been working for Ryback for years.'

Nate paused. 'Nothing yet helps me understand why they wanted to set me up. It can't just be so that the cops don't look elsewhere for a killer. They tried to give me to the cops at Ryback's apartment, and that doesn't make sense. The police already think I'm the killer, so why risk having me tell a different story? Why not do what they originally tried to do and bury me?'

'You're right. There's more to this. You see the answers written on these walls?'

He actually looked. Damn drug addling his mind – yet again. 'No. I don't understand.'

'So, the answers are outside this room. To get them, we need to be outside this room also.'

He understood. A convoluted way of saying they should escape. 'How?'

'Smash a bottle of wine and get a shard to my feet. I'll hold it and saw through your ropes, and then you do mine.'

It seemed like a good plan, but they never got the chance to see if it would work. Because right then the cellar door opened.

Nate hopped back to where they'd dumped him and lay on his side near the chair, just as a man came down the stairs.

Yet another new face. This guy had dark olive skin, just like Damar. He had a face that looked fifty, shiny black hair that seemed twenty years younger, and so Nate put his age at right in the middle: forty. He also wore a monocle, as if he considered himself gentry. But that didn't sit well with the tracksuit he wore. He thumped down the stairs with a clear plastic bag in one hand and in the other a rope tied in a noose at one end, which he swung like a pendulum.

'Hey, killer,' Monocle said to Nate. He got to the bottom of the stairs and held up the bag. Nate saw that the monocle was just a tattoo, even including a piece of string running down his face. Strangely, Nate wondered if the guy had a necktie tattooed under his shirt. 'You ain't done yet, killer,' he said. 'I need some prints on these babies. And then it's dying time.'

Monocle stopped as he noticed that Toni's mask was free. 'Cheeky.'

He approached her and stroked her breast, then replaced the mask, but not the ear defenders, and she didn't object, as if there was no fight remaining in her. He returned to Nate and shook out the items from the bag onto the carpet, ten inches from Nate's eyes. A mobile phone and a kitchen knife. He picked both up and stepped over Nate, and then Nate felt him press the cold plastic of the phone into his hand, followed by the warm wooden handle of the knife.

'Killing your own friends, eh? Bad boy.'

Friends? Plural? Achala Kaushal and Carl Webber, of course. And of course they would want to set Nate up for those killings as well. The knife put images of their cut throats in his mind.

Monocle held up the knife by using the bag like a glove, careful not to leave his own DNA on it. 'And her over there. Now, since you'll be blamed for her bloody death, I'll give you a choice. You can do it, if you want. Slit her throat. At least then you won't be blamed for a crime you didn't commit. This one tried to kill you, remember. You want it?'

He saw a chance. If Monocle cut his bonds and handed him that knife...

Then Monocle laughed. Just a joke, then: he was aware of what thoughts his bogus offer would put in Nate's head. 'Nah, you don't get to steal my thunder, killer.'

Next came the noose. Nate tried to avoid it, but there wasn't much movement allowed by his condition, and Monocle easily slipped it over Nate's head and pulled it tight around his neck. Nate felt his breath restrict.

'Here, boy,' Monocle said, laughing. And like a stubborn dog he pulled Nate closer to the chair. He threw the loose end of the rope over the ceiling pipe and yanked, hauling Nate to his knees.

Nate struggled to his feet to relieve the pressure, but breath was still a chore.

'Thanks for the help,' Monocle said, and leaned back and pulled, like a guy in a tug of war, and Nate's feet left the ground, and there was no breath at all.

Nate tried to shout for help, or mercy – he wasn't sure which – but all that came out was a long, gurgling noise. Toni started yelling, asking what was going on.

With eyes that were staring to blur, Nate watched Toni force herself to her feet. She tried to yank the pipe away from its split clamps, but they refused to give it up. She couldn't generate much power because turning towards the pipe had forced her forearms to cross.

Monocle pulled on the rope again, hauling Nate higher. Then he used a leg to pull the chair under Nate's feet. Nate got his toes on it and managed to raise himself two inches, which allowed him to suck in a tiny portion of air. Monocle stepped closer, feeding the rope through his hands in order to keep it tight, and then used Nate's weight to help pull himself up onto the chair. They stood side by side, their faces just inches apart.

'Don't piss yourself just yet, wait till I'm clear.'

He started wrapping the rope around the pipe until only two feet hung free, and then he tied it off. Toni, Nate could see, had freed the mask by dragging it against the wall. Seeing Nate, she yelled a promise: the guy was going to suffer unimaginably unless he let Nate go right now. Whether he laughed at the threat or the fear in Nate's eyes, Nate didn't know.

Nate's consciousness was going. As if sensing this, Toni's next words were delivered with low volume and pleading, and they stung Nate's heart: 'Please don't kill him.'

'I ain't, he's killed himself,' Monocle replied. 'Guilt, girl, guilt. All those killings, broke something inside him. He even wrote a sweet suicide note.'

Out came the note, a crumpled ball of paper. Monocle stuffed it into one of Nate's jacket pockets. Toni abandoned the begging route and started fighting the pipe again, screaming at it while trying to wrench it right off the wall. But still it held.

Then, amazingly, Monocle reached behind Nate and snipped the ropes binding his wrists.

'There. No-one's going to believe you hung yourself if you're tied, right?'

Up came Nate's arms, and he wanted to fasten his hands around the guy's throat, but something inside him that knew only survival instincts instead directed them to the pipe. At full stretch, he just managed to lock his fingers together on top of it, and raised himself from the chair like a man doing a pull-up. The crushing pressure on his throat was beautifully reduced, blood again able to flow freely to the brain.

'Thanks again,' Monocle said. As he stepped off the chair, he kicked his back foot and sent the chair bouncing away even before he'd landed. It looked like a move he'd done before. Nate hung there, already feeling the burn in his biceps. 'Two minutes maximum, I say, then your arms will go.'

Without his legs to help, he could do nothing. Already his fingers were slipping apart and his body was lowering as the strength in his arms sapped. Two minutes was a wild fantasy: Nate knew he'd start strangling to death in a quarter of that time.

Monocle folded his arms, just watching the show now. 'I'll cut the feet ropes after you're dead. Try not to get shit on them when you die because I forgot my gloves.'

Nate's dead arms gave way. He dropped five inches and the jolt tore his fingers apart, and the crushing band of fire was back around his throat. His legs kicked uselessly and his body swayed and the pipe vibrated like a plucked guitar string, causing one of two clamps in front of him to shear its worn bolts. Rust rain pattered onto Toni's upturned face.

Nate saw black dots dance across his cataract vision. The pain was horrible. Air was a distant childhood memory. A distorted Toni turned to the pipe, slid her hands up high, lifted a flexible leg, put a foot on the clamp, and launched herself towards the ceiling. She flipped her bonds over the elbow joint and grabbed the horizontal pipe. The last thing Nate saw before everything dissolved into a toddler's experiment with coloured paints: she flipped up her legs and planted them on the ceiling, like an upside-down squat astride the pipe.

The next thing he knew, there was a screech of metal and the ground powered upwards into his feet. He threw his hands around the pipe to hold himself upright. The pressure on his neck was gone, and Monocle shouted, 'What the fuck?'

His vision immediately started to clear as blood and air were returned to him. He saw that the pipe no longer ran along the ceiling, but angled down to the floor. The vertical section was still in place. He understood: the weak flange joint had been torn away. Toni.

She was on her knees where the ceiling pipe dove into the carpet. The big guy was rushing her. Nate watched her stand and turn towards him. In her hands was the cast iron elbow joint, and in his was the knife that had Nate's prints on it.

Nate struggled to his feet, cracking his head on the angled pipe. Black dots again. He dropped again to his knees. His eyes found Toni, and for a second he didn't understand what he was seeing.

She was piggybacking Monocle, legs locked around his waist, the rope between her wrists across his throat, and his nose was a bloody, ruined mess. He was making the same gurgling sounds that had leaked from Nate's own restricted airway. He found himself liking that sound.

Monocle fell over backwards, hoping to dislodge her that way, but while the impact made her grunt as she hit the carpet and her head bounced off it, it served only to drive him into her harder, allowing her to strengthen her grip. Any Brazilian jiu-jitsu practitioner will tell you that falling onto your back is a mistake for this reason.

Still wobbly, Nate stood again, this time leaning against the pipe for support. He grabbed the knot in the rope and started to untie it. It was done in thirty seconds. He slipped back down to his knees, removed the noose from his neck, and clutched the rope tightly in both fists, as if it might all by itself try to snare him again.

Toni and the guy were still locked in that embrace, but unmoving. Monocle's arms lay limp, eyes wide but unblinking, blood around his lips and chin. Toni's face was a grimace as she continued to tug the rope hard into his throat. Nate could see he was dead already, but she couldn't tell, or could and was just making damned sure. She held on for another minute and then shoved him off. Watching, getting his bearings back, Nate didn't say a word as she got up, found the knife, and slit the guy's throat. Nate looked away.

'That's for Damar,' she said.

'How do you know it was him?' Nate said. His voice came out like a smoker's rasp.

Her look said she didn't. But he knew she would cut many a throat, just to be sure.

'I'm guessing they touched you inappropriately,' he said, because he could think of nothing better.

'They did,' she said. She approached Nate, and started rifling through his pockets. He was too disoriented still to work out why, until she extracted the note the guy had stuffed in there. 'But he wasn't even the one who did it. That guy's upstairs.'

'He better pray he has a fatal heart attack in the next two minutes.'

'I pray he doesn't.' She unfolded the note and showed it to Nate, who read, in a script that was surprisingly like his own:

I am sorry for everyone I killed

That was it. Short and sweet. 'At least they didn't put that I was sorry for touching kids and robbing from charity collection boxes, just to make me even more hated across the world.'

'Just backup for the suicide story. No need to elaborate. Anyway, this is like a horoscope. Universal. They could mass-produce these.' Toni laid the note on the dead man's chest.

'Not great for repeat custom. And that's not going to fool anyone,' Nate said.

'Maybe his mother will be comforted to know her son wasn't murdered.' She checked the pockets of his tracksuit bottoms and found something, which a second later skidded across the floor and into Nate's knee.

'Half-witted bozo,' he said as he lifted Buzzcut's revolver and checked that it was still loaded.

'Bozo? His mother?'

'Doesn't matter. Can we leave now, please?'

Holding Monocle's knife, she climbed the stairs and opened the door, no pause, no concern for who might be just beyond. No-one was, of course, because she waved him on.

Nate struggled to his feet. He felt confidence returning. He knew it was because he had Toni by his side again, and he didn't feel embarrassed by that. He could no longer deny that she was the tougher one. That he was a wet businessman and he needed her. As he joined her at the top of the stairs, he knew that, if he had to lose one, Toni or the gun, he'd toss the lump of metal and feel safer for it.

But he was the only safe one. 'Any chance you can leave one of these guys breathing long enough to get some answers?' he said.

'I'll think about it.'

They were in a short corridor that ran left and right. To the right was a porch and a front door of frosted glass that let in a lot of light – so, daytime still. To the left were a set of double doors in each wall and a set at the far end, open. A kitchen beyond. They could hear music from in there, and see the back of a guy in jeans and a T-shirt at the stove, cooking with two or three pans. He was wiggling his hips to the music. It was the guy from the van.

'That's not him, either,' Toni whispered. 'So this won't take long.'

It didn't. Naked, wearing blood from Monocle across her legs, oozing all the confidence ever created, she stormed into the kitchen and right up behind the cook, and paused, as if thinking how to do this. In the end she dropped the knife and grabbed his head and slammed into onto the stove, sending pots and pans clattering and water and chopped vegetables flying. He thrust backwards, screaming, and she stepped aside and left her leg there, tripping him. He had no sooner landed on his back than she had grabbed a hot pan and slammed it hard into his head, three times. When he was out, she held the hot base against his face. Nate heard flesh sizzle.

'We're not exactly sneaking about here,' he said, shocked.

She was holding her bad arm. The swinging motion must have irritated it. 'Take a look out the window if you think we're making too much noise.'

'Thought I told you no baseball with that arm,' he said. He

entered the kitchen. There were French doors leading into a garden. Beyond the hedges, he saw fields and trees.

Behind him, he heard the scrape of her picking up the knife from the tiled floor, and three seconds later heard her say, 'That's for Damar.'

He did not want to look round.

'We're in a cottage in the Essex countryside,' she said. 'No-one around for miles.'

He turned to look at her, but kept his eyes high. She had a fresh coating of blood now. Legs and hips and waist, and a line like a gash running up to her shoulder. She looked like some maniac from a slasher movie. She turned and opened a set of double doors into a lounge with a spiral staircase.

'You know where he is?' he whispered. He followed her and tried not to look at the body as he passed it, but he saw a pool of red out of the corner of his eye.

'They gave me a guided tour, sort of,' she said as she mounted the staircase. Not a whisper. 'Don't worry. Number three said he needed to wash my juices away not long before you got here. He heard nothing.'

Have they raped her? he wondered. He didn't want to think about it. He followed her up the stairs. There was steam coming past an ajar door off the first-floor landing. Bathroom. More music playing. She pushed into the bathroom nonchalantly, as if she lived here.

Nate heard water splash as someone in a full bath jerked in shock. Nothing said for a few seconds, as if the guy's brain couldn't understand why his naked captive was standing in the doorway. Seeing the knife probably got him going:

'What the fuck? Danny!'

'Reach for it and I'll cut off those balls.' Nate heard in reply.

'Danny!'

'Go search the house, Nate.' Then the door slammed shut.

Nate didn't hang around. He had no doubt that Toni would be okay, and he didn't want to hear any of what was about to happen. He went back down the stairs.

He knew it would make hearing the approach of a vehicle or pedestrian harder, but Nate turned up the music in the kitchen while he searched the house. Even so, the thumping bass of rap music didn't drown every scream. He didn't like to imagine what was going on upstairs.

The kitchen had a rack on the wall full of paperwork, but it was mostly junk mail and old magazines. Nothing of use, but he did note the names on the mail: either Joan or James Ryback. So this cottage was probably the Rybacks' private retreat. But where was the man himself?

As he passed out of the kitchen and into the lounge, he heard Toni laughing, and guy number three moaning.

The lounge was old-fashioned, but by design in order to give a bit of character. He got it. Technological sophistication didn't gel with what the countryside was all about.

There was a bookcase with the top shelf dedicated to paper-work, some of it in plastic zip-lock folders. He pulled one out. It seemed full of utility bills. Another held insurance documents.

The music stopped as a track ended. Upstairs, he heard the shower running. The next track started.

There was a library, and here, slumped in a chair, he found Ryback. The man himself. The kingpin. The guy who had orchestrated all this. The fellow Nate needed to get hold of in order to clear his name. Only it was clear now that Ryback hadn't been the top dog after all. Or he wouldn't have been sitting there, dead.

Arms lashed to the arms of the chair, feet tied to the legs, stab wounds to the chest and groin, and blood everywhere. Tortured and killed. Nate had waited what seemed like a long time to stand in front of this guy, but it wasn't Ryback's body that drew his shocked attention. It was the coffee table in front of him.

Evidence, evidence, evidence, a whole host of it, like a table of exhibits in a murder trial.

A bloody bayonet. Nate's. He knew it. Part of his army uniform, which he'd kept locked in a cupboard. Until he decided to bring it out to kill Ryback before hanging himself in the cellar, or so the cops would believe.

A Polaroid photo of Achala Kaushal. On her front in wild grass, hair bloody, face in lakeside mud, one arm in the lake itself, skirt hiked up to reveal red knickers. Soon to be taking an eternal swim. If he'd had doubts about the hitman's story, 'had' was the important word now.

A Polaroid photograph of Carl Webber. Puzzle over. Carl lay gored and dead in an unknown living room with one leg up on a sofa. That explained that.

A Polaroid photo of Pete. Laying in a living room that Nate knew well. His very own, pre-fire. Pete was on his back, blood all over his chest and throat, eyes closed. One arm was up over his head. The other, the left, was down by his side, the forearm slightly raised, fist resting on his hip. Nate knelt on the floor and stared at the photo, which shivered in his shaking hands. The bastards had taken a photo after killing Pete, maybe laughing while they did so. While another of their number got the petrol can and the matches. While yet others stuffed Nate into the boot of his own car.

He heard Toni call out from upstairs.

He went up, slowly, still in a daze. He tried to clear his mind.

As he passed a bedroom, he glanced in through the ajar door and saw a leg on the bed, surrounded by blood. Blood and death everywhere. Too much. An unforgettable amount. He had a future of nightmares ahead, however long his future lasted.

She called out again. Bathroom. Come in.

Guy number three was gone, of course. Three baddies in the cottage, and that meant number three was the guy on the bed. Just Toni here. She was in the shower, wet and clean. The glass of the shower door was frosted, but he could see her wet tan colour, and, amazingly, he felt a little turned on. A far cry from his emotional state downstairs, when she had been dirty and angry and they had faced death. The sudden onset of lust appalled him.

She saw him and put up a hand, as if telling him to wait. So he waited, just inside the doorway. Staring at the floor and the walls, and noting that there was no blood. None at all. She hadn't killed the guy in here after all.

She stepped out of the shower and remained naked before him, clean and sexy, everything animal and maniacal about her gone. Even the facial bruises and the laceration seemed somehow innocent now, like nothing more than the result of walking into a door. She pointed at a towel and he threw her one. But he did it slowly.

'Your turn. You stink,' she said.

He took his eyes away from her glistening body. 'Ryback's dead downstairs.'

She stopped towelling herself. He had her attention.

'I also found proof that Carl Webber's dead. Ryback was killed by a weapon the cops can link to me, and I bet when the cops find whatever was used to kill Kaushal and Webber, well, guess fucking what.' He did not mention the photograph of his brother.

She continued towelling, as if his news hadn't been news to her at all. Then she said, 'That's good.'

'Good? Ryback's sitting dead downstairs. Someone killed him. That means this isn't about Ryback getting revenge. We were on a wild goose chase. Don't you understand? We're back at square one. There's someone else out there who was behind all this, and we have no idea who.'

She put the towel around her hair, looked at him, and said, 'Get in the shower and it might wake you up. You're not thinking straight.'

Like a robot under programming, he stripped naked and got in the shower, hoping hot water would... he didn't know what. He could see her pixelated form standing where he had stood.

'Now think,' she said. 'We were on "square one" until you found Ryback's body. Someone else was behind this, and we never knew that. But now we know that, don't we? So we've made forward progress, haven't we? So it's a good thing, isn't it? You understand?'

He did. She was right – again. And he had been cloudy-headed – again.

'Did you get any information?' he said, turning away from her to hide his genitals.

He heard the shower door slide open, but did not turn. She touched his back. He heard her step in, and the door shut.

'He knew nothing. He was told by his boss to come here and watch a woman they brought in. Me. Then go collect a guy. You. His boss, unfortunately, is the guy in the cellar. That's all he knew, and he gave that up before the pain got too bad.'

'Then we have nothing.'

She turned him. He was still rotating when she kissed him.

'This is bizarre,' he said, pulling away. 'You just killed people, and now you want...?'

'Yes.' She kissed him again, and this time he didn't pull away.

'You've seen what I'm capable of, so are you really going to try to stop me?'

Afterwards, they moved to an empty bedroom and lay on the bed, side by side, staring up at the ceiling. There were packed suitcases near one wall.

'That was to unstick your mind,' she said. 'Did it work?'

He looked at her. 'What? You didn't want that, it was some trick?'

'Not a trick. A theory. I wanted to try to fill your mind with other emotions. I get the impression women aren't plentiful in your life.'

'I don't miss a woman's company or need it, if that's what you think. I work a lot, so there's not much time spare. And I've had relationships. Four long-term relationships and a bunch of short ones. I don't miss it.'

'Must be true. You said it twice. No wife in the past?'

'No wife in the past. I was army from seventeen until I was twenty-eight. Since then I've been kind of with Pete most of the time, and we were working hard on the security business, and Pete was gay, so it wasn't as if we could go out and pull together.'

'But you don't want to die a lonely old man, do you?'

'Half of that, yes. I want to die as an old man. But I'm not thinking that far ahead. And at the minute, women are the last thing on my mind. More pressing worries.'

'And yet with all those pressing worries, you found time to have sex.'

He laughed. 'And you did that so easily. Makes me think you're quite experienced with men.'

'You're only the second man I've ever had sex with. The first was as a teenager, so quite a long time ago.'

'But you've been married?'

She laughed. 'No.'

He touched the ring finger of her left hand, where there was an indentation. 'Doing a Sherlock Holmes.'

'That was a ring Damar gave me, for luck. Not marriage. He took it off me so I wouldn't lose it when we...'

'Were burying me. Fair enough.'

'Besides, like you, I never had time for relationships.'

'Too busy killing people, eh?'

'I don't do relationships.'

'Yet you hate being alone.'

She looked at him. She tried to look puzzled, but he saw guilt there. And she didn't meet his eyes.

He said, 'You need people with you, even if they aren't really friends, and even if you don't care about them. I think that's part of the reason you teamed up with me. Once Damar was gone, you needed someone to replace him. Even if the only guy left was the one you'd just tried to kill.'

'Don't mention Damar like that,' she said, hard. 'Don't compare yourself to him, because I don't want to insult you. Let's just say no-one will replace Damar.' She got up to emphasise her annoyance.

He tried some damage control: 'How come you and Damar never became a couple?'

She had been walking towards the window, but now she stopped and glared at him as if offended at the mere prospect. 'He never showed an interest, which I liked.'

'How do you know him?'

She approached the window and stared out. He watched water slowly drip from her wet hair and stain the towel around her waist. 'I don't want to get into my history. Let's just say I was forced to leave home at sixteen. I liked the sound of England, so I came. I ended up sleeping rough and Damar found me and took me under his wing, and he never once tried it on. So yes, Sherlock, I want people around me. Since sixteen, I've been surrounded by people and I've never been lonely. I don't want to be. But I don't *need* people around me. I choose it. The people I surrounded myself with were not what you'd call friends, but they'd smash your skull in if you looked at me wrong. But Damar was a friend. My best ever.'

He didn't buy her claim that it was a choice rather than a need, but didn't say so. 'So, Damar got you into crime?'

'Don't say that like he did something wrong. Damar was on the streets from about twelve and he was nineteen when I met him. Like me, he stowed away on a boat to get here from Turkey, so he was here illegally and had no prospects for a normal job, and he had this rather silly idea that he didn't want to starve to death. So, taking what he couldn't buy with money he didn't have was the only way to survive. And it was the same for me. He didn't push me into anything. I made a willing choice. We stole cars and robbed houses and sold stolen items, but we didn't hurt anybody.'

'Victimless crime, eh?'

'I meant that we didn't hurt innocent people to get what we needed.'

'Something changed, though. Because you seem quite comfortable around violence, and you're good at dishing it out.'

'Yes, something happened.'

He waited, but she didn't elaborate. He knew she wasn't going to. But she did say, 'I learned that danger is like cancer. Let it progress too far and you're in too deep. Kill it early, that's the way to survive. Put down a threat long before it becomes one, and don't leave roots that can regrow.' She'd admitted as much recently.

'Damar teach you that?'

'My people need to stay constantly defensive.'

'Turkish people? Certainly all the ones we've come across have had attitude problems.'

She laughed. 'You racist bastard. I meant street-dwellers. It's a tough...'

She stopped, and he worried that he'd upset her. But she clutched her head and said, 'I've been so stupid.'

'What is it?'

She began to pace alongside the bed, worked up now. 'You think all Turkish people are criminals?'

'No, I didn't mean–'

'Get dressed and let's find my clothes,' she interrupted. 'We just made another step forward.'

Edmonton, a street with a pub on the corner, just past six in the evening. She told him to stop the car outside the pub. He turned off the engine.

'He lives in a pub?'

He was Puzzler, an Edmonton-based crime lord. Puzzler had often recruited Damar, and through him, Toni, to steal or break or threaten. And sometimes these jobs had required a large crew. And always the crew had been made up from the Edmonton criminal fraternity.

Turkish criminals.

'I was so stupid,' she had said as Nate unlocked a 2005 Nissan Almera parked alongside the stone cottage in Essex. 'Damar never mentioned Puzzler, but I should have realised that Puzzler was the one who had sent us to kidnap you.'

Nate couldn't help but picture a supervillain in a daft outfit. 'So, you think this Puzzler's the guy behind everything just because of all the Turkish people involved?' he had asked.

'Doesn't add up. Not everyone has been a Turk. Lazar for instance.'

'Maybe Mr Big needed help and sub-contracted Puzzler to supply extra men. Damar and me, we were invisible people. For us to be part of this thing, it had to have come through Puzzler. Puzzler was the only guy Damar ever did jobs for. So Puzzler's involved for sure.'

Now, Toni said, 'I don't know where Puzzler lives. I never met him. I just accompanied Damar on jobs that Puzzler gave him. The guy who lives here is called Olcay, and he's Puzzler's right-hand man.'

'Okay, so Olcay lives in the pub? Or works there?'

She shook her head. 'There's a phone in there. You need to do something before we move on. Then we go to number 18a, just down there. Just open the door and walk in.'

'What? None of that made sense.'

'Then I'll explain for your sleepy head.'

Five minutes later, against better judgement, Nate entered the pub, which was empty apart from four young guys in suits playing pool, their ties hanging loose after a tough day's work holding a phone to the ear. They ignored him, and the cute bargirl ignored him, so obviously they weren't big local news fans. He went to the payphone and slotted in a fifty pence piece and called a number.

Hello? said a gritty female voice with clear frustration, and he knew right then that she had been getting a lot of calls from people she didn't want to speak to. Cranks and journalists and cops, probably.

'Mum, it's me.'

He was nervous, visibly shaking. The world's press could

label him a killer and berate him, but if his mother scolded him for his recent actions, he would probably burst into tears.

'Nathan. Lord. You ran away and I understand. But don't you dare ever ignore your mother again, understand?'

He was speechless. He had not expected that reaction. She sounded angry, not ashamed.

'I had nothing to do with the fire,' he said. He couldn't bring himself to mention dead bodies. 'Or anything else.'

'I know, of course I know that. Are you in England?'

'Yes.'

'Then stay here. Don't you be running off where I can't get to you, understand?'

He did, and it appalled him. She meant prison. She was telling him to stay in this country so she could visit him in prison. Did that mean she thought he was guilty?

'I haven't done anything,' he said, his voice cracking.

'The truth will come out, Nathan. It will. You just stay in England. Promise me.'

'Do you believe me?' he said. He needed to know. Her words so far had not unfolded her mind to him. Did she think he was guilty of killing his own brother?

'You want your mother to be well, I know that, Nathan.'

A hammer blow to the heart. She was saying she knew that, guilty or not, he would deny any wrongdoing because that was what mothers needed to hear, to believe.

Then, the first crack in her voice as she said, 'Is it Pete?'

He almost fell over. Guilty or not, there was still a dead man, and a good chance that that man was her other son. He couldn't think of the right response. Both *yes* and *no* seemed wrong.

'The police wanted my DNA,' she said. 'I said no. I don't know why I said no. They don't know if it's Pete yet, do they?' Then, more sternly: 'Is it Pete?'

So, the authorities hadn't yet announced that the dead man

was Pete, despite the sesamoiditis angle. Perhaps they still wanted DNA to officially confirm it. He understood, even if she didn't, why his mother had refused to give a sample. If the burned body was never identified, then she could convince herself that Pete was still alive somewhere. And so could Nate.

'Are they threatening you about the DNA?'

What would they do if she continued to refuse? Slap a court order in her face? Scour the ruined house for some tiny item, a hairbrush or toothbrush, that might hold Pete's DNA? If they needed Nate's cells for analysis, he would find a way to give them all they needed. His blood posted in an envelope to the police station, maybe.

'No. I haven't heard from them since that first visit yesterday. Nathan, is it Pete?'

So, they hadn't pressed her on the issue, and they would have because DNA analysis took time. Nate could fathom only one reason why, if indeed the police had decided not to chase up DNA collection. The sesamoiditis discovery. They had all the proof they needed.

'Nathan!'

He snapped back to the now. 'I don't know,' he said. 'I don't know, Mum, but probably. Probably.'

Silence as she digested this. The crack was gone from her voice when she returned. 'But you would know for sure, wouldn't you?'

Now he was silent. He had no idea what that meant. Did his doubt tell her he was innocent? Or was she mocking his doubt?

Before he could speak again, she said, 'I do not know if the police can somehow bug my phone, Nathan. I don't know what they're thinking and if they would do such a thing or not. Let's speak no more for now. I will see you. I will see you in England, make sure of that.'

And she hung up. He slammed the phone down, hard. The

bargirl yelled at him for it. The pool players glared at him with smirks. He was angry, and a big portion of that was his goddamned failure to grab a hold of knowledge. His constant fumbling about like a blind man. He gave the girl the finger and told the suits to mind their own fucking business. Then he stormed out. Before he hurt someone.

Number 18a was a basement flat with its entrance in a litter-strewn pit next to the front door of the main house. Nate clumped down the steep stone steps and opened the door, as instructed. He moved through a grimy hallway that had no carpet and wallpaper on only one side, as if the decorator had given up. Three rooms ran off the hallway, with voices billowing out of the open doorway dead ahead. He entered a living room lit by three standing lamps because the main window was whitewashed for some reason.

Toni was here, standing before a man Nate assumed was Olcay. Nate had expected a crime lord's right-hand man to be a behemoth with no neck, but Olcay was a skinny runt with a beer belly and too much facial hair and a nose that would keep the rain off his chin. He was cowering on a crappy sofa.

'I ain't seen him for days,' he said as Nate entered. 'He'll wipe you away for this, Nesrin.'

He saw Nate. And somehow managed to look even more shocked and scared than before.

Ten minutes. Nate figured she had been here for ten minutes already, and still hadn't gotten any information. She had cut throats earlier today, yet had hardly touched this guy. Some kind of remnant loyalty? Maybe Olcay had done her favours in the past, or she felt bad for him because he'd had a hard life. But Nate knew nothing about Olcay's struggles, and the guy hadn't done Nate a single good turn. So there was no loyalty staying his own hands.

He grabbed one of the standing lamps and smashed the shade and the bulb against a wall bearing football posters. Feeling weak and helpless under his mother's scrutiny had loaded him with anger. Like a bully beaten down by an abusive parent, Nate now needed a soft target to unburden upon. 'Where the fuck is he?' he snarled, maximum effort put into an angry face.

'I don't know!' Olcay yelled. Louder than necessary: perhaps trying to alert the neighbours that he was in trouble.

Nate didn't care. Not all of that rage-face was fake. 'Then die!' He felt a sudden explosive itch to crack open the guy's head, and raised the lamp like a woodcutter with an axe.

Toni grabbed him, pushed him away, said they needed Olcay alive, and he saw the look in her eyes. Like she thought he was playing good cop, bad cop. He hadn't been playing at all. He really thought he might have crushed Olcay's head. But there was no need now, because the skinny runt was nodding furiously.

Nate leaned against a wall and tried hard to concentrate on Toni and Olcay, and ignore what had just happened. To pretend that he hadn't been about to really hurt the guy.

Toni knelt before Olcay and coaxed answers out of him, and they came like a waterfall: a rave, tonight, don't hurt me, some old warehouse, Puzzler might show up, don't hurt me, the address is on a piece of paper on the TV, don't hurt me.

The words continued. Nate pushed away from the wall and staggered into the kitchen. He grabbed the first glass he saw, even though it was dirty, and filled it from the tap. He drank the lot in one, refilled and repeated. His hand shook so badly that water spilled out and down his chin. When he returned to the living room, Toni and Olcay were sitting together like good friends, although the interview was ongoing.

'Puzzler wanted a bunch of people for a recent job,' she said. 'What do you know about it?' She was staring at a piece of paper that looked like it had been torn from a spiral notebook.

Olcay said he knew nothing. Promised on his mother's life that he didn't. Nate stood in the centre of the room to make sure Olcay knew he was listening. Olcay stared up at him.

'What do you know about these people?' Nate said, then reeled off names: Kaushal, Webber, Agar, Nathan Barke, Pete Barke, Ryback, Lazar.

And Olcay's shaking head stopped shaking. Lazar. A name he'd obviously heard before.

'Tell us about Lazar,' Toni said.

Olcay seemed delighted to talk now, probably eager to give them what they needed in order to get them out of the house. And because he didn't mind stabbing Lazar in the back.

'All I know about Lazar is stuff I heard. I never met him. I don't know him. But I know he's a copper. I heard about the arrest of a guy in America, who told the cops over there something to get himself a deal, and they called the cops here. Lazar was one of those cops. Puzzler knows Lazar. Puzzler was helping with whatever it was Lazar was doing. But I don't know what it was. And that's all I know. Honest.'

Nate and Toni stepped aside. Olcay watched them as if he thought they were discussing which of his eyes to bite out first.

Nate said, 'Agar tells the Americans something to get a shorter sentence, and then they call Lazar? I think Agar might have seen something at HyperX. Something illegal, something Ryback was up to. HyperX could be a chop shop, or those Rolls-Royces could have been stolen.'

Toni shook her head. 'No.'

'Why?' Nate snapped. Olcay heard his raised voice, and Nate

saw the guy perk up. Maybe he hoped Nate and Toni would fight, allowing him to escape.

'Look, I know you want an input, but you're wrong again. Two reasons. First, the Americans didn't call Scotland Yard. They called the people dealing with the murder case. They called Lazar. That means Agar's information was not about HyperX in general, but about *that night*.'

Nate let his emotions subside. She was right. Maybe he just wasn't very good at detective work.

'Second, if Agar volunteers information about HyperX, the Americans will look into it and realise that they've got themselves a wanted murderer. He'd get extradited and he'd go to prison for a lot longer than if he just kept his mouth shut and did his time in America. So he– What?'

Nate had raised his hand, stopping her. 'But what if he wasn't a murderer?'

Toni stayed silent.

'I always wondered where Agar got the money to suddenly flee to America. The guy had nothing. What if Ryback gave him the money and told him to hide and keep his mouth shut? And he did, for four years. Then he gets arrested and he's facing prison, so he tells the Americans, "Hey, I have a deal for you. Give me a lighter sentence, and I'll help you get some glory by clearing up an unsolved murder in Britain".'

This time she didn't shoot him down. She rubbed her chin, like a thinking cartoon character. 'If not Agar, then who do you think killed the robber that night?'

'Someone who might not trust three idiot security guards with half a million pounds' worth of flash cars.'

'Ryback?'

'I think he was there. I think he was too paranoid to leave the cars alone with three people he didn't know. So he stayed with them that night. And he had a gun. And he shot someone. And then he got Agar to flee with the blame. Agar was unlicensed as a security guard, and maybe the cops were after him for some other stuff, and he knew he'd be screwed. So he agreed. And then Ryback got the others to go along with his bullshit. Remember, the CCTV footage was missing. Why hide it if it shows Agar shoot someone? I think that footage captured Ryback killing a man. I think Lazar helped to cover it up. And I think Lazar and Ryback panicked when, four years later, when it's all but forgotten, some cops thousands of miles away called to say they had a guy in custody who was telling a different story, or was planning to.'

Toni thought. He waited. 'It would explain why the others were killed. To silence them. Maybe Ryback suspected that Kaushal or Webber had told you and Pete the truth, so he decided it was safer to kill everyone involved with HyperX that night. But the Americans might have already heard Ryback's name from Agar, and they would suspect something fishy if the entire crew involved with HyperX that night, including a man in their custody, suddenly got murdered...'

She let that last sentence hang. *A test for him: explain that one, Sherlock.*

'But one of that crew isn't dead. He's on the run, and the English police have evidence that he's the killer. Lazar is one of the cops who investigated the case, and he can convince the Americans that Agar was lying. There are no witnesses left who can testify differently. The Americans will not involve themselves too deeply in a case that's light years from their jurisdiction, and they'll move on. There might not be a clear motive as to why the dangerous fugitive Nathan Barke killed everyone, but the evidence against him cannot be ignored.'

She was thinking. Looking for holes in his theory, he suspected. So he was surprised when she said, 'That could be it, Nate. That brain of yours finally woke up when it mattered most.'

But already he'd found a crater in his own hypothesis: 'Something doesn't add up, though. Puzzler. He was supposed to be hired help. Brought in from outside, he should have no connection to HyperX, yet something about that place and that night must be so damaging to him that it forced him to kill Ryback.'

'The jigsaw is not complete, but the last piece is in the hands of a man that we know might be at a warehouse later tonight.'

'Puzzler's going away tomorrow,' said Olcay from behind them. They turned. He looked somewhat smug, and they knew he had heard some of their conversation. Their voices must have raised a little as they got carried away and forgot about him.

'He cut his ties with me, Nesrin. I suspect he's going away, and I don't imagine he'll be back. You want him, you better go now, get out of here or he's gone. You got tonight to get him, or he's a ghost, and then you're fucked.'

Tough words from a frightened guy. But potent, because he was right. Toni and Nate looked at each other, and both sets of eyes said the same thing. They knew their next move. Tonight. Some old warehouse.

'Now we have to tie you up,' she told him. 'No struggle, no pain. But it's happening, so accept it in your mind right now. And lead us to some rope or something, or I'll leave you here with him while I go to B&Q for barbed wire.'

Olcay wanted them gone quickly, and was eager to help. He told them he had a drawer full of phone charger cables in the kitchen, and asked if they didn't mind tying him up on the bed. They allowed him the cable, but insisted on the bathroom, where there was a thick metal pipe running behind the sink and toilet.

Later, back in the car, Nate said, 'Nesrin?'

'You guessed it. I lied to you about my name. We were ten minutes out from trying to kill each other. It's Nesrin, but I always liked the name Toni. So you'll call me that.'

'Is this why you don't carry ID? In case people see your real name? What's Nesrin mean?'

'I've never had ID. So no. And it means wild rose.'

'As in unpruned, left to grow in disarray, without order?' He laughed.

'What's that supposed to mean?'

He just laughed again. She gave him the finger.

She told him she wanted to drive, and he gave her the seat. He put his seat back and focused his eyes on a stain on the ceiling, and tried to make shapes with it. The next thing he knew, she was shaking him awake.

He sat up. It was dark. They were in a McDonald's car park. She held up a tea and a wrapped burger. He was reaching for it when he noticed something, which he stared at for a few seconds. When he looked at Toni, ghostly cornflakes floated across her face.

She had hidden her emotions back at Olcay's flat, but not now. Her expression was grim, her mind obviously in turmoil, and he understood why.

'Ryback or Puzzler must own the warehouse,' he said.

She nodded.

'Are you okay with this?'

She nodded.

'His body will be gone, you know.'

She nodded.

They ate, and then they drove. Eight minutes later, she made a turn. The residential road. The palisade fencing. The industrial park.

After hours, the place was empty and quiet. Streetlights illuminated the road, but apart from a lit sign or doorway, the buildings either side sat half-hidden in the gloom. No activity anywhere except ahead, on their right: Saturn Printworks.

Five vans were parked close to the doors. Men moved around them, unloading bags and boxes, which they carried inside via a loading dock at one corner. Nate saw a guy carrying tall lamps, and another with crates of alcohol. They were preparing for the rave.

Toni drove past, said it was risky to stay within sight.

A couple of hundred metres along, the road ended. 'This helps us,' she said as she turned in the road and drove back.

On the way past Saturn again, they heard intermittent music. Someone testing the sound system. The loading dock now had a pair of Tensa barriers blocking it and a guy was stacking pallets to create stairs up to the lip.

They left the park and parked between the fenced areas of scrubland, near a padlocked gate that led nowhere. Through the back window, they could still see the warehouse. Toni killed the lights and the engine.

'Now what?' Nate said.

'If Puzzler's coming to oversee his great show, it won't be until it's in full swing. So we wait.'

It got darker. Twenty minutes into their wait, they saw pinpricks of light ahead as a car turned into the residential road. A taxi rolled past them, three made-up girls giggling in the back. It stopped outside Saturn, out they got, back it came. It passed two other cars coming this way. Each had all seats taken. Only one of them returned, minus its passengers. The other parked near the warehouse and all living things exited.

Pedestrians next. Six young men in crisp shirts walked past the Almera, laughing and staggering. They nearly got hit by the arrival of yet more cars. The party was starting.

Half an hour later, the place was getting busy. Parking spaces near the warehouse were dwindling and neighbouring car parks were being used. People were walking down the road in ones and twos and groups. God knows what the residents thought.

Toni started the car and turned it. She drove past the warehouse again. There was a queue at the loading dock now. Two guys in long black coats, like genuine doormen at a legit nightclub, searched them and let them in. The music was thumping. Coloured lights starburst beyond the doorway.

'What's the plan?' Nate said as Toni pulled up again by the gate that led nowhere.

'Watch for Puzzler. Maybe he'll come in a cavalcade, like a king.'

Another half hour passed. A steady stream of cars and pedestrians went by. Nate was surprised the warehouse had room for everybody. He was surprised some old dear in one of the houses hadn't called the cops.

His ears registered the sound of a motorbike. Bikes had played a part in this thing a few times, and never in a good way. So, bikes he was wary of. He thought he might never again relax if he heard one. He sat up. Three headlights coming his way. Beside him, Toni was asleep.

He had the snub-nosed pistol liberated from Buzzcut, then liberated again from the living room of the Essex cottage, and he held it now in both hands. He was ready to use it – hopefully. But Puzzler would not come by bike, surely?

The bikes approached fast. They entered the roofless tunnel created by the palisade fencing. They passed the Almera in single file. The first had a single rider, as did the third, but the middle bike carried a pillion. Nate nearly fired a shot right there inside the car as the second bike blew past. He had seen that bike before.

He shook Toni awake, but he did it too fast, too much panic in his hissed words, and her hand grabbed his throat. He did not fight it, but waited. Three seconds, and then her sleepy eyes registered his face. Her hand fell away.

'Lazar just went past,' he said.

She looked in the mirror, watching the bikes recede. Then she looked at the gun Nate clutched. Then she shook her head.

'We could have had him right here.'

He felt guilty, but defensive. 'It was too late. He was past. It's bloody dark and he had a helmet on. There's only one way in or out, so we get him when he comes back.'

'No. Now.'

Now? Lazar was a big scalp for her, but surely she didn't plan to enter the warehouse? That was the lion's den, and entering a den of lions was a dangerous idea.

She got out of the car.

Many in the queue were already drunk. They laughed and shouted, fidgeted and wobbled. Most would have been turned away from a licenced nightclub, but these bouncers didn't care. And they were not searching people for drugs or weapons. One guy had a bag of weed, but he was let in because he had a wallet stuffed with cash. Another guy couldn't produce any money and was forcibly ejected from the queue. It seemed the organisers didn't care if people took drugs, but were outraged by those who attempted to enter and didn't have cash to spend.

Nate and Toni were just ten feet from the loading dock now.

Toni asked if he recognised either of the bouncers, who were Caucasian, not Turkish.

'No, but I'm more bothered about them recognising me. And they're searching people. I've got a damn gun and you've got a knife.'

'Don't worry about that. They won't be searching us. Hawaiian here will get us in nice and search-free.' She pointed at the guy in front of them. He was short, young, and wore an outrageous blue shirt with palm trees all over it, like he thought he was on the beach.

'How?'

Two girls got let through and the crowd moved forward. They were six feet away now, eight or nine people ahead of them. Toni reached past Hawaiian deftly when he was looking elsewhere, pinched the back of the upper arm of the denim-clad guy in front of him, and jerked her hand back quickly. The guy yelped, turned, determined that only Hawaiian was within pinching range, and raised his fist and dropped it like a hammer onto the top of the shorter man's head.

All hell broke loose. The two guys grabbed each other and went down, intertwined like squabbling cats. The crowd bust apart as the bouncers stepped in. Everyone behind the fighting cats just watched the action, but those who had been queueing ahead of them rushed up the pallet stairs and into the loading dock. Toni grabbed Nate's arm and pulled him, and moments later they were inside.

Last time he'd been here, this place had been a dusty old room, and the difference tonight was surreal. The floor heaved with bodies like a bag of maggots and thudding music seemed to shake the walls. Pulsing lights gave everyone's movement a robot-like appearance, like in a movie shot at ten frames per second. People were shouting, laughing, stumbling, groping; drinks fell, people fell, intelligence fell.

Nate had never been to an illegal rave before, but it was everything he had expected. He wished he could have been here another night, drunk, not hunted by killers and cops. With Pete.

Toni pulled him through the crowd. Most of the partiers were young and inebriated, but his alert eyes locked onto older men who were clearly sober. Puzzler's men, circling and selling drugs and being obvious about it. And orbiting these dealers, protecting them while watching the rest of the room, were bigger men in suits. Some had Nate's skin tone and some had Toni's.

'I think Puzzler soaked up Ryback's men after he had him killed,' Toni said, mirroring Nate's thoughts. Two teams working as one: a far bigger kill crew to hunt him. And a big slice of it right here, surrounding him.

They moved deeper inside. They passed one of the bars, which was simply a foldaway table with an old cash register and rows of cans and bottles, and headed towards the mezzanine at the back of the room. The busted floor beneath had been covered by a large tarpaulin and the three open sides sealed off by manhole barriers. Nate wondered if Damar's body was still there. He wondered if Toni was wondering the same thing.

A meaty white guy sat on the metal stairs. He tried to appear casual, like some guy just having a sit down, but Nate knew he was one of Puzzler's minions. His job was probably to stop drunken fools from trying to gain access to the offices atop the mezzanine. Did that mean Lazar and Puzzler were up there having a private party?

A white guy in a black T-shirt, which all the barmen wore, was heading towards the stairs with a cereal box. The guy on the steps let him up. Box guy stopped outside one of the office doors.

Nate saw the word STAFF printed on his back. A Turkish colossus opened the door, took the box, slammed the door. Box guy scuttled away. Nate saw a logo on his T-shirt's front: a three-dimensional diamond made up of coloured squares.

'I bet that was money from the bars,' Nate said.

'Did you see beyond the door when he opened it? No roof on the offices.'

She seemed very delighted by this. He had a bad feeling about the reason.

When she looked up at the roof of the warehouse, he said, 'Tell me you're joking.'

'We have to get into those offices. The guy on the steps is an alarm. He'll go off if we try to get up, and then anyone up there with a gun will have time to pull it out. We have to take them by surprise.'

Her plan was loco, but he looked up anyway. The roof was flat, corrugated iron, some of the panels twisted, some hanging loose and exposing the night air. Six feet below it was a grid of rafters. The rafters were only ten feet above the top of the office building. So, climbing a pillar and working across the rafters and dropping into the roofless offices was possible. Daft, but possible.

'But you don't know how many guys are inside,' he said. 'You can't take out ten by surprise, unless you're invisible and they're all blind and deaf.'

She wasn't bothered by this: 'That's not the problem. The lights are.'

The disco lights were painting coloured swirls not just on the floor and walls, but amongst the rafters, too. People would be looking up. She would be exposed.

She told him to go to a specific bar, and then she waved her phone at him and walked away. He understood. Also liberated from the country cottage in Essex: a second mobile, which Nate had. A burner, no numbers stored. Except that Toni's was in its memory now. They would keep in touch by phone.

Keeping his eyes on her, he approached one of the bars and joined the queue, and watched the barman work himself into a lather. Twenty metres away, she stopped at one of the pillars. He couldn't believe she was going through with this lunacy. He couldn't believe he was helping.

His mobile rang. He answered it. Above the noise, he barely heard her say, 'This is what you do–'

'Toni, listen carefully,' he cut in. 'Name a puzzle involving a cube.'

'What? Rubik's Cube. Why?'

'Swap the U in Rubik for a Y.'

'Rybik... Ryback? Okay, that explains why Ryback picked the nickname Cube to give to the hitman. A play on words. What's your point?'

Nate was still staring at the logo on the barman's black T-shirt. The 3D diamond wasn't a diamond at all – it just looked like one because it was balanced on its corner.

'I'm staring at a Rubik's Cube on a barman's T-shirt *here*, in Puzzler's warehouse rave. Now think of another nickname that's a play on words.'

She got it quickly. 'My God. Ryback is also Puzzler? But he's dead.'

'Exactly. So who the hell are we chasing?'

'Remember the packed suitcases in Ryback's cottage?' Toni said. 'Olcay said Puzzler was going away. It's true, then. Ryback is Puzzler. Playing games with names.'

'Ryback is about the right age to have been at school when Rubik's Cube became popular in the eighties. Because his surname sounds similar, Cube might have been a nickname given by classmates. When he hired the hitman, maybe Ryback thought nothing of using that nickname. The hitman operated out of Scotland, and they weren't going to see each other again. No risk.

'But for Ryback's criminal activities in London, there was a bigger risk of Cube the gangster being connected to James Ryback the successful local businessman. All it would take is one guy to say, "Hey, I knew a guy called Cube at school". So he adopted an alter ego, like a supervillain persona. He chose a name that was along the same lines, but distinct. Puzzler.'

She sounded horrified when she said, 'I can't believe me and Damar were working for Ryback all this time. I never met him, but I thought Puzzler was Turkish like us. My God.'

'Well he's nothing at all now, except dead. So, who's running this show? Lazar? Did he double-cross Ryback?'

'I hope so, but I doubt it. Lazar's a gofer. He hasn't got the brains to match his balls. And he won't have blood in about two minutes. But if he's working for some faceless boss, I'll get the name from him. But if Lazar is the top dog here, do I have your permission to kill him?'

'I'm not sure I could stop you, Toni.'

'I'm not sure you would if you could, Nate. Which is why I asked. It's been a long time since you mentioned wanting to clear your name. Seems to me you gave up on that.'

Nate didn't respond. Of course he wanted to clear his name. He just wasn't sure that it was a realistic premise now. Staying out of jail even less so. So why not get himself some vengeance for Pete while he at least had the chance?

She took his silence as consent. 'I'm going up. This is what you do...'

Despite their fight outside, Hawaiian and Denim had gotten inside, and here they were at the bar, right in front of Nate. And making up. Shoulder slaps and handshakes and slurred apologies. Then Denim, standing in front of Hawaiian, turned away, and Hawaiian looked at a short skirt and legs to his left. Nate reached over Hawaiian's shoulder and flicked Denim's ear and quickly stepped back. Denim spun around with a sneer, and, lo and behold, once again only Hawaiian was within range.

Down they went, tugging, elbowing, rolling. As if a bag of shit had dropped out of the sky, nearby merrymakers backed away, and a clear space was accorded the combatants for their ungraceful duel. The music thumped to each grunt and punch, like some odd soundtrack. Conversations faded and dancing faltered as the entire room tuned in.

Fuelled by a desire for action, two bouncers thundered across the warehouse, taking the path of most resistance just so they could elbow people aside for added effect. They tore apart the duellers and dragged them away. Moments later, the cavity left by the fighters filled and the bar queue reformed, minus Nate. Conversations resumed and dancing restarted. And nobody noticed that the young woman standing by the pillar had vanished.

Except Nate. He watched her go up the pillar like a monkey and into the rafters, where she was painted by colours. Across a thick beam, and over the office building. By this time the Turkish colossus had appeared at the door to see what the commotion was, but although his head was only ten feet below Toni as she passed above him, his eyes were cast down. A second later she was out of range of the lights, shrouded in darkness.

Toni stared down. Six rooms in two rows of three, no roofs,

which was like looking at a cross-section. Internal doors connected them all, but only four had external doors: the three at the front and the centre back one. And that door was a fire exit in the back wall of the warehouse. That would be her handy flee route if she couldn't get down the stairs. She needed to warn Nate that he might have to escape without her when the shit hit the fan, but she couldn't risk using the phone. Not with four men just a few metres below her.

They were grouped in the front centre room, the only one not in darkness. It was lit by a single construction floodlight in a corner. The beam was angled towards the floor so as not to be blinding, but this also meant the light did not reach the rafters. Knowing she was hidden from any quick glance, she scrutinised the occupants of the room.

Two Turkish guys, two white guys. One was Lazar, and even though he was six feet tall, he was the smallest by far. The others were muscular beasts doubtless hired for their intimidating presence. But they didn't intimidate Toni. She was aware of the negative effect that heavy muscles had on stamina and speed.

Plus, no-one looked geared-up for action. One mammoth white guy sat on the floor with his back against the wall and his legs crossed, reading from a tiny diary. The two Turkish brutes were on wooden chairs and playing cards on an upturned wooden box between them. Lazar sat on a battered and grimy two-seater sofa, playing on his phone. All four had cans of lager, which would further inhibit their reaction time to her attack.

She heard a knock at the door. From her angle, she couldn't see who was there, but wasn't surprised when it opened to reveal a black T-shirted bargirl with another cereal box. She was gone ten seconds later. The Turk who'd answered the door took the box to a sports bag by Lazar's feet and tipped in the contents. Money. Notes and coins poured out like a jackpot breakfast to join a mountain already inside the bag. Beer and drugs revenue.

A lot of it. And they expected a lot more throughout the night, because there were three similar but empty sports bags on the arm of the sofa.

Damar, and now riches to boot? No. Her plan had been to try to get Lazar alone to take him down, but there was a rising bloodlust inside her that she couldn't deny. Nate had been right about something being wrong inside her head. But whatever it was that sometimes gave her seizures – a cancerous tumour or a faulty connection, maybe – it only unleashed her violence on bad people. And she could live with that.

She pulled out her knife.

Nate moved closer to the mezzanine. Toni hadn't told him what to do while she was off playing Supergirl. He had thought about going outside to wait for her, but that seemed like running out on her. So he was doing this, although he had no idea what 'this' was. So he approached the stairs, and the guy who was just having a sit-down saw him coming and got up and came down. Nate grabbed the handrail and lifted a foot and pretended that there was something wrong with his lace. The guy just watched him. His job was to watch the stairs, so he had every right to be there, and Nate didn't. Couldn't just play with his lace all night. He moved away and tried to think of another plan.

That was when he noticed the women. Two of them, young girls in killer dresses, staring at him. Three days ago he would have gotten all hot and hopeful about such a thing. Because there would have been no chance that they were staring because they'd seen his face in a newspaper.

That was when he noticed the men. Two of them, young men in crumpled shirts, staring at him. Nothing good about such a thing, now or three days ago.

He turned and walked, threading his way through the crowd, around a puddle of vomit. He looked up at the mezzanine, but nothing was happening up there.

A tap on the shoulder. He turned. The two guys were right there, with the two women a safe distance behind them.

'How's things?' one said. He had a ring in his lower lip. The other one said nothing.

'All good,' Nate replied. 'You?' He felt the weight of the gun in his pocket, but knew he could not use it here.

The speaker handed his drink to his pal. Then he reached up to his lip. Going to remove the ring, Nate knew.

Kill a threat early, he thought, and drove his head forward. The guy's head snapped back. The two women were yelling even before the guy had hit the deck. His pal backed away and shouted:

'He's that bloody killer guy off telly!'

'Gone and chopped up his brother!'

Nearby heads turned his way. Shit. Two bouncers heard. One went running for the stairs. The other sprinted towards Nate.

Toni heard the shout, even above the thumping music. She saw Nate immediately because there was a clear space around him. And a fallen guy at his feet. She knew he had been recognised by someone. Wouldn't be long before some have-a-go-hero grabbed him, or the entire room, like a pack of wolves, fell on him.

Below her, the men jumped to their feet, having heard the shout, too. And realised that the 'killer off TV' had to be Nate.

And right then, another shout. Something beautiful at this moment: 'COPS!'

The flashing lights and music instantly died, plunging the whole warehouse into gloom.

Except for the room below. In the aura from the floodlight, Toni watched Lazar slap one of his men on the back. 'Get down there, all of you,' he yelled. And they obeyed instantly, almost fighting to see who could get out of the door first.

Lazar wasn't planning on going down there himself, though. The moment the last of his cronies had gone, he grabbed the bag of money and launched it over the back wall, into the room behind. The one with the handy flee route.

The door into that room must have been locked, because Lazar stood on the sofa and hauled himself up the wall, which wobbled under his weight. He was sitting astride it, about to flip his back leg over and drop down, when Toni wrapped her hands around a beam. Ten feet. Seven for her with her arms extended, and three for Lazar's upper body. Just enough. Praying her bad shoulder would hold out, she swung down, fully extended, and her feet caught his head like a table football figure whacking a ball.

He fell into the back room, tried to get his feet under him like a cat, and half managed it. But his landing was ungraceful. Toni dropped onto the top of the wall, then down into the room, and her transfer had all the grace that Lazar's had lacked. Which meant she was on her feet before Lazar had even gotten to his knees.

He saw her, and his hand slipped into his jacket, pulled out an extendable baton. She stepped forward, grabbed it, and lifted a knee into his face. He fell back and the baton stayed where it was, now in her hand, not his.

She planted her feet, waist twisting, arm thrown back, ready to deliver a home run to his head. The baton extended at the end of the back swing. She hoped the blow would not kill him:

she wanted him alive, watching, feeling, as a blade opened his throat.

His hands came up to cover his face. The baton powered forward. Halfway through its lateral arc, though, her shoulder jerked and pain jumped through her entire arm. The baton jumped off its arc and ruffled Lazar's blond curls as it passed over his head. She stumbled and dropped to one knee, clutching her shoulder.

Seeing his chance, Lazar twisted on his knees and grabbed the bag, and at least two thousand pounds sterling cracked her in the head and shoulder. The world swam as she fell onto her back.

He was standing over her a second later, showing how well-equipped he had come tonight. First the baton, and now a knife.

'You know it was me who slit your boyfriend's throat, right?' Lazar said, staring down. 'Let me show you–'

Shouting, bellowing, screaming. Laughter and whistling from some of the more inebriated of the merrymakers. Then the threat of 'COPS' took hold in another voice, and another, until it ran rampant throughout the entire crowd. People bolted. The loading dock soon got crammed, so people headed for any nook or cranny that looked like it might offer a way out.

Nate found himself forgotten, thankfully. He looked up at the offices and saw Lazar's men fleeing also. They thundered down the stairs, and he thought they were coming for him, and maybe they had started with that intention, but they joined the rush of escapees. There was no sign of Lazar.

In the gloom high above, he saw a black shape swing down from the rafters and drop out of sight. Toni. He ran up the stairs and booted open the door of the middle office.

This room was lit by a lamp. He saw three doors, but concentrated on the one in the back wall. Because that was the room he thought he'd seen Toni drop into. The door was padlocked.

'Let me show you–' he heard Lazar say from beyond, then the door burst inwards under Nate's foot, the hasp torn away from the wood.

Lazar was standing over Toni, with a knife. Their gazes met. Nate pulled Buzzcut's revolver, but he was too slow, and he saw Lazar's hand delve into his jacket at the same time. He knew the guy would draw quicker, and so he ducked behind the doorway. But no shot was fired.

Nate stuck his arm through the doorway, made sure he aimed at least six feet high because Toni was laying down, and fired two bullets. He hadn't expected to hit Lazar, but to buy a second in which to poke his head out and see what was what. And what he saw was the night sky beyond an open fire exit in the far wall.

And Toni, squatting, hands over her head, looking his way. And much closer than before to the fire exit. 'You damn lunatic,' she yelled, angry and shocked. He knew what had happened.

Lazar had had no gun – why pull a blade if he had a firearm? Delving into his jacket had been a tactic to scare Nate, and it had worked. Lazar had then fled. Toni had started to pursue Lazar, and then hit the deck when Nate started firing blindly.

She rushed through the fire exit and onto a metal landing. Nate joined her. Below, in the grassy area between the building and a dark river, sat the three bikes that had brought Lazar and his henchmen. No sign of Laz–

'There,' Toni said, pointing.

A black shape with a bag running along the riverbank, already thirty or forty metres away.

Toni ran down the stairs and Nate followed.

The cops had arrived out front. Six cars, their spinning roof lights washing the building's walls, reflecting off the glass of the nearby buildings. It was as if the police were throwing their own party. Nate heard shouting and the thud of running feet, and saw uniformed officers chasing inebriated revellers who had no chance of escaping. Nobody came down the side of the building, so without fear of being seen, he and Toni darted towards the neighbouring establishment and behind. Shrouded in blackness, they pounded along the riverbank.

Lazar was fast, despite carrying a bag, and showed no signs of slowing. Forty metres became sixty. They could see him in the moonlight reflected off the river.

'We're losing him,' Nate said. He was dropping behind Toni. But as the noise from behind them faded, Lazar seemed to slow. Toni slowed also and ducked behind a bush. Nate did the same, and just in time: Lazar stopped, turned, paused. Looking for pursuers. They waited. Thirty seconds later, he continued along the riverbank. But now he was walking, not running: obviously he thought he was home free.

'Hopefully he'll go right to the big boss in his incriminating evidence-filled lair,' Nate said.

'If we run along the front of the buildings, we can get ahead of him,' Toni said.

'The cops will see us out there.'

'You just want to see if he leads us to the big boss.'

'That's right. There's no point leaving Lazar dead in a river if we never find the man paying him.'

'If he gets away, I'll blame you.'

'So will I.' She looked at him. He saw something in that look that he thought was admiration. She did not say anything else.

They continued to follow Lazar, but slowly, moving amongst

the thicker undergrowth closer to the buildings in case he turned to look again. But he believed he had escaped, so he didn't do anything more than throw the odd look back, and it was too dark for a quick glance to expose them.

Then he moved off the riverbank and vanished down the side of a building. Nate and Toni copied, two buildings separating them from their quarry. Fifty metres. No cops down this end of the industrial estate. Lurking at a corner of the building, they watched Lazar rush across the road like a scared cat and down the flank of a building on the other side. They scarpered across once he was out of sight.

Behind this row of buildings was a chain-link fence, a sports field beyond. They could see a school in the distance. Lazar was sixty metres away, climbing the fence. They watched him walk across the field.

A much greater risk of being spotted if they followed him across the field: brighter, nothing to hide behind. But Lazar got halfway and he hadn't looked back once. They decided to risk it.

Soon they were treading mown grass out in the open, and even a quick glance back from Lazar would expose them. No glance came. His tradecraft was bad, or his ego dangerously bloated. He reached the playground and aimed for a gap between two buildings.

'Right here,' Toni said. 'Give me the gun. We make him tell us where the big boss is. If he gets to a busy main road, game over.'

Nate sidestepped to create distance between them. He didn't want Toni trying to wrest the gun from him. 'No. We follow.'

'You came full-circle. From wanting to clear your name, to revenge, and back to doing the right thing.'

'Lazar's not waking up tomorrow,' Nate said. 'You'll get your fantasy. Try a little patience for once.'

She said nothing further, and there was no attempt to wrestle the gun from him.

From behind a stone bike shed, nervous as petting schoolkids, they watched Lazar climb a set of wrought-iron gates in a brick wall as high as his head. Beyond was the main road: they could see the aura of headlights, and the passage of bigger vehicles.

'Last chance,' Toni said. 'If he gets away...'

For the first time in a long time, her threat carried a serious tone. He believed she might try to hurt him if Lazar got away. But Nate had endured so much over the last few days that he wasn't bothered. Civilian life might have mellowed him, but he'd re-entered the fog of war recently. He told Toni to shut up, and his tone wasn't that of a wet businessman. She opened her mouth to object, and he said, 'I want the big boss. If *you* let *him* get away...'

Lazar dropped over the gate and was gone. They broke cover and ran to the wall, avoiding the gate. They peeked over like nosey kids. Lazar was on the other side of the main road. At a bus stop!

A bus arrived.

Blocked from his view by the vehicle, they clambered over the wall and darted across the road. Lazar was already on the bus. Through the windows, they watched his brightly lit form vanish up the stairs to the top deck.

They got on behind a black guy with a guide dog. Nate paid with loose coins from his pocket. They found empty seats near the back, same side as the stairs so they'd be beyond the peripheral vision of anyone coming down to the lower deck.

Nate took the window and expected Toni to sit beside him, but she knelt across his lap, facing him.

'What are you doing?' he said, aware of glances from the few other passengers. But they looked away quickly. In London at night, you didn't stare if you wanted a peaceful life.

'Playing the role of a loved-up couple.' She linked her fingers behind his neck.

'Cool it,' he hissed. It was too intense. People kept glancing. He waited for someone to recognise him as that bloody killer guy off telly who had gone and chopped up his brother.

'My arm's dislocated again.' He looked at her face, saw it creased in pain. 'Damn baseball you warned me about. Use your basic knowledge of physics again.'

'Not here.'

'I'm not getting off until you do.'

An old couple on the other side had their faces turned to the window, but he suspected they were watching his reflection. He put his hands on Toni's breasts. And pushed. He felt the jerk of her shoulder. She yelped. Heads turned. With her ass on his lap, and that noise, God knew how this looked. She collapsed into him, head on his shoulder.

'You went two inches lower,' she said into his neck. 'I should crush your nose with my forehead.'

Lazar got off just a few minutes later. He came down with his head bowed, as if, like Nate, he feared being recognised. No look around the bus: no fear that he had enemies close. Again, bad tradecraft or bloated ego. He got off. Nate and Toni let three other people get off, then stepped onto the street behind them. Lazar had turned left, so they turned right. From behind a free-standing digital advertising board, they watched the bus move away to reveal Lazar crossing the road.

They followed him along the road, staying on the opposite

side. Here, there were restaurants and late-night shops and the trade was bustling, which was good because Lazar had either suppressed his ego or remembered a couple of Robert Ludlum novels he'd read: he kept glancing around. But they hung back, walked alongside pedestrians, and kept street furniture between them and their target, and he had no chance of spotting them unless he stopped and really stared. Which he didn't.

Three minutes later, he turned down a side street. At the corner, they glanced down a road of terraced houses, and just in time to see him take another turn. They gave him thirty seconds and then followed.

It wasn't a corner as such, but a break in the terraces where a recessed building sat behind a flower-bordered lawn. A three-storey block of flats, pale red brick, with blue window frames and a bright green door of glass. And a key fob entry system. As they arrived, the door was just closing behind Lazar. Two seconds later he was gone.

As one, they looked up. They were waiting to see if any of the dark windows lit up. But nothing had changed five minutes later. Either the guy was sitting in the dark, or he'd already left his light on. Of course, he might not have entered one of the flats at all.

A guy in a British Gas uniform appeared at the door, opened it, stepped out. But then he watched the door swinging closed.

'Stay here,' Toni said. She rushed towards the gas man, waving her hand, saying something about a lost key. The gas man stopped the door with his hand. She went in and thanked him and vanished. The gas man let the door swing shut, and pushed it to make sure it was locked, and then left. Ten seconds later, just as Nate was beginning to think that Toni had abandoned him so he wouldn't stop her killing Lazar, she reappeared and opened the door.

There was a lift and a set of stairs, and a list of residents. The names were on pieces of card slotted behind glass. Sixteen spaces. The flats were all on the first and second floors, eight at the front, eight at the back.

'Back row,' Toni said. Nate nodded. No light had come on in the front-facing flats.

Of the eight at the back, only two didn't have names written on the cards. The others were in different scripts, suggesting the residents had written their own. Both empty ones were on the second floor. And both were at the end of the row. Nate tapped the one on the corner.

'That one, because he wouldn't want neighbours.'

They went up the stairs and into a corridor lined with blue doors. They approached the nameless end flat. In the end wall was a window looking over the back gardens of the terraced houses.

The front door had a lever lock door handle, surprisingly. Luckily. Toni grabbed it and turned it slowly before Nate could stop her. The door was not locked.

'Maybe–' he said, and that was all he got by way of a warning before Toni opened the door all the way and stepped inside.

A hallway. Bare, not even a carpet. Instantly, Nate knew that this was a temporary place for Lazar. Just a place to crash so he could be closer to... who or whatever. Or maybe it was a hub for something, a hideout for many. They heard no voices, but the noises of movement.

Two doors in the right wall, two in the left, and one dead ahead. Similar design to Olcay's cheaper flat, which would make the room ahead a living room. The only open door was in the right wall. They approached slowly, careful not to make a noise on the tiled floor.

Nate pulled the gun, and Toni snatched it off him.

'We get information first,' he mouthed at her. She ignored him and turned away and stepped ahead of him. He couldn't do anything about it in case he alerted Lazar.

It was a bedroom. Lazar was facing the bed, sideways on to them, bent over a suitcase laying on the quilt, stuffing the money from the other bag into it.

'I hear hell's hot this time of year,' she said.

Lazar jumped and went for his knife even as he turned his head to see who had accosted him. The shock on his face when he saw Nate and Toni was a picture. Toni was already pointing the pistol at him. He froze, then put his hands up. One still held the knife.

'You caught me just doing an overnight bag for my sick mother. Hospital.'

'Back against the window. Face it. Knife down.'

Lazar moved back until his ass touched the sill. Then he turned around, but corkscrewed his neck so he could still watch his unwelcome guests. His hands were still up, and still he clutched the knife. 'What was the third one?' he said with a grin. You couldn't doubt the guy's balls. But he dropped the knife two seconds later.

'Search the case,' she told Nate. He tipped it out. Nothing but money and clothing. Nothing else. Lazar was planning to flee the city, maybe the country, just as Ryback had planned to. Before he got killed.

'I don't know what you think you know,' Lazar said. 'But you've got a gold-standard in wrongness.'

Nate said, 'I know you killed my brother, and Toni's partner, and that puts you in a world of shit.'

Lazar turned around. No-one objected. Still that grin slicing his face. 'Enjoy jail for that, won't you?'

'I'm not going to jail. Because you're going to tell the police, your brothers in blue, all about what you did.'

Surprise there, as if Lazar hadn't known that Nate knew he was a cop.

'What happened at HyperX, Lazar?' Nate said. He saw Lazar's eyes drop to the knife. No, not the knife. Higher. Something on the bed. Nate looked. He saw, amongst the clothing, a tiny flash drive. He picked it up.

'Fuck it,' Lazar said, still grinning. 'Why not, eh? Can't hurt. Laptop's in the living room. Grab some popcorn.'

'Get it,' Toni said to Nate.

'Screen's knackered,' Lazar said. 'It's hooked up to the TV. Can't bring it in here.'

'Living room it is,' Toni said. 'But I'll check it first. Make sure there isn't a pit of snakes trap waiting for us.'

She gave Nate the gun, told him to hold it on Lazar and to shoot the guy's balls of if he moved. She took the knife and left the bedroom.

'She's only using you, you know?' Lazar said.

'Keep going. You're close. Another couple of sentences designed to make me turn on her, and I'll probably be unable to stop myself going in there and shooting her dead.'

Lazar said nothing further. A minute later, Toni was back. She took the gun from Nate.

'Clean,' she said. 'No secret gun that he can shoot us with.'

Nate went first and waited just inside the doorway while Lazar came, on his hands and knees like a dog, as ordered. Behind him, at a safe distance, Toni followed with the gun aimed at his ass.

The living room had no furniture apart from a two-seater sofa and a coffee table with a TV and a laptop on it. No carpet here, either. The room stank of cigarette smoke and there were overspilling ashtrays around, and empty beer cans. Lazar looked too fresh-faced and healthy to be a smoker and a heavy drinker, so maybe he held parties or meetings.

Lazar climbed onto the sofa like a naughty dog before anyone could object, as if he thought all three of them would sit side by side to view whatever was on the flash drive. He sat right in the middle, so that the seam between the cushions was between his spread legs. He put his hands on his knees.

'What's on this?' Nate asked him, holding up the flash drive.

'Watch the video,' was all he said.

Toni turned the coffee table so that the TV and laptop faced away from Lazar, so they could watch without giving Lazar their backs. Nate knelt before the TV, but Toni remained standing, off to one side, so that her view of Lazar was unrestricted. The gun barrel never stopped pointing at him.

Nate fed the flash drive in the laptop. A list of folders popped up on both screens.

'Oh look, the laptop's fine,' Toni said sarcastically. 'It's almost as if he wanted us in here.'

'Keep that gun on him,' Nate said.

'I can't be held responsible if something happens because he tried a cheeky move.'

'Don't think I don't know that you want him to try that cheeky move.'

Knowing that Lazar would understand exactly what Nate meant by that, Toni winked at the police officer. *Please try*, she mouthed at him.

'Third file down,' Lazar said. 'Then the second video in the list. I could go out for popcorn while you watch?'

Nate followed the instructions. A video started to play. Nate instantly knew what he was seeing. CCTV footage from inside HyperX. A certain night four years ago. Footage that had been stolen, according to the police. According to Lazar. But here the footage was.

Lazar watched them as they watched the screen.

It was hi-def video with timestamp but no audio. Location: the workshop, where Ryback's three glossy Rolls-Royce Wraiths wait, wrapped in plastic. And here come the robbers: four machete-wielding men clad head-to-toe enter. They're identical except for the hands: each wears different coloured gloves.

They enter behind two of Nate's crew. Carl Webber, thirty-three, a tall white guy, someone who looks older than his years because he sweated the small stuff, said it kept him alert. Dead now in a living room. And Achala Kaushal, twenty-six, a handsome Indian lady who looks younger than her years because she was obsessed with make-up and the small stuff never intruded into her happy-go-lucky attitude to life. Dead now in a lake.

Nate knows the story, so he knows the missing guy, Agar, is already hiding under the table, because the video has started just after he heard the robbers coming his way. He will remain hidden until found, after the robbers have cannibalised the three cars. And when found, Agar will shoot one of the robbers dead in self-defence.

But that was the official version, as told by the police, as told to the police by Webber and Kaushal. As Nate watches, the four men in black and the security guards calmly walk in, and there are no raised machetes. The raiders carry them down low, hanging by their sides. The guards walk ahead, but uncon-cerned, not pushed, not forced, not rushed. In the centre of the floor, they all stop, and the two guards face their captors. Kaushal's face is away from the camera, but Nate sees Webber's mouth moving, and knows the six are talking. And then one of the men in black leans back, laughing. Webber slaps his own forehead. Kaushal covers her mouth, which was a habit Nate remembered: she didn't like to show her oversized front teeth when she laughed.

Okay, so the raiders didn't manhandle their prisoners in quite the way the official story had it. But here comes the part where they cannibalise the cars, and kick over a table, and one of them gets shot by Agar.

Nope. Agar isn't under the table at all. He climbs out of one of the Wraiths and joins the group. More chatting. If ever you've gotta be robbed, these sweet guys are the ones you want to do it.

Here, though, we get back on track as the robbers dismantle the cars. But with help from Webber, and not the coerced kind. Kaushal just watches and smokes a cigarette. Agar fidgets on his toes, like he's got something on his mind.

But it's not about stealing car parts to sell. What the men take out of the cars are beige-coloured packages about the size of house bricks. Drugs. Lots of drugs. These packages go into bags, and the bags get hauled outside. Afterwards, the car parts make the same journey and thus create a cover story. Throughout, Red Gloves chats to Kaushal and Webber, while Agar stands apart, still fidgeting.

When everyone is back at the party, White Gloves points at the camera and Blue Gloves gives a thumbs-up and leaves. This would be the guy who busted the CCTV and took the tape. More milling in the centre now, three guards facing three raiders with six feet between them. Agar's still twitchy, but so is Green Gloves. He's got his machete in his hand for some reason.

It's done, and all that's left are the goodbyes. Except, that's not what happens, is it?

Green takes a step closer to Agar, but at that exact moment Agar pulls out his gun. Up it comes, quick, and Nate sees the muzzle-flash. Two shots aimed at the same area, the trunk, but Red Gloves drops to his knees after the first, so the second takes him in the face. Everyone jerks in shock.

Except Green Gloves, who clears up any wonder about why he's holding his machete: he swings it hard at Agar, and it's clear this isn't just a reaction to his friend's death. He's had this planned for a minute or so.

Agar darts back, out of range, and the machete cleaves only air. And then Agar is running for the door. No-one knows it yet, of course, but that's him gone for the next four years. Everyone else freezes for a second. Then both remaining living raiders look at the body, and then the door, and then each other, and Nate knows mouths are moving behind those balaclavas. Webber and Kaushal are just standing there in shock.

The raiders run, leaving their dead comrade on the floor. Right then, with what you could be forgiven for thinking was too coincidental to be coincidental timing, the picture dies, because this is the point at which the guy sent to fetch the tape pulls a wire or flicks a switch.

Lazar looked pleased with himself.

'A drug-trafficking business,' Nate said. 'That's what was going on with HyperX. Drugs get shipped from the branch in Dubai to England, hidden in luxury cars.'

Lazar nodded. 'It's beautiful. The guys who overhaul the cars are experts at hiding drugs so well that you have to strip the vehicles to get the stuff out. The cars slip through customs easily because it tends to be lone cars they suspect, not profitable, legit businesses. Plus, they'd have to pay for damages, so who really wants to take apart a half-million pound motor?'

'But Ryback set-up his own place to be robbed. And he had my people in on it. Why? He wasn't being paid enough?'

'He gets a pittance compared to what HyperX's owner in Dubai makes. And don't ask me about her, okay? I only know she's some reclusive businesswoman called Xiomara, hence the X. Ryback wasn't happy with his cut of the business. That latest drugs run was worth ten figures and he gets six.'

'Drugs,' Nate snapped. 'So that's what my brother and the others died for?'

His anger was bubbling up, and only just kept in check when Lazar laughed. He felt Toni's hand on his shoulder, as if she were trying to calm him.

Lazar said, 'There are people out there who'd kill for the price of a pack of cigarettes, and this was about a lot more. Anyway, that wasn't the reason people started to die. It was because everything was about to go belly-up.'

'Because of Agar,' Toni said. 'We know all about Agar. We know he was captured in America, and threatened to tell the world the truth. Which we now know is about a big drugs operation. So, witnesses started to die. But the planned deaths started earlier, didn't they? On that video, it didn't look like something went wrong and a guy got shot.'

Lazar didn't seem surprised by their knowledge. 'I'm a cop. First thing I think in an armed robbery: insider job. And Ryback knew Xiomara would think that, too, so he had to make it look real.'

'By having Agar kill one of the robbers?' Nate said. 'And then having one of the robbers retaliate and kill Agar. On the tape, the man with the machete wasn't reacting to the death of one of his comrades. He was gearing up for it. It was planned from the start.'

'Well spotted,' Lazar said. 'There's no honour amongst thieves. Ryback would have been suspected by Xiomara even if the robbery was genuine. This was the only way Ryback would avoid getting the truth tortured out of him. We picked Agar because he had a criminal record and was known to be hot-blooded. He was told to shoot one of the robbers after the job was done. And we told one of the robbers to kill Agar. Neither team knew about both plans. If someone from each side died, how could anyone suspect a set-up? Except that Agar got away.'

'But you could have hidden the body,' Toni said.

'The cars were above board. They had insurance. With the police involved, Xiomara could get a pay-out to mellow her a little. And if Ryback suddenly got killed, the police would dig a little deeper, and he knew Xiomara wouldn't want this. So Ryback stayed safe.'

'Except he's now dead,' Nate said. 'And your role in all this? Kill the investigation?'

Lazar nodded. 'Reason I became a cop, my friend. From the start, I wanted to get on a rich bad guy's inside and start earning. That might sound a bit clichéd, but I earned, didn't I? There's enough normal cops out there to keep the country from imploding. They could miss me. Ryback needed me. Armed robbery and a dead guy – nobody's going to do a cursory investigation into this. I was needed for deflection.'

Nate said, 'Ryback bought himself a team of robbers. Easy for him, I guess. But what about my people? How did you turn them?'

'I wasn't in on that, so I don't know. You should have asked Ryback.'

'So, Ryback decided to kill everyone who knew about it once Agar threatened to talk. But why me and my brother, when we knew nothing?'

Lazar laughed. Then he got all serious, but Nate could tell his serious expression was faked. He was trying not to laugh some more. 'That would be called tying up loose ends.'

'Why set me up to look like the killer, though? Why not just kill me?'

Lazar thought. A long time. *Not to create a lie,* Nate thought, *but to carefully word his answer.*

'These people didn't spontaneously combust. There had to be a killer,' said Lazar.

'But me? I'd need a motive. A whacked-out heroin junkie would have had more motive. It makes no sense, and that's because you're hiding something. What was my motive?'

'Were you whacked out on heroin?' Lazar said.

Nate had been avoiding asking his next question. Saving it for the end. He suspected the answer would explain everything that was still so puzzling about the whole episode.

'Who was Ryback's partner in this?' Toni said. Nate looked at her. 'He couldn't have set all this up by himself. Who was he working with?'

Now Nate looked at Lazar. The man didn't deny that Ryback had a partner. In fact, he seemed to confirm it when he said, 'On the laptop. There's a video called *Truth*.'

Nate found it with shaking, impatient fingers. Toni did not watch, never took her eyes off Lazar.

'You'll need the TV sound right up to max,' Lazar said. 'And watch and listen very carefully. And then get ready to apologise to me.'

A blue background. REMEMBER THESE WORDS in bold text popped up, filling the screen. The text vanished a second later. There was no sound other than the hiss of speakers turned up to full.

MOON appeared next. Big, bold, but smaller than the previous text. It vanished.

OCEAN. Smaller again.

'What the hell is this?' Toni said, flicking a glance at the screen.

'Haven't you worked it out yet?' Lazar said, shaking his head.

Nate was puzzled, but he watched with fascination as more words appeared on the blue background, each smaller than the last. Eight words in and Nate had to lean closer to read them. Still no sound but the hissing of a million snakes.

Then, suddenly, a beast's face appeared on the screen, filling it, some horned demon with jagged teeth, and it roared, and the noise was tremendous, shockingly so. Nate jerked back from the screen and swore. Even Toni jumped, and the gun flicked away from Lazar.

Even as it happened, Nate knew he had been tricked. He had seen such prank videos on the Internet before. Designed to get the prankster a laugh. But Lazar's intention hadn't been to get a laugh.

But he'd had an intention. Had planned it right from the start. His placement on the sofa allowed him to delve a hand into the seam between two cushions, and return a second later with a gun.

He raised it, no attempt to get up because that would take concentration that could be better spent on the shot. He continued to sit back, almost leisurely, and raised his hand and fired, casual but fast, like a man so confident in his aim and his invincibility that he believed all his troubles would go away following a couple of presses of the trigger. As if knowing that she would be too late, Toni's gun lowered. Nate, sitting on his ass, acutely aware that he could do nothing, put up a defensive hand and turned his head away. It was all he could do, and he knew it would do no good.

Lazar's gun clicked on empty.

'Didn't I tell you there was no gun that could kill us in here, Lazar?' Toni said. From her pocket came the magazine for his pistol. She tossed it into his lap. He looked at it, sitting there on his crotch, then back up to see Toni's gun aimed right at him.

'You damn bitch. Damar screamed for his life, you know.'

She fired.

The gun clicked on empty.

Lazar reacted instantly. He grabbed the magazine and slammed it into his gun, but before he could aim the weapon, Toni fired again, and this time, instead of an impotent click, there was the boom of a powerful weapon doing its job correctly.

The bullet hit his raised hand, knocking it and the gun aside in a splatter of blood. He thumped back against the sofa. His eyes stared at them. His busted hand lay on the sofa, one shattered finger bent unnaturally under the back of his hand.

Her gun lowered to aim at his groin.

'Say that again about Damar,' she said.

'He's dead,' Nate said. He got to his feet, staring at Lazar. He remembered the way Toni had laid in the van, busted arm bent under her. No way she could have been faking, because her arm would have been killing her. She would have shifted to make her arm comfortable. Same thing with Damar, back in the woods. Lazar, if playing possum, would not have let his finger come to rest like that.

Toni wasn't convinced. Still aiming, she circled to one side, then stepped closer, aiming at the side of Lazar's head. Lazar didn't move.

'Your damn bullet must have deflected off and into his body.'

Lazar didn't move. Toni moved in front of him and looked into his wide eyes, still aiming that gun right at his face. And then she reached out and grabbed his jacket's zip and yanked it down. Beneath, he wore a white T-shirt that was stained red. It had a small hole right where his heart would be.

'You set him up,' Nate said, angry. She lowered the gun.

On the TV and the laptop, the loud beast was still laughing.

Nate pulled the cable that connected both devices and the noise died.

'I left one chamber empty,' Toni said, still staring at Lazar, as if finding it hard to believe that he was dead. 'It was a trick to see what he'd do. And he tried to kill us.'

'It wasn't a damn test. You wanted him to go for the gun. So you could justify killing him. You wanted to shoot him.'

She looked at Nate finally. 'I wanted to cut his throat.'

But Nate couldn't take his eyes away from Lazar. From that blasted finger, bent under his hand. He thought about Damar lying unconscious in the woods.

'I'm sorry,' she said, stepping close to Nate. 'We didn't get a name from him.'

He thought about Toni lying asleep in the van.

'We take the video to the police. That clears you, surely,' she said. A hand dropped onto his shoulder.

He thought about Lazar sitting dead on the sofa.

'There will be evidence somewhere, and the police will find Ryback's partner, and this Xiomara bitch. Hell, I'll go to prison for you if someone has to. I don't care about prison. Are you listening to me?'

He wasn't. A hot wave of dread came over him and he had to grab the coffee table to avoid falling over.

'Nate? You hear? This could be what you need.'

'I have to go,' he said, and started for the door.

'Where?' Toni said. 'The police?'

'No,' Nate said. 'Atlantis.'

Halfway to 'Atlantis', he drew up at the kerb near a petrol station on a country road. Toni was asleep beside him, her mouth moving. When the car drew to a halt, the tiny jerk was enough to wake her. Her fingers went to her mouth.

'You were chewing in your sleep,' he said.

'I dreamed of chocolate,' she said. 'Where are we?'

He pointed out the petrol station. The only two vehicles on the forecourt were a sandwich delivery van and a taxi. He told her to go inside and buy a map.

'Pull into the forecourt, then.'

He said no: CCTV. The car they drove had been stolen from outside a pizza shop near Lazar's flat and was probably already reported, since they had taken it when the owner, leaving the engine running, went inside to collect pizzas for delivery.

Lazar's bag of cash was in the back seat, and he reached in and took a handful and gave it to her. Far too much for a map. She took it all, looked at it, and looked at the petrol station.

'You seem... distant,' she said. He said only that they needed the map, quickly. Didn't look at her.

'I have epilepsy,' she said. 'Partial seizures. Some medical student Damar knew called it Jacksonian March. Like you, he liked to Internet surf to find out what makes me tick. He was worried because I act out my dreams sometimes, and my right arm shivers, although that hasn't happened since my shoulder dislocated. There's the cure, eh?' She laughed. It was forced. 'But he didn't worry about the rage inside me. He looked beyond that. You can't, I know. Maybe my anger is tied to the epilepsy. But I don't want you to worry that I'm dangerous... to you.'

He told her again to get the map.

'I'll see you later, Nathan Barke.'

She got out before he could say another word. Walked towards the shop, cash right there in her hand. She did not look back. The taxi driver came out of the shop and looked at her, and he saw her mouth moving. They passed each other. Nate let her get ten more feet, right to the doorway, then spun the wheels and tore away.

His phone rang just seconds after he'd left the garage. He had expected this. He had even *wanted* it. He remembered her face in the leisure park, when he had offered to go out alone to steal a car. She had been upset that he was leaving her side, in case he didn't return and she was left all alone. It was a strange childish weakness in a woman who was otherwise as tough as God made them. Her Kryptonite. For that reason, despite his plan to never talk to her or see her again, he could not abandon her without an explanation.

He answered with, 'I'm sorry to leave you alone. I just can't do this with you, sorry. Use the money for the taxi and go home. Maybe we'll hook up again when this is all over and we no longer have to run.'

Surprisingly, she said nothing. It worried him. The silence was deafening. He said, 'This, I need to be on my own for,' and then hung up. He pulled the battery from the phone. He drove for half a mile with the handset and the battery clutched in his fist, that fist hanging out the window. It took all his will to finally let go of them.

He stamped the accelerator, feeling like a parent who'd dumped his baby on the doorstep of an orphanage.

Port Werbergh in Kent, only about eight miles from Sunny Dream Leisure Park.

Maybe it was because of an over-abundance of cheery holiday resorts with the word 'Sun' in their names that the owners of the marina called their site 'Frosty Breeze'. Maybe they were practical individuals who didn't see the point of a blatant lie to people who knew British weather. But Nate was puzzled by the illustration on the gates leading to the road that sloped down the hill into the marina: a family of four on the deck of their houseboat, the woman at the rail, enjoying the sea, ignoring her ball-playing kids and the husband reclining on a deck chair, all of them in shorts, a bright blue sky above them, crystal clear green water below. Cold wind off the North Sea or not, it seemed the fun was endless here.

Not at two in the morning, though. Most of the houseboats were as dark and dead as the calm black sea. Those with lights on showed no signs of life, either, but maybe that was because their owners were at the disco.

The marina's entertainment complex consisted of seven or eight commercial structures and a handful of outbuildings on a shelf of land poking into the sea. All were dark and dead also, except for a large white Victorian-looking house with a black timber exoskeleton. Music throbbed and light pulsed behind curtained bay windows. Out front people drank at long wooden tables, while behind, sea-side, they milled on a large patio, warmed and illuminated by tall heaters.

Nate watched the partiers only for a moment. Long enough to feel the first pangs of jealousy. No-one down there had nowhere to go tonight, and no-one down there had no friends to turn to. No-one down there faced a bleak future of hiding under a rock or rotting in a cell. Then he turned his attention to the houseboats again.

They were a mix of styles, some large, some small. Some appeared to be typical boats given a soft makeover to achieve a homely veneer, while others, monstrous mongrels with chimneys and gardens and bay windows, looked like actual houses that had been craned in and dumped on floating bases.

They were arranged either side of a large jetty curving around the tip of the shelf of land and along five twisty piers shooting out from it seaward, like gnarled fingers on an arthritic hand. The boats were tightly packed together, just a few metres between neighbours, and Nate didn't get the attraction. For him a houseboat should mean peace, solitude. This place was a flat, floating tower block.

But he wasn't here to buy one. He was here for a man who'd bought one.

At the entrance to the main jetty was a map of houseboat positions. There was a tiny guard hut, but no guard. Maybe when everything was closed for the night, the managers put a guy here to make sure dangerous fugitive killers didn't get to the boats. But the party at the skeleton house meant residents were still coming and going even at this late hour. So Nate strode onto the jetty without worry. He passed a couple coming his way, and neither screamed about intruders into their world. He passed a drunk woman leaning over the rail, maybe trying to vomit. She waved him away as if determined to have no help with this one, even though he was already trying to ignore her.

He turned left at a junction, heading along a thin, wobbly pier. Here the houseboats reared up high either side of him, swaying and groaning like snoring giants. Only two of them had lights on. He passed the first. The second was near the end of the pier. That was the one he needed.

He stopped at the ramp leading up to the boat. And there was the name on a sign: 'Atlantis'. Who decided to name a boat after something that had sank?

The house was on two levels, one smaller block atop a larger, all in white painted wood. The entrance was a patio door. A kitchen beyond, lit. No-one there. He tried the door and found it unlocked, which he expected. Dangerous fugitive killers didn't lurk around here.

He pulled Buzzcut's revolver, even though it was unloaded, and stepped inside.

The kitchen had all the amenities you'd expect. Nice, except that the windows looked out onto other houseboats. There was a glass door leading to a dining area, and at the back of that a patio door leading onto a terrace with a floor of artificial grass. Beyond was the sea.

The patio door shrieked as it slid open. He stepped into the kitchen. On a worktop he saw coffee, sugar and tea jars arranged in a line just like that, in that order, which some might assume was alphabetically, but which he knew was in word size, high to low. He knew for sure then that he had the right place.

Entry to the top deck was by ladder, which the brochure probably called stairs. Actual stairs nearby led down to a lounge. Three levels, then. That explained a price tag of just short of £190,000. Nate, pointing the way with his useless revolver, took the stairs without secrecy. If anyone was here, they had already been alerted to his intrusion by the noisy patio door.

Since the lounge was below decks, it obeyed the oval shape of the boat instead of the oblong form of the house. Here, again, everything you'd expect from a room in a typical house, except for three portholes giving a view of nothing but black water. There was a pillar right in the centre, which he thought was awkward. The décor was soft, hinting at relaxation, but Nate didn't think he could ever unwind in a room that was underwater.

In the far wall was a door. He opened it to see a thin corridor with a bedroom either side, a bathroom and, at the end, a ladder leading to a trapdoor in the ceiling – probably access to and from the terrace at the bow.

The rooms off the corridor were empty, so Nate climbed the ladder and pushed opened the trapdoor. Night air was sucked in and all around him. He stepped out onto the terrace. He looked at the black sky, with its twinkling of stars, and the black sea, with its twinkling of reflected moonlight, and tried to see the line where they met. For a moment he understood the attraction. At night, here, you could fool yourself into thinking you lived aboard a luxury yacht moored at St Tropez. If you ignored the frosty breeze.

He could see the skeleton house off to one side. The party seemed to be winding down because people were leaving in droves, headed this way. Drunk, tired, needing their rocking beds. So, it shouldn't be long now.

Nate went back to the lounge and sat on the sofa to wait.

Eighteen minutes later, he heard footsteps climb onto the boat. A voice he knew shouted a goodbye to a man who replied with a kissing sound. The back door opened, and above him he heard the fridge open, a beer bottle cracked, keys slamming onto a worktop. He didn't stand or even sit up straight, simply turned his gun towards the stairs. The big man who came down froze halfway when he saw that gun and the person holding it.

Then his shock subsided and he gave one laugh, like a bark, and continued down. Nate waited. The man went to the stereo and pressed a single button, and it lit up and began to play rock music, low, fifties of course. Nate waited. The man sipped his drink and sat in an armchair that faced the sofa. Nate waited.

'Clearly the false sighting of you in Gibraltar tonight was, well, false,' the man said. 'I followed the news. Some expats thought they'd seen you in a Sunglass Hut outlet. Then there were sightings in London, a couple in Wales. All sorts. The cops even went in guns first into a B&B in Nottingham. Of course some had to be false. Not ever Superman gets around that quickly.'

Nate said nothing.

'How long have you known?' the man said.

Nate said nothing.

'Okay, *how* did you know?'

Nate pointed the gun at the coffee table, and the man leaned forward. On it was the photograph of Pete that Nate had taken from a similar table in Ryback's country cottage. Pete on his back, throat bloodied, one arm raised over his head, one loosely curled on his waist. The man looked puzzled.

Pete Barke picked up the photograph and studied it. He dropped it after a few seconds and rubbed his face. Bare, smooth, like his head. Shiny, curly hair that got the ladies interested – gone. Thick greying beard that got drunken men wanting to fight him – gone. Nate recognised him easily despite the drastic change, but knew others wouldn't associate this chemo-looking guy with the portraits of the dead man shown on the news.

'The elbow bursitis? They got me to lie down before they applied the fake blood, that was the problem. It started killing my elbow, so I had to rest my hand on my belly. But that's not what gave it away, Nate. A damn photo. What else?'

Actually, it had been. A simple theory based on how he had seen three people posed in uncomfortable, painful positions they would not have maintained had they been able to manoeuvre their bodies. But he said nothing. He wanted Pete to simply... explain.

'I didn't kill that guy, by the way. The body in the house. That was Ryback's men. For a long time we feared the day Agar would tell his story, and we made contingency plans. Ryback found me a guy with sesamoiditis. Bone surgery, evidence of which would survive a fire. That was a good touch. We kept tabs on that guy for four years, never knowing when we'd need his body. If the body was sufficiently destroyed that identification would be very hard and lengthy, and if the police were under enormous pressure to get it done quickly because there was a killer out there, then they might take anything they could get and run with it. The teeth had to go, of course, and the guy had lost part of a finger in some industrial accident, so his hand had to go – that wasn't mentioned in the news. We were ready to release the sesamoiditis information if the police somehow missed it and went straight for DNA testing, but then an anonymous caller did us a favour. You, of course. Did you see the ten o'clock news? Alongside your Gibraltar sighting, they confirmed it, Nate. Right there on the national news. Peter Barke, dead. They showed some of my old army photos. It was like some beloved celebrity had died. I almost cried. So, thank you for that.'

Nate said nothing. Pete looked at the gun. He sipped his beer.

'Maybe you're speechless with shock that your brother could get involved in such a thing. Don't be. Ryback came to me with a plan. I'd had nothing to do with the man before, and I thought he was taking a risk suggesting it to someone he didn't know, but he told me his plan, and it sounded foolproof, so I agreed.'

Pete gave him a rehash of Lazar's tale: a staged break-in at HyperX, and car parts taken to hide the very existence of a serious amount of cocaine.

'Of course, I lied to you about the windfall I got in my ex-fiancé's will. There was no will. I made excellent money from the drugs. I bought the house, and in secret I bought this boat. You remember viewing this with me four years ago, of course, since you're here – well done for your memory and guesswork. But look at the house, look at this place, and tell me it was madness to agree to join Ryback's plan.'

Nate told him nothing.

Actually, Pete admitted, there *was* an element of madness, a serious risk of the police somehow finding out about the drugs once they got involved. Because of Agar.

'You knew what Agar was like. The violent sort, liked to run his mouth. The original plan was for Agar to kill one of the robbers, to make the set-up look genuine, and then hide abroad. But we saw a problem. Kaushal and Webber we could keep close and under control, but we didn't trust Agar not to resurface somewhere and shoot off his mouth, especially if he got arrested. Rightly guessed, as we now know. So, we decided Agar had to die as well. No more risk of his runaway mouth, and we get to add a little bit of excessive force just to make sure the police kept their attention outside, not in. And we had Lazar to obstruct the police at every turn. Foolproof.

'So, new plan. One of the robbers is told to kill Agar. We told everyone that Agar was going to shoot a bullet into a wall to make it look like the guards fought back. And we told the robber to kill Agar after he shot that bullet. But Agar we told to shoot a robber instead, then run. I saw the video, too, and must give praise to the robber, because even though Agar killed one of them, that guy still tried to chop Agar's slimy head off.'

Nate waited. He wanted more.

'Ryback and Lazar thought Agar was trying to cut a deal by selling us out when he got arrested in America. But I believe differently. The night of the shooting, Agar didn't run home to collect his bags. Nobody saw him again. I think he knew that the other robber had been ordered to kill him, which meant he knew we wanted him dead. So he didn't risk going home. He just ran. And, credit to him, he kept his mouth shut. For four years. But when he got arrested, I think he feared that we'd learn of his location and go after him again. And he was right. He sold us out, not to cut a deal, but to see us locked up so we couldn't get to him.'

Pete sipped his drink. He looked at the gun. He shrugged, as if to say, *So there you have it.* Nate just stared, wanting more. He had been trying to intimidate his older brother, but the silence and the scrutiny and the gun started to have the opposite effect. He could see Pete starting to get impatient, even annoyed.

'Maybe I started this conversation the wrong way. Maybe you're more interested in why I didn't bring you in on the plan? You wouldn't have agreed. It was safer to keep you in the dark. And I didn't think you'd hold up under police questioning.'

Nate waited.

'Or why I didn't tell you the truth when we learned that Agar was about to sink us? That's it, of course. I'm sorry, I'm drunk, not thinking straight. Your concern, understandably, is why your own brother faked his death and allowed you to take the blame for it.'

Pete's own anger was beginning to rise now. 'I had just days to organise things. How was I supposed to start that conversation? "Sorry, Nathan, I fucked up four years ago and I'm afraid we're going to prison, but how about we fake our own deaths and flee the country?" Besides, it would have meant finding another body for you.'

Nate said nothing.

'It was the only way, Nathan. I had no idea what Agar knew, or what evidence was out there. Maybe he even still has the gun I gave him. Ryback was quite happy to uproot and flee, but I wasn't. I could have run and lived out my days as a rich man on a foreign beach. But I'd be looking over my shoulder for the rest of my life.'

Nate said nothing.

'Besides, back home everyone would think I was a despicable criminal, wouldn't they? And I've got some pride, haven't I? So this way, rather than a despicable murdering thief, I'm the poor bastard who got killed–'

'By his despicable, murdering, thieving brother,' Nate snapped, unable to contain his silence.

Pete threw out his arms like a man basking in applause. 'We needed a bad guy, Nate. Ryback had no-one else to blame, but there was one person who could get *me* out of trouble. You. You and me ran Acorn Security together. We lived together. We were inseparable brothers. I needed the police to believe that Agar's orders came from you, despite what Agar told them. And how could the police deny the guilt of a man who killed his brother and burned down his house to cover the crime, and then fled the country?'

'I didn't flee the country, though, did I? I went six feet underground. At least, that was the plan.'

'No it fucking wasn't,' he snapped. 'You were never supposed to die. You think that was my plan? To kill my own brother? You arsehole. You were never going to go along with what I had planned, so I forced you into it. The plan was to give you a couple of weeks in that damn warehouse, fed and watered, and then be shown the world as it had become. One in which you were a fugitive hunted for the murder of his brother, nowhere to turn, no-one to help you. Alone and desperate. No memory of that night.'

Pete put his right foot on top of his left toes, digging the heel in. A habit Nate remembered: the dull throb from the ball of Pete's big toe, because of the sesamoiditis, could be alleviated for a time by a blast of sudden, sharp pain. Pete said, 'Then a man would step in and offer you a new life in some other country, and a small business to run, and new friends, maybe even a girl.

And then, after maybe a year, I'd turn up and say hello. You'd punch me, of course, but then you'd remember all the money you had and you'd laugh at your brother's deception and hug me. All's well that ends well. And if you're wondering about Mother? Well, imagine her joy a year down the line when she would have learned that both her sons are alive and well and living in luxury.' He sipped his beer, using the time to calm himself. '*That* was the fucking plan.'

Nate said nothing.

'Ryback changed that plan, Nathan. He told his two goons, including that girl you were running around with, to bury you, because he didn't want loose ends. He wanted you dead, and when I found that out, I had him killed for it. See, brotherly love.'

'Brotherly love? I was drugged and kidnapped.'

Nate's mind went back to the night of the kidnapping, armed with missing pieces. The memories were vivid, having been rescued from the depths. A simple, normal night in–

'I'm not into crappy fantasy, Nate.'

'We'll flip this. Heads it's "Game of Thrones", tails it's "Breaking Bad".'

Pete fixing him a drink...

'This tastes funny, Pete.'

'A little something I added.'

Somehow realising that it had been drugged... *'What do you mean?'*

'I mean stay sat down or you'll crack your head when you fall. Don't fight it, Nate.'

Tossing the cup at his brother, then fleeing. Intention: hospital. Last memory of his life at home: flinging open the back door to find intruders blocking his path.

'Just stop, Nate. Trust your brother. You won't be hurt.'

'You were never supposed to be hurt, Nate.'

Pete's words pulled Nate back to the now. 'Never supposed to be hurt? Your people have been trying to kill me ever since.'

Pete laughed. Actually laughed. 'Do you really think they tried to kill you, Nathan? You damn idiot. How many times would you have been dead already? You would have never woken up that first time. They used tranquilliser darts, not bullets. Think about that.'

Nate tried not to let his emotions show on his face. Because his emotions said he believed this.

Pete said, 'After you escaped and started running around the country, the plan threatened to fall apart. When my men didn't capture you at the holiday park, I knew there was no chance of getting you out of the country as planned. There would have been sightings of you. The cops might get you first, and when you started denying everything, they'd dig deeper, and I had no idea what they'd find. So I had no choice.'

Pete leaned forward, fixing Nate's eyes with his own. 'It really hurt to do it, Nate, but I had to cut you loose. Let you go down. And make sure that when you went down, there was enough evidence against you to sink you forever, no matter what story or proof you might have to the contrary. *I* sent the police to the holiday park.'

Pete finished his beer and tossed the bottle behind him. It bounced off the wall.

Nate just waited.

'So I left a guy behind at the park, his orders to keep out of sight, but to give you a postcode. The idea was that you'd hopefully write it down, so that when the police came to the holiday park and arrested you, they'd find it. Then they'd find Ryback's smashed flat and a clue about a cottage in Essex. And at the cottage they'd find your latest victim. Ryback.'

'And evidence that I'd killed Kaushal and Webber, right? Nathan Barke, the serial killer.'

Pete nodded almost apologetically. 'But our guy at the park didn't check in, and you got out before the cops could get you. I didn't know if you'd seen the postcode on the guy's arm, so I had Lazar send you down to Ryback's London place. But yet again you escaped the cops. Once my men finally captured you, I decided to let the cops have you at the cottage. Red-handed, so to speak.'

Pete indicated the photograph of himself, apparently dead. 'I wasn't happy about having photos of the dead floating around, but Ryback insisted. Extra proof, he'd said. But I had an afterthought that turned into a brilliant idea. I decided to leave the photos near Ryback's body to make the police think you'd showed them to him before killing him. Think about that, Nate. Why show them to a man before killing him?'

Nate said nothing.

'The police would assume Ryback killed them and you were there for revenge. Understand? Ryback killed Kaushal and Webber and me, and tried to kill you. Because we learned about his faked robbery and drugs hoard. But you escaped and found him, and got revenge. I did this because I didn't want that scumbag getting mourned, but mostly because I care about you, Nate. This way, the only deaths on your hands are those of a hitman and Ryback, criminals the world would be glad to see dead. I did this because I didn't want you to be hated by the world.'

'He's lying,' said a new voice, and both heads turned as Toni came down the stairs, holding a pistol of her own.

Nate recognised the pistol. Lazar's. He hadn't seen her take it from the dead cop's flat.

'I got to live one of my dreams tonight, Nate,' she said. 'I always wanted to jump in a taxi and say, "follow that car".'

'Toni, put that weapon away,' Nate yelled.

'Both of you, sit with your backs against that pillar. Ask him this, Nate. If the plan was to have you arrested after you escaped, then why the noose? The suicide note?'

Nate's head snapped back to Pete. 'That was Ryback,' Pete said, his calm now gone, his eyes unable to meet Nate's. 'That was his plan, but he didn't know I had already signed his death warrant. I had already turned his own men against him with a simple magic trick involving making money appear out of thin air in their pockets.'

'Those men at the cottage were turned against Ryback, yet still they had the noose and the suicide note ready to go? He's lying. It's obvious. He's telling you what you want to hear so you let him live. But what he doesn't realise is that it doesn't matter what you believe, Nate, because I'm here to kill him for killing Damar. And then I'm going across the sea out there, and I'm going to kill Xiomara.'

'Damar?' Pete spat. 'Your loyalty's misplaced. That fool set you up. You were supposed to die as well.'

She aimed the gun, angry. 'More lies.'

'He gave you no money up front, did he? He took your ID away, didn't he? He said it was in case you dropped it, didn't he? Did you really buy that, you daft bitch?'

She paused. Nate could see her mind struggling with Pete's claim of betrayal by Damar. 'All lies, Nate. That's what people backed against a wall do when facing a gun. They lie to try to save themselves.'

'What about the ring he gave you?' Pete barked. 'He took that away, too, right? What, in case you lost dropped that as well?'

She said nothing.

'He knew more about all this than he told you. He knew quite a lot. He was one of Ryback's main bitches. Answer this: why didn't he tell you everything he knew?'

She shook her head, but Nate could see she wasn't totally convinced that Pete was wrong. 'If Damar had planned to kill me, he would have told me the truth. Just like the bad guys in movies. Just like you, right now, although your reason is that you think it's going to allow you to see a new day.'

'No, he would have told you the truth if the plan had been for you to *live*, not die. You were his good friend. Of course he wouldn't keep such a secret from his good friend. The truth is, you didn't need to know because you were not going to survive the night.'

She stepped closer. 'But I did. And unlike you, I'll survive tonight, too.'

Nate stood up. 'The police, Toni. That was the plan.'

'Your plan. I told you mine. Go outside if you don't want to watch.'

'If you don't put down that gun, I'll turn mine on you, Toni. And then we'll have a serious problem.'

'Nate, listen to me,' Pete said. 'I can probably never convince you that I never wanted you hurt, but you can never prove that I did. So, the choice is yours. Ryback was the criminal mastermind with the damn stupid supervillain alter ego, but his men work for me now. I have a lot of contacts, and I can get us out of the country quite easily. It was all set-up. Spain. You and me, we can go there tomorrow morning. That was the plan and it still is. Make a choice, because if you turn me in or let this woman kill me, everyone loses. There have been deaths and someone's got to go down for those. Make that choice right now.'

'It's not his choice,' Toni said.

Nate turned the gun on her. 'Don't make me shoot you, Toni.'

She said, 'This was what we expected from the start, right? You'd want to kill me, and I'd want to kill you. That's what we both feared. Is this what it comes to?'

'I guess it is. You are not killing my brother. Despite what he's done. Remember I came all this way to get revenge for him, so don't think at this stage, despite what he's done, I'll let anyone just shoot him dead.'

'Your gun is empty, Nate. I put the last bullet into Lazar.'

Pete looked at the gun, and Nate saw his hopes drop. Nate tossed the gun away as if it were dirty.

Toni said, 'Are you seriously thinking about it? Running away with him?'

Nate nodded.

She stepped closer to them. 'Against the pillar. Now. Hands behind your back.'

Pete moved first. He sat with his back to the pillar and put his hands behind him. Nate didn't move.

'Do it, Nate,' Pete said. 'She won't admit as much, but she isn't killing anyone. She would have shot already.'

Pete obviously didn't think Toni could be as callous as killing a man who was tied up, but Nate knew better. But he sat by the pillar and put back his arms. With one hand holding the gun on both men, she extracted two cable ties from a pocket. Nate's right arm was locked to Pete's left, and then Pete's right to Nate's left on the other side of the pillar.

'So, what now? Kill us both?' Nate said.

Toni knelt beside them both. Heads turned, Pete's to the left, Nate's to the right, they watched her.

She showed them her phone. 'I know the whole story, okay? I recorded it for the police.'

Her head cocked, as if she was listening for something. Or to something. Nate strained his ears, and heard it.

A police siren.

'You'll go to prison, too,' Pete yelled.

Nate calmly said, 'I'm not sure she'd mind. Nobody's lonely in prison.'

Toni kissed Nate on the cheek. He tried to avoid it, but she grabbed his hair and held him still, and planted her soft lips once on his skin. Then she got up and sat on the sofa, and put the gun on the table. 'Now listen carefully, both of you.'

Wandsworth arson death victim found alive – woman arrested

Today, Metropolitan Police announced an arrest in the Wandsworth house fire murder investigation – even though the victim has been found alive and well.

In a shocking twist to this story, police yesterday raided a houseboat in Port Werbergh, Kent, where they found not only the man believed to have perished in the fire, but also his brother, the man suspected of his killing. Both men were discovered handcuffed and incapacitated aboard the vessel.

Following the fire last week, which destroyed a large house in Putney Village, Wandsworth, police discovered the body of a man believed to be Peter Barke, 48, and were seeking to question his brother, Nathan Barke, 42, who fled the scene and was the focus of a nationwide manhunt.

But today police arrested a 26-year-old Turkish woman on suspicion of arson, murder and kidnap. The woman is suspected of kidnapping both brothers and setting fire to the house to cover the crime. It is alleged she was working with a local businessman-turned-gangster and a rogue police officer, whose identities have not yet been released. The three co-conspirators are also being investigated about a drugs-related murder four years ago.

During their time as captives, Nathan Barke was allowed to leave the boat to buy supplies. He managed to escape and return to London, but was recaptured at Sunny Dream Leisure Park in Kent by their kidnapper's co-conspirators, who are believed to have killed an unidentified man at that location, a crime that Nathan Barke was originally suspected of.

Although information from the police so far is sketchy, they have said the woman faked Peter Barke's death in order to access funds in his bank account. Police are trying to establish the identity of the man whose body was found in the burned house.

The woman, who had been living rough on the streets of London, is fully co-operating with the police.

ACKNOWLEDGEMENTS

For my partner, Jen, who kept me grounded while writing this (more free time because I'm not allowed to watch the UFC).

Many thanks to the entire Bloodhound Books team, for hard work, dedication, fine editing and patience. Especially Betsy, Tara and Clare, who gave me a lot of their time (clearly not UFC fans).

And a final thanks to all who read this book. I hope you liked it. If not, I'll get you next time.

9 781913 419110